HERE STANDS
A MAN

Books by Blaine M. and/or Brenton G. Yorgason

Here Stands a Man
Dirty Socks and Shining Armor
Tales from the Book of Mormon
And Should We Die
Into the Rainbow
Sacred Intimacy
Little Known Evidences of the Book of
  Mormon
Decision Point
Pardners: Three Stories on Friendship
In Search of Steenie Bergman
  (Soderberg Series #5)
The Greatest Quest
Seven Days For Ruby (Soderberg
  Series #4)
Family Knights
The Eleven Dollar Surgery
Becoming
Bfpstk and the Smile Song (out of print)
The Shadow Taker
The Loftier Way: Tales from the Ancient
  American Frontier
Brother Brigham's Gold (Soderberg
  Series #3)
Ride the Laughing Wind
The Miracle
The Thanksgiving Promise
Chester, I Love You (Soderberg
  Series #2)
Double Exposure
Seeker of the Gentle Heart
The Krystal Promise
A Town Called Charity, and Other
  Stories about Decisions

The Bishop's Horse Race (Soderberg
  Series #1)
The Courage Covenant (out of print)
Windwalker (movie version—out of
  print)
The Windwalker
Others
Charlie's Monument
From First Date to Chosen Mate
Tall Timber (out of print)
Miracles and the Latter-day Teenager
  (out of print)
From Two to One
From This Day Forth (out of print)
Creating a Celestial Marriage
  (textbook—out of print)
Marriage and Family Stewardships
  (textbook—out of print)

"Gospel Power Series"

1: Binding the Lord
2: The Sword of Testimony
3: Receiving Answers to Prayer
4: How to Repent
5: Satan and His Host
6: Obtaining Priesthood Power
7: The Problem with Immorality
8: Agency, Spiritual Progression,
  and the Mighty Change
9: Seeking Wealth
10: A Gift of Dogfood
11: To Mothers, from the Book of
  Mormon
12: Cory and the Horned Toad

HERE STANDS
A MAN

BLAINE AND BRENTON YORGASON

Deseret Book Company
Salt Lake City, Utah

Library of Congress Cataloging-in-Publication Data

Yorgason, Blaine M., 1942–
    Here stands a man / by Blaine and Brenton Yorgason.
      p. cm.
    ISBN 0-87579-311-8 (hardbound)
    1. Bennett, William Hunter, 1910–   –Fiction. 2. World War,
1939–1945–Fiction. I. Yorgason, Brenton G. II. Title.
PS3575.O57H47 1990
813'.54–dc20   90-37959
                                                              CIP

Printed in the United States of America

10   9   8   7   6   5   4   3   2

For Bill and Pat Bennett—
who share an eternal love

THE SOLDIER

For my brother Bill

In the summer months
When he was just a boy,
He played war games with his brothers and friends,
Refighting history's battles with a wooden gun
And a polished branch for a bayonet.
In wintertime, with the others,
He fired bullet-hard balls
From snow forts,
Perfecting his aim,
Learning ambush and counter strategy.

A few years passed.
The boy learned about long hikes and weariness,
About survival skills,
About fair play and love of country,
About goals and commitment
In a scout troop.

Time went on.

He learned more lessons on a track field
When he matched his practiced skills,
His months of discipline and training,
And his will to win
Against the best opponents;
And he felt the heady joy of victory.

When drought and dust and economic depression,
Those giants of despair,
Held the western farmlands in their paralyzing grip,
He fought them with the zest and optimism of youth.
He toiled, he struggled, he saved, he sacrificed.
He severed the shackles that threatened his dreams,
And pushed his horizon back
Into the wide world of education and learning.

Years later when madness gripped the world
The games became real,
The foes, formidable,
The weapons, sophisticated tools of death and destruction.
It was then he learned the final lessons in soldiery
In tropical jungles.
By the things he suffered did he learn
About ambushes and counter strategy,
Of meeting cunning with cunning;
Learned to endure physical pain and deprivation,
Separation from home and those most dear,
And loneliness in the midst of raucous comrades.

In the end he knew of a surety,
Whether in a forest of camouflaged enemy,
Or on an exposed slope,
Or during the long night watches before a blood-red dawn,
All battles are fought in the heart and mind,
And the soldier who wears God's armor,
Having faith his breastplate,

And wielding the sword of the Spirit,
Fights the good fight,
And stands tall,
A man.

Lila Bennett Spencer

ACKNOWLEDGMENTS

We would like to thank Leslie and Dorothy Milam for their help with this manuscript. Lila Bennett Spencer has spent much of her life gathering and recording family records. We relied heavily on these, and we thank her for her work as well as for the introductory verse in this volume. Clifford Bennett's memoirs were invaluable, as were the memoirs of William Alvin and Mary Walker Bennett, parents of the family. We also acknowledge the incredible value of Elder William H. Bennett's personal writings.

Finally, we express deep love and appreciation to Sister Patricia Bennett, who invited us to share this journey with her, and who then shared, read, studied, compiled, worried, prayed, and, finally, joyfully, accepted. To her and to each of the Bennett children—Camille, Brad, Mary Ann, Julee, Deborah, and Jacqueline, each of whom also gave us invaluable counsel—we express deep gratitude.

INTRODUCTION

World War II, at least to the date of this writing, has been mankind's greatest cataclysm. What we did to each other is almost beyond human conception. More than fifty million people were killed. In fact, more than twice as many civilians died as did uniformed soldiers, sailors, and airmen. Young and old of all races and religions perished as innocent victims of the juggernauts of war and genocide.

Additionally, the economic cost can never be fully calculated. However, the conservative estimate of at least $2 trillion indicates the war's dimensions. There is hardly a person alive today—whatever his or her age—who has not felt the impact of the conflict. Even those who were not directly involved, including today's youngest children, have been touched by the political, economic, and social consequences of the world's first total war. However, for the 85 million men and women who served as combatants and survived, the influence of the war was direct and profound. Many were never again able to function as whole human beings. Either their bodies were torn apart and maimed, or their minds and hearts suffered similarly.

INTRODUCTION

Yet there were others, both wounded and otherwise, who seemed to grow from their experiences. These individuals became wiser, more compassionate, more understanding. Somehow they were able to pull only good things from the horror that surrounded them, and to walk away better people themselves, lifting others as they went.

The following account is based upon the handwritten journals of one such person, a remarkable young man who walked through the human devastation of war unscathed save for personal growth, and who quite unintentionally carried many others through on the strength of his faith, lifting them with him as he climbed.

PART ONE

AMBUSHED

January 1931–October 1944

THE WAR

Though the United States did not enter World War II until the Japanese bombing of Pearl Harbor on December 7, 1941, the war had already been in progress for ten full years. In 1931 Japanese militarism in Manchuria first kindled war flames, and in that same year the obscure leader of the National Socialist German Workers' (Nazi) Party, Adolf Hitler, was granted a meeting with German President Paul von Hindenburg, thus granting Hitler a measure of respectability previously denied.

Through 1932 and the initial throes of the world-wide depression, Hitler gathered power with other European nations; meanwhile, the Japanese widened their base of operations in China. By 1933, Hitler had risen to position of chancellor, and all of Germany had acceded to his dictatorial rule. That year the first of Germany's Aryan Laws were passed, making it illegal for people of Jewish descent to hold public employment. Further, Hitler announced publicly that he planned "to eradicate Christianity in Germany, root and branch."

Because Hitler's dreams and policies were also expan-

1

sionist, and because he spoke openly of taking over other lands and peoples for "the good of the Third Reich," neighboring nations grew nervous and through 1934 and 1935 frantically sought security through new alignments of power. Some, like Mussolini's Italy, aligned with Hitler, while Great Britain became the standard-bearer for those who opposed him. France for a time became a divided nation, the Vichy French going pro-Hitler and the Free French otherwise. And even Russia found herself on both sides of the mounting conflict, supporting Germany until the very moment that she found herself under attack by Hitler's forces.

Yet the United States desired to remain neutral and in 1935 passed the U.S. Neutrality Act. Roosevelt supported the act but worried that its inflexible provisions might drag the United States into the war instead of keeping her out.

In 1936 war did break out in Europe, but it remained essentially a civil conflict, confined to Spain. However, all European nations hastened to arm themselves further and to align themselves more tightly with those who seemed to hold the most power or security.

By 1937 this alignment had formed what came to be known as the Axis Powers, based upon an imaginary line between Berlin and Rome that Mussolini considered an "axis round which all European states animated by the will to collaboration and peace can also collaborate." The Axis powers were opposed by the Allied Powers, which consisted of Britain, France, the Netherlands, and numerous others.

Meanwhile, the Japanese continued to press the war in China, and for the first time they spoke publicly of turning all of the Asian and Pacific theaters into a vast Japanese empire.

In 1938 Austria and Czechoslovakia fell under the Nazi jackboot, while the Nazi party newspaper wrote: "Jews, abandon all hope! Our net is so fine that there is not a hole through which you can slip." Thus was launched an anti-Semitic

2

campaign that culminated 9 November in "The Night of Glass" or "Crystal Night," when 267 synagogues were plundered and six million marks worth of crystal windows were shattered. Also that night, 815 Jewish shops were wrecked, 36 Jews were killed, and 20,000 more were arrested.

In 1939 Hitler attacked Poland, launching World War II proper. As a preface to that attack, he said: "On the whole, there are only three great statesmen in the world; Stalin, myself and Mussolini. Stalin and myself are the only ones that see the future. So I shall shake hands with Stalin . . . and undertake with him a new distribution of the world.

"What weak Western [Europe] thinks about me, does not matter . . . thus for the time being I have sent to the East only my 'Death's Head Units,' with the order to kill without mercy all men, women and children of the Polish race and language. Only in such a way will we win the vital space that we need. . . .

"My pact with Poland was only meant to stall for a time . . . [and the same with] Russia. After Stalin's death, we shall crush the Soviet Union. . . . Our enemies are miserable worms. Be hard . . . be without mercy. The citizens of Western Europe must quiver in horror."

On September 3, 1939, Britain finally declared war on Germany, and a few days later Roosevelt proclaimed a state of limited national emergency and began building up U.S. military strength at home and abroad. However, public opinion did not turn against Germany until October 9, when Germany captured and would not release the U.S. cargo ship *City of Flint*. Shortly thereafter Congress repealed the U.S. neutrality law.

Through 1940 the Germans appeared unstoppable, invading Denmark, France, and Norway and shortly thereafter the Low Countries. When England launched a few tentative air strikes against Germany, Hitler ordered into effect Operation Sealion, which was the invasion of Britain. Beginning

3

in early September, German aircraft began bombing London; and from then until November 13, between 150 and 300 Luftwaffe bombers dropped at least 100 tons of explosives on London every night. About a million incendiary bombs fell. Yet the British rallied, and after a horrific German daylight raid on September 15 (now celebrated as Battle of Britain Day) when Royal Air Force pilots downed 60 German planes while losing only 26 of their own, the tide slowly began to turn in favor of the British.

In October, however, Hitler, still confident of absolute Nazi victory, proposed that Russia and Japan join with Italy and Germany in a virtual division of the world. Russia and Japan were agreeable, and at least the Russians met secretly with Germany to plan the division.

In January of 1941, U.S. Ambassador Grew, United States Ambassador to Japan, first advised Washington that reports were circulating in Japan of an impending attack on Pearl Harbor. Yet the reports were labeled "too fantastic," by both himself and Congress, and nothing was done to prepare.

In April, Hitler met with the Japanese and advised them: "England has already lost the war. It is only a matter of having the intelligence to admit it." He then encouraged Japan to go to war with Britain and the U.S., promising German support should they do so.

In May, Roosevelt proclaimed an unlimited national emergency, stating: "What started as a European war has developed, as the Nazis always intended it should develop, into a world war for world domination. . . . The war is approaching the brink of the Western hemisphere itself. It is coming very close to home."

And then in June, Hitler launched the greatest military attack in history, hurling more than 3 million troops, 600,000 vehicles, 750,000 horses, 3,580 tanks and 1,830 planes against the Russians along an 1,800-mile front that extended from the Arctic to the Black Sea.

At the same time, Hermann Goering, president of the German Reichstag, issued the first known written order for the elimination of the Jews living under Nazi rule. Ultimately, of 8,851,800 Jews living under German rule, 5,933,900, or 66 percent, would be put to death by the Nazis.

Taking advantage of the almost global confusion, the Japanese military began expanding southwest into the Pacific, and so Roosevelt returned General Douglas MacArthur to active duty and nationalized the armed forces of the Philippines.

Yet not all the Japanese wanted war with the United States. In September, Emperor Hirohito was told by certain of his government ministers that a war with the U.S. could not possibly be won. But it was hoped that England's hoped-for surrender and Japanese successes in the Pacific would influence American public opinion and draw the war to a close. So the decision was made to go ahead.

In November, Ambassador Grew again sent a cable from Tokyo, warning Washington that Japan was doing more than saber rattling, and to be prepared for all-out war. Worried, Congress voted to stay in session, and U.S. Navy commanders were warned to be ready to expect an attack either on the Philippines or on Guam. Hawaii's Pearl Harbor still seemed too fantastic to consider, and so it wasn't.

On December 6, 1941, Roosevelt approved research funds for an atomic bomb, and a day later, in a daring daylight attack on Pearl Harbor, Japan forced America to enter the war, making it truly a global conflict.

Through 1942, the Allies, with America now pouring in millions of men and dollars, held their own in Europe and very nearly halted the Axis Powers in Africa. But in Asia and the Pacific, the Nipponese ruled, overrunning the Philippines, orchestrating the infamous Bataan Death March, eliminating the Allied combatants on Corregidor, and taking Singapore and the Dutch East Indies. But they also experienced losses, in the Battle of the Coral Sea and the Battle of Midway, which became a turning point in the war in the Pacific as Admiral Chester Nimitz, using cracked enemy codes, turned the attack back upon the Japanese.

By August 1942, MacArthur's promise to the Filipinos, "I shall return," was being fulfilled as a U.S. force of 11,000 men invaded Guadalcanal and the Solomon Islands. But the Japanese resistance was terrific, lasting better than six months on Guadalcanal alone. By December 9, 40,000 American troops, including a crack unit called Carlson's Raiders, were raising havoc among their 25,000 Japanese enemies. On December 31, the Japanese, shocked at their own incredible losses and that the Americans could be as adept at jungle warfare as themselves, determined to evacuate Guadalcanal and establish a new defense line in New Georgia.

Still, the war in Europe continued unabated. Hitler was lashing out on all western fronts; Russia had finally aligned with the Allies and with Allied help was holding the Germans out of Moscow; the Finns were dealing with startling strength against a surprise Russian invasion; Rommel's activities in Africa were at a standstill; and Italy was reeling under increased Allied pressure.

The United Nations announced to a world-wide audience that crimes against the Jews would be avenged.

And it was also in 1942, on September 9, that the only air attack against the continental United States occurred. On that date, a Japanese submarine-based plane dropped incendiary bombs in a forest near Brookings, Oregon. A small fire was the only damage, and the plane escaped.

The year 1943, horrendous in terms of human loss, nevertheless saw the Allied forces on all fronts turn the tide of battle. Italy, invaded by the Allies, capitulated after 32,000 German and 131,900 Italian casualties on Sicily alone, not to mention casualties north into Italy itself, and switched sides.

However, German troops in Italy continued their fierce resistance.

Montgomery's forces, after see-sawing back and forth for years, finally took control of North Africa. Allied bombing of Hamburg killed 41,800 and wounded another 37,439, while destruction of property was beyond comprehension. The German offensive in Russia was stopped cold at the Battle of Kursk (which became the greatest land battle in history, and which saw 25,000 German soldiers killed in a two-month period), after which the Russians began their rapid sweep back to the west. And in the Pacific, American forces fought their way across the Gilbert Islands, clearing the way for a hoped-for American invasion of Japan.

Finally, U.S. Army Air Force pilot Capt. Fred M. Smith sent this alliteratively imaginative report after sinking a Japanese destroyer-mine sweeper with his P-38 during the Aleutians campaign: SAW STEAMER, STRAFED SAME, SANK SAME, SOME SIGHT, SIGNED SMITH.

Through 1944 the Allied offensive continued, both on the continent and in the Pacific. In January, 37,000 British and American troops stormed onto the beach at Anzio in Italy, where they began pushing relentlessly toward the German Gustav Line. German resistance was terrific, and it would take them until May 13 to breach the line. On that day, French Colonial troops would finally push through in the Abruzzi Mountains. The Poles alone, in the two-week battle for Monte Cassino, lost 1,200 dead and 2,500 wounded. At their cemetery is the following epitaph:

> We Polish soldiers
> For our freedom and yours
> Have given our souls to God
> Our bodies to the soil of Italy
> And our hearts to Poland.

Late in May, the first of 380,000 Hungarian Jews were deported to the concentration camp at Auschwitz. More than 250,000 of them would be gassed there. Also, in one of the most savage actions of the war, a company of the SS *Das Reich* Division killed all the inhabitants of the French village of Oradour-sur-Glane. About 600 people, including women and children, were executed on the spot or burned alive in the village church because the SS had been unable to find one of its commanders who had been kidnapped by the French Marquis.

In June, Germany began launching V-1 rocket bombs against England. Eight thousand were fired at England, with 2,300 hitting London. These "buzz bombs," named for the noise they made during their terrifying descent, had a profound psychological effect upon the civilian population. The V-1, 25 feet long and carrying a one-ton warhead, killed 5,479 British, wounded 15,934, and destroyed or damaged 1,104,000 houses, 149 schools, 11 churches, and 95 hospitals.

On June 6, D-Day, General Dwight D. Eisenhower led more American and British troops across the English Channel and onto the beaches at Normandy. In the greatest amphibious operation in history, the Allies, under Churchill, Roosevelt, and DeGaul, put ashore 176,000 men from 4,000 ships. These men were aided by 9,500 aircraft and 600 warships, and by nightfall they had established beachheads on Utah, Omaha, Gold, Juno, and Sword beaches. While Russia pressed in from the east with 555 divisions, the Allies marched from the west across France toward them, and more and more Hitler began to feel the pressures that would build toward final defeat. Ninety days later, the Allies had landed 2,086,000 men in France, as well as 3,446,000 tons of goods to support them, and had liberated nearly the entire country.

German losses were staggering. In the three months after D-Day, 1,200,000 German soldiers died. Fifty divisions were destroyed in the east, 28 in the west. In addition, 230,000

German troops were surrounded in pockets in France, and most of these ultimately surrendered.

Meanwhile in the Pacific, MacArthur convinced Roosevelt that it would be wiser to honor his promise of returning by first invading the Philippines before moving on to Formosa. Advancing that plan, he landed troops in New Guinea, Kwajalein, the Marshall Islands, the Admiralty Islands, the Solomon Islands, New Britain, and Saipan in the Marianas.

On July 9, Saipan's last Japanese defenses fell as U.S. Forces secured the island. U.S. casualties were 3,674 Army and 10,437 Marines (including 3,126 dead), but the Japanese garrison of almost 27,000 was eliminated.

From there, invasions were staged on Guam and Tinian Islands, and then on Peleliu Island in the Palau group, where progress was measured in yards as the Japanese hid in caves and pillboxes and fought suicidally for an entire month. Finally invasions were launched on Okinawa in the Ryukyus and Morotai Island, just off Halamahera in the Moluccas.

THE MAN

William Hunter Bennett, known as "Ben" throughout his military experience, was born in Taber, Alberta, Canada, on November 5, 1910. Baptized a member of The Church of Jesus Christ of Latter-day Saints at age eight, he grew up in a home where the Church was important, and so throughout his life he also considered it a pearl of great price. Educated in Canada at the Raymond School of Agriculture, he came to Utah in 1932 and attended Utah State Agricultural College. He graduated in 1936 with a degree in agronomy, soon thereafter entered graduate studies, and in 1938 was elected to membership in both Sigma Chi and Phi Kappa Phi.

A proficient amateur athlete, Ben competed in numerous track and field meets, in Canada and also at Utah State. Winning numerous ribbons, medals, plates, and trophies in the shot put, discus, and javelin throwing, he lettered twice at

9

Utah State, set a conference record in the shot, set numerous Canadian records in the shot and discus, and won gold medals in both the shot and the discus in the Canadian Olympic Trials in 1936.

In 1938, while he served as assistant county agent for Salt Lake County, Ben obtained his master of science degree in agronomy, again from Utah State. A week later, he was appointed as county agricultural agent for Carbon County, Utah.

For the next four years, Ben lived in Price, Utah, where he instituted the 4–H programs in the county and worked tirelessly to improve agricultural conditions and understanding for the citizens of Carbon County.

In 1940, though still a citizen of Canada, Ben was required to register with the Selective Service for the draft. On May 4, 1942, he was ordered to report for induction into the Armed Forces, but that call was deferred for one month, giving him time to apply for citizenship. He did so immediately, and on May 15, 1942, he became a naturalized citizen of the United States of America.

Inducted at Fort Douglas on June 5, 1942, Ben was almost immediately made a corporal and given leadership responsibilities. Soon he was a Tech 4, and in December he was accepted for Officers Candidate School at Fort Benning, Georgia. Graduating as a 2nd lieutenant in April, Ben was assigned as a platoon leader in "E" Company of the 31st Infantry Division and within hours was on his way to Camp Shelby, where he became involved in extensive training for overseas jungle warfare.

By the end of May, he had become supply officer for all of "E" Company, and for the entire balance of the summer he was involved in tactical training maneuvers in central Louisiana and eastern Texas. That summer he also discovered that another Mormon was in his company, a sergeant named Leslie Milam, from Natchitoches, Louisiana. The two quickly became fast friends, and Ben visited Leslie Milam's home during a leave in August of 1943.

Ben wrote: "About 10 pm I went to the Milam home and visited with the family until midnight. I was very much impressed with Sergeant Milam's blind brother Vernon. He read to me in braille, played some of his symphony records for me, then played the piano and talked with me on various subjects. I was thrilled with his cheerful, pleasant, wholesome outlook on life, and really felt like thanking God for my opportunities and blessings. It was a delightful evening, and it so happened that the entire Milam family was together for the first time in years. There were Mrs. Milam, Brother Milam, Noble, Leslie, and Vernon, and Veonca the charming sister. I stayed with the family for the night and slept with Noble on a feather-like spring mattress (the first time for ages). Noble is a Lieutenant in the Navy. About midnight I bathed, shaved and retired."

In September the 31st Infantry Division was moved to Virginia, and Ben was promoted to first lieutenant. In Virginia there was more training, and that continued until January 8, 1944, when he and the others were loaded aboard ship (the *Cape Neddick*) and the journey to the South Pacific began.

Traveling through the Panama Canal, the ship struck out across the Pacific, and Ben, overwhelmed at the vast expanse of ocean, penned the following: "Anyone who has sailed o'er the broad expanse of the Pacific Ocean for days and days — for weeks and weeks — without sighting land, cannot help but feel impressed with the thought that all the military might of all the warring nations in the world today — Germany, Russia, Italy, Great Britain, Japan and the United States — with all their allies and associates — all their ships, planes, tanks, guns and ammunition — singly or collectively, could be sunk in the waters of this mighty ocean, without so much as raising its level *one single inch* — without so much as affecting in the least, the play of the tides upon its surface."

11

On February 21, 1944, Ben reached Goodenough Island and with others established a bivouac area eighteen miles inland. For a month, Ben and the others participated in more training, and then they were all shipped out to Oro Bay, New Guinea, where Ben and "E" Company would experience their first combat with the Japanese.

From April through the first part of September, he and his men patrolled the Aitape area of New Guinea, following the treacherous rivers, scaling the incredibly steep mountains, and slogging through the bottomless swamps, ever in search of their dangerous enemy. Occasionally the Japanese were encountered and firefights ensued, but by-and-large the experience of Ben and his company in New Guinea was one of sheer hard work and drudgery—mud, insects, and exhaustion being the lot of every man there.

On September 10, the men boarded ship once again, and off and on during the next five days, Ben penned the following:

"Archibald F. Bennett

"Salt Lake City, Utah

"Dear Uncle Archie:

"It has been almost eight months since we left the shores of the United States. It was also on a Sunday, as is today. What a long eight months it has been. What will the next eight months bring? For the first time I have seen death in war, and it is very sobering to me. I hope and pray that it is the will of God that my life and health might be preserved so I can at the end of that time send you another report. How wonderful it would be if that letter could be written in peace!

"Even though we are on ship we had a grand L.D.S. meeting this morning. We sang 'Come, Come Ye Saints,' Bro. Leslie Milam offered prayer, we sang, 'Jesus, Once of Humble Birth,' I gave a scriptural reading from 1st Cor. 2:16–21, Bro. Caulder and Bro. Milam administered the Sacrament, Bro. Lindsay gave a talk on administering to the sick and wounded, and Elder Caulder bore his testimony and talked on the healing of the sick. Bro. Cragun, the mail clerk for 'F' Co., offered the benediction. It was a grand spiritual occasion. I also read "Voice of Warning" by Parley P. Pratt last night. It is a wonderful presentation, and gives the gospel picture so clear that one's testimony of its truthfulness is greatly strengthened.

"Uncle Archie, the Church is growing rapidly in importance in my mind as I become more involved in the war. The nervous strain on a man at night as he sits in his foxhole in a battalion perimeter is terrific. The long tropical nights, with their weird noises and sounds, can almost make a man's heart stand on end. Add to that the danger of a Jap creeping up on you, and you have an ideal stage set for a nervous breakdown. What a horrible thing is war!

"I do not desire to shed the blood of my fellowmen, Uncle Archie, no matter who they might be. But if God so wills that I do more active fighting, it is my duty to fight and I hope that I can discharge my duty as befits a man and a Latter-day Saint. It is my constant prayer that my life and health be preserved, that I be protected from harm, danger, evil, sickness and disease. But God's will be done, not mine.

"However, as you predicted in the Priesthood blessing you gave me on the occasion of our last visit, the promises of the Word of Wisdom are becoming daily more important to me. How thankful I am that I have refrained from such things as coffee, tobacco, alcohol and other things that are harmful to my body. Not only is my body stronger for it, but even more importantly, the Lord is pleased with me, and because of my obedience He is more able to bless me. Truly am I learning to lean upon those promised blessings.

"But I have had one very unusual experience, Uncle Archie, at least for a Mormon boy who has such a strong feeling about the necessity of living the Word of Wisdom. Let me tell you about it.

"On the morning of July 30th, we boarded trucks and

proceeded to the vicinity of the Driniumor River where we established a battalion perimeter on the beach. The field order stated that a coordinated attack would be launched across the Driniumor River at 0800 the next morning. Four Battalions were to participate in the attack, with the 2nd Bn. [battalion] of the 124th Inf. Regt. on the left next to the beach, the 1st Bn. (124th) on the right, and the 2nd Bn. (169th Inf.) in reserve, and following our 3rd Bn. A 700 yard gap would be between the 2nd and 1st Bns. Our objective was Numen Creek, about 1 1/2 miles east of the Driniumor River. In the 2nd Bn. zone, 'E' Co. was to be on the left next to the beach, 'F' Co. on the right, and 'G' Co. in reserve and following 'F' Co.

"My first platoon was assigned to lead 'E' Co. and to have responsibility for the left sector. Three LCM gun boats armed with rocket guns and 50 cal. machine guns, and four tank destroyers, were to support the attack. I had a patrol operate just outside the woods so that the position of the front-line troops would be indicated at all times. We crossed the Driniumor River st exactly 0800. Tow guides from the 32nd Division pointed out the trail to us on the other side of the river, after which we were entirely on our own. As we crossed the river we passed within a few feet of the body of a Jap major who had been shot the night before. It was my first view of a dead Jap, and it gave me a strange feeling. We proceeded very cautiously, my two scouts and squad leader from the first squad proceeding me. We carefully searched every tree, crevice, and depression for snipers, and proceeded very slowly.

"We encountered no enemy until we reached our objective, the Numen Creek, when all at once a shot rang out. It came from Sgt. Tommy Dabbs' rifle. Investigating I found that he had looked directly into the eyes of a Japanese sniper who was hiding in a well concealed position, and had shot the Jap before he could shoot him. Grenades were thrown and a BAR and heavy machine gun opened up. We immediately commenced setting up a defensive line along Numen Creek. 'F' and 'G' Cos. soon put in an appearance. They had tougher terrain to go over than we did, and the 1st and 3rd Bns. had hit more enemy resistance.

"We worked on our defensive positions for several days, and a number of patrols were sent out. I was assigned on the night of August 2nd to go on a special patrol up the beach to Yakamul. I was to be in complete charge of the patrol which would have two gun boats, 4 tank destroyers and a 284 radio assigned to it. It looked to be a dangerous mission, but about 7 P.M. word came down that the patrol was called off until further orders.

"A change in plans had been made, and we were to go into an attack, into the jungles and mountains after the enemy. On the afternoon of the 3rd we moved out in a south direction. 'G' Co. was leading the battalion and killed about 15 Japs as we proceeded up the trail. 'H' Co. was ambushed as it crossed the creek, and killed four Japs without losing a man.

"A very foolish thing took place on this march. We had been taught from the beginning that no Allied movement should take place after dark, but we made a night march into enemy territory. To make matters worse, the head of the column moved too fast and lost the trail. 'E' Co. was bringing up the rear and as we crossed the creek we lost the 3rd and part of the 4th platoons. They did the only wise thing for them to do—go into a perimeter for the night and proceed back to the beach the next day and reestablish radio contact. They did so, and on their way back they killed one Jap and captured two more.

"The rest of us proceeded on and went into a perimeter for the night with the 3rd Bn. arriving there about 9 P.M. The next morning we moved out at 0800 with the 3rd leading. They hit a lot of sniper activity and there were quite a few casualties.

"My platoon and part of the 2nd (50 men) were delegated to carry casualties back to the aid station. We did this. There were eight litter cases and the trail was very muddy. One man weighed 250 pounds and only four men could carry him at a time. It was exhausting work.

"We failed to arrive at our destination before dark, and it was necessary to send a scout on ahead to advise them that we were coming and that we needed relief. By full dark no relief had arrived, but we dare not stop with our litters of wounded men. Carefully we moved forward, and relief came just as we reached the river. I was informed that our scout had only just arrived at the Bn. aid station, stopping plans to drop mortars and artillery fire in our general area. The relief party further instructed us on how to identify ourselves in the dark as we crossed the river.

"Accordingly I gave orders (and this I find humorous, coming from a Mormon such as myself), and told all the men to light up their cigarettes so that the sentries could see the line of red glowing embers as we crossed the river. That was to be our signal. My men did as directed, and a little later we reached the aid station in safety—because I had ordered my men to smoke! Please rest assured that I do not intend to ever issue such an order again.

"I could write of many more harrowing experiences in New Guinea, Uncle Archie, but as you have also seen war first-hand, I will not do so. But please know that I am very thankful to my Heavenly Father for his guidance and care. He has answered my prayers and the prayers of my loved ones, and I am very thankful for this. As you know, it is hard to describe one's feelings on the battlefield, especially when one is up front on the point in enemy territory, for you never know which tree, bush or rock may be hiding a Jap. I have no desire to shed the blood of my enemy, the Japanese, but in time of war it may become one's duty to do so.

"Now we are off to a new destination—I know not where.

But I do know that I will continue to live the Word of Wisdom. Thus I will be worthy of the divine protection afforded me thus far."

On September 15, Ben and the other men of "E" Company participated in the amphibious assault on White Beach, Morotai Island, the Halamaheras.

SWPA Maptalk, for September 23, 1944, states: "The area U.S. troops have inhabited, the southwest coast, is the only large plateau on the island and the only region of military importance.

"It was here in an area known as Doroeba that the Japs had started the Pitoe airstrip, but abandoned it because they couldn't solve the drainage problem. The terrain, however, presents no problem that Yankee know-how and modern machinery can't solve. Probably by the time you read this, General Kenney's bombers will be taking off for raids on Davao, 395 miles to the north.

"Morotai is about 40 miles long and 30 miles wide, and is 90 percent mountainous. The interior is completely so. Two main ranges trending from southwest to northeast form the backbone. Separated by a depression and covered in thick virgin rain forest, one range rises to a height of 4,100 feet and the other to 3,000 feet. Spurs from the mountains extend all the way to the coast, and the terrain is steep and difficult.

"Morotai is only two degrees above the equator and has the humid climate to be expected. It is no more unhealthful than any other island Allied forces have occupied, however, and considerably more healthful than some. Tropical ulcers are common and leprosy is occasional among the natives (a simple and primitive people who have been left in a destitute condition by the Japanese), but there's no reason to expect our men to catch either."

It is on Morotai Island, on October 10, 1944, that we take up our story.

CHAPTER

ONE

It was hot, hot and humid! Inhaling deeply, Lieutenant William "Ben" Bennett wiped the perspiration from his forehead and peered into the jungle. He was a big man, six feet one inch in his socks, 180 pounds, and with shoulders as broad (his brothers had always said) as the handle of an axe. Yet in the waist and hips he was lean and trim, and he had the legs and feet of the true athlete.

In the distance a bojong bird sounded, and then the only noises he could hear were the insects. These hummed and chirped and buzzed and clacked, near and far, creating an endless cacophony that somehow over time blended into the background until it became, at least for him, no noise at all.

Unless it stopped. Then, when something disturbed the insects and they grew still, the silence became deafening, and Ben and the other men of his patrol knew that danger lurked nearby.

But now the noisesome hum continued unrelentingly, so Ben allowed his mind to consider more where he should lead the troops than he did the possibility of an enemy ambush.

Unconsciously he pulled at the sweaty, clammy clothes that clung to him, and then he wiped again with the back of his arm at the salt sting of sweat in his startlingly blue-green eyes. It was October 10, 1944, the season of spring on Morotai Island, though truthfully it felt more like midsummer than it did spring.

Glancing at the map in his hand, he noted without seeing that Morotai was part of the Moluccas chain of islands, just off Halamahera in the South Pacific. A beachhead had been established on Morotai on September 15, 1944, by the 31st Infantry Division, part of General Douglas MacArthur's campaign to return to the Philippines. And now Ben's patrol, part of "E" Company, was doing outpost duty and patrolling up the Sambiki and Asangoiviki Rivers, doing their best to protect the radar station at Poesi-Poesi from attack by the Japanese.

Their objective today, a hill called 745 — 1,800 incredibly difficult yards of tortuous terrain from the station and a reported location for an enemy supply dump. Three days earlier, he and his patrol had discovered another dump near hill 745, unknown to the natives, who had been allowed to loot it of rice, canned rations, and munitions before it had been destroyed.

His platoon had been commended for that, as well as for the pack of maps and orders they had captured from the enemy. But now they had this next supply dump to locate, loot, and destroy, and so Lieutenant Bennett examined his map carefully, pinpointing exactly where he was and where he wanted to take his men in the next few moments.

"What do you think, Lieutenant?"

Ben turned at the soft, drawling voice and for a moment regarded his tall, skinny acting platoon sergeant, Tom Dabbs. "I don't know, Dabbs. How about you?"

"I don't like it, Lieutenant. I got me a bad feeling, like something's coming that's big and awful, something I can't stop."

Ben grinned. "You did all right with that Jap sniper two days ago, Sergeant."

"Luck, Lieutenant, and you know it. Just like it was luck that he was carrying those papers we captured."

Ben looked back at the surrounding jungle. "Maybe, Dabbs, but to tell the truth I don't think so. I think the Lord is protecting us."

Sergeant Dabbs gave Ben a quizzical look, then pulled free a long stem of grass and began chewing on it. "You really believe that?"

"I do."

"Wish I did. Trouble is, I've seen a few people die, good people, and I just don't think the Lord cares which Jap bullets hit which American soldiers."

"*You* haven't died, have you?" Ben asked quietly.

"Not yet, Lieutenant, but like I say, I have me a bad feeling about today . . . "

Ben adjusted his M-1 on his shoulder and hitched up his pack. Then he looked keenly into the eyes of the gentle but battle-toughened sergeant. "Dabbs," he spoke quietly, "the Lord knows we're here, and He knows that we wouldn't be here fighting the Nipponese if we had a choice. So I have the assurance that He is watching over us. So does Sergeant Milam, by the way. Now, I have prayed earnestly for protection, not only for myself but for all the men I have been assigned to lead, and I've been given a feeling of peace. We'll be all right. Leslie Milam feels the same — told me so just this morning."

Sergeant Dabbs shook his head. "You're a wonder, Lieutenant. So's Milam. You guys of the same faith?"

Ben grinned. "We're both Mormons, if that's what you mean. However, I suspect that Les has more faith than I do."

"Well," Dabbs said, shaking his head, "you couldn't prove it by me." Dabbs then swung his arm in a wide arc. "Where to from here?"

Ben looked across the Little Mira River at the steep and heavily wooded terrain that climbed steadily upward in sharp ridges and jagged gashes of ravines. "There," he said, pointing, "is hill number 745. After we cross the river and get up the bank, I think we should follow up that long ridge. But first I want to check with Lieutenant Kempainen—"

"No need to, Ben."

Spinning in surprise, Ben and Sergeant Dabbs stared at the other officer, who was weapons platoon leader. "For a northern boy, Lieutenant," Dabbs drawled in admiration, "you sure do move quiet."

"My dad took me hunting a lot," Kempainen replied.

"It shows. We get home, you'll do to take out running a few coons."

Kempainen nodded. "Sounds good to me, *if* we get home."

"We will," Dabbs replied, grinning mischievously. "Lieutenant Bennett here says he has prayed us all to safety. Now if we can just get the Japs to go along with that there prayer . . ."

"You've prayed for us, Ben? Seriously?"

Ben nodded without speaking.

"Well, I'll be. Milam told me after that skirmish with the Japs the other day that he had been prayed over and promised he would come home safely. He isn't worried, not even a little bit. Is that what you did?"

"Not exactly," Ben replied. "Leslie got what we call a blessing, a patriarchal blessing from a priesthood leader back home. In it he was promised—"

"What's this . . . this patri . . . "

"A patriarchal blessing, Dabbs, like Abraham gave to Issac, or Isaac gave to Jacob. More or less, it is a personal message to someone from God, delivered through a worthy man who is called a patriarch."

21

"Lawsy," Sergeant Dabbs breathed. "Imagine hearing personally from God."

"And you believe that?" Lieutenant Kempainen asked incredulously.

"Les does," Ben replied. "That's why he isn't worried. He has faith, and a prophetic blessing or promise upon which to base that faith. That's why the Lord grants such things as patriarchal blessings."

"What about you, Lieutenant? Do you have one of those blessing things?"

"I do."

"Were you promised that you would come home safely?" Ben shook his head. "No, I didn't get a promise like that."

"Too bad," Dabbs said sincerely.

"I'll say," Kempainen agreed, grinning. "I don't know if we should follow *you* anymore or not."

Ben grinned back. "Maybe you shouldn't. But on the other hand, I was promised some things that haven't occurred yet, so I believe I will be going home so they can happen later. Besides, I do have a separate promise of safety that the Lord made me, a promise that He also made to anyone else who wants to have it. Its found in the 89th section of a book of scripture we Mormons call the Doctrine and Covenants. Based on that, I'm sure I'll be taken care of. Now, shall we get across the river and see what's on that hill over there?"

"You aren't going to tell us what that other promise says?" Kempainen groused half teasingly.

Stepping forward toward the river, Ben answered back over his shoulder, "Not now, not until you are both sure you really want to hear it. Now, jack up the men and let's move it out."

With a look that showed at least as much admiration as it did confusion, Dabbs nodded at Lieutenant Kempainen and then signaled up the men. With sighs and groans and mumbled oaths they stood, four squads of infantry and one 60 mm. mortar squad, the latter headed by Sergeant Leslie Milam, the only other Mormon, besides Ben, in the entire outfit.

Silently the men of "E" Company moved down through the thick foliage toward the river, the nettles and grasses of the underbrush lashing the blood to the surface of their arms and legs. Quickly spreading out and positioning themselves on the bank, they covered each other in a single-file advance across the river, a maneuver they performed to perfection.

Ben, who was leading behind Private Haines, his Nica interpreter, found himself noting the men's proficiency and then forgetting it almost instantly as he sighed with the blessed cool feeling of water breaking through his shoes, running fast and tickling like cool little mouse paws all over his feet. It was hot, too hot, and he doubted that a Canadian boy like himself would ever get used to such ridiculous temperatures and humidity.

Thinking of it, though, put him in mind of the endless days he and his older brother Cliff had spent with their father out on the dryland. He had been thirteen then and had driven six horses pulling a two-bottom plow, while Cliff had driven eight horses pulling a three-bottom. The dust and heat had seemed unbearable, and he had persevered only because he had been able to think of no other alternative, and because he couldn't let Cliff call him a quitter.

Now it was the same. The situation was horrid and impossible, but he could think of no other alternative, and the men all looked to him for leadership. Therefore he kept on, one exhausting step after another —

Coming out of the water, the men ran at the hill, scrambling up, and Ben watched with admiration. Truly these were good men: Garic from New Orleans, the lead scout; Milam, who was also from Louisiana and who was the epitome of a true southern gentleman; Tom Dabbs from Alabama, as were Timmerman and Thrasher; Green, who was another scout

23

from West Virginia; Grisson from Texas; Fulton and Harmon from Virginia; Pitre and Tiffin from Mississippi; Handshaw and Garvilla from New York; Weiner, who was a volunteer from battalion headquarters and who had seen action in Spain fighting as a loyalist against Franco; and of course Lieutenant Kempainen, who hailed from Minnesota, nearly as far north as Ben's own home in Taber, Alberta, Canada.

Then there were the others, fifty or so, most from the southern United States where the unit had originally been formed, and every man of them was a fighter.

Ben enjoyed watching them, listening to them, working beside them, pitting his strength against theirs. And because he was so much older than most of them, in most ways he enjoyed leading them. But the responsibility for their welfare and safety was heavy, for with the slightest mishap they could all be faced with disaster. Of course, that was the way of war, but it didn't make it any easier . . .

Ben's reverie was cut short by the loud, angry snap of a fired gun. Looking up the steep slope past the other men who were already on their faces in the grass, he saw that the culprit was Garic, his lead scout. Garic was shaking his head in consternation, for it had been accidental. But as Ben scrambled up the hill toward him, he knew that wasn't a good enough excuse.

"Well, Garic," he questioned as he got close, "do you want to tell me what happened?"

"It was an accident, Lieutenant," the man replied softly, plaintively.

"I assumed as much. But we can't afford such accidents, and you know it."

"But sir, these tommy guns—"

"That's enough, Garic! I know about tommy guns, and I also know that you have been well trained in handling them properly. But you were careless, and now that carelessness has very likely alerted the Japs to our presence and location."

"Yes, sir."

"Are you prepared to bear the responsibility for what the enemy may do to us?"

In anguish the man looked at his comrades, who were now on their feet, listening quietly. "N-No, sir," he finally faltered as he looked away.

"But you will," Ben said flatly. "Should we lose any of these men, your conscience will see to that."

"Yes, sir."

"You know," Ben went on, "your carelessness reminds me of a horse named Butte that my father used to have. She was a lazy cuss, Garic, but she was also careless, and that carelessness laid me up for an entire summer. Because of her carelessness, that horse had to be shot, Garic. She just wasn't worth keeping around any longer."

"I . . . I get the picture, Lieutenant."

"Good. Now lead out, and let's carry this war to the real enemy rather than to ourselves."

Eagerly Garic saluted, turned, and started up the slope, and with even greater caution than before, Ben and the others followed.

"You going to bust him?" Kempainen asked as they stood together a little later at the top of the steep river bank. "I'd say that sort of prank deserves it."

"No," Ben said as he gazed up the ridge that loomed ahead of them. "I reprimanded him fairly severely, and that should be enough. Besides, he's a good scout, and this is his first mistake."

"Well, I hope you won't regret it, Ben."

"I hope so, too. But I'll take a lesson from my father and let it go this time with a scolding."

"You place a lot of faith in your father, don't you."

Ben nodded. "I do. He wasn't highly educated, but I have come to understand that he was amazingly wise. He seemed to know how to get more out of his children, day to day and year to year, than most other parents ever could. It was the same with his hired hands. He was a true leader, quiet but always out in front. So, it just seems smart to take a few pages out of his book of life and apply them here."

"Like with Garic?"

"That's right."

"What'll you do if he blows it again?"

Ben scowled. "After working with the horses in the fields all morning, Kemp, my father used to bring them in at noon for a drink and some feed. We had a water tank on wheels, and he would turn the water from it into a half barrel on the ground. Since the water had to be hauled a long distance, any water left in the barrel would be held until the next watering.

"My brother Cliff and I were quite young, but we liked to play in the water left in the barrel. Of course, if we had fallen in, we could have drowned. But we didn't think of that. Father did, though, and told us to keep away from it.

"One day, however, he came in for lunch and there we were, playing in the water barrel. He didn't say a word, just walked over and picked us up and, one at a time, gave us a head-first ducking in the barrel, holding us under until we knew we were there. We didn't play in the barrel again."

Kemp nodded. "So his rule was to give a fair warning and then lower the boom?"

"I couldn't have said it better," Ben replied, grinning. "Garic will be handled the same way. Now take a look up there, Kemp. That's the same trail we were following day before yesterday when we found that other dump. If you were the enemy, wouldn't you expect that we would follow it again, since we had such great success with it the first time?"

Kempainen studied the hill thoughtfully. "Probably," he finally replied. "Especially since Garic's round let them know we were back in the area."

26

"Amen," Ben said as he readjusted his pack. "So let's make the best of a bad situation and see if we can fool the Nips. Instead of following up the trail, we'll make a sweep to the right, wide out, and see if we can flank them."

"That's thick jungle, Ben."

"We've been through worse, and I think the extra effort will be worthwhile. Dabbs, deploy the men, and we'll make a wide sweep to the right of that trail. A hundred yards maximum. And tell them to be careful."

Dabbs grinned as he lifted his lazy salute. "No need to worry on that count, sir. These boys are nervouser'n foxes in a hen house with the farmer coming through the door. They'll go quiet."

And they did, silently filtering through the dense growth as they crawled and dug and pulled their way up the side of the ridge. Sweat built on their bodies and rolled down their spines in sticky rivulets; sweat stung their eyes and burned the myriads of lacerations that the sharp-edged grass had inflicted on their arms and legs; and sweat matted their hair under their helmets and caps until it nearly drove them crazy with its itching. Yet still they pressed forward, two or three yards of effort, a pause for gasping breath, then two or three more yards of lung-burning climbing.

But besides the torturous climbing, always there was the threat of the enemy. Snipers hid in the trees and in the shallow foxholes that the men called spider boxes, unseen until they chose to open fire. And the jungle growth was so thick that squads and entire patrols of the Nipponese could be ready for a full-scale attack and remain undetected. So the men went carefully, not only watching where they were placing their feet but also watching the trees above them, the growth around them, and the very ground beneath them where spider boxes might be concealed.

Suddenly the sound of a bird's whistle pierced the humid air. Lifting his head in recognition of a signal he had taught his men, Ben pursed his lips and replied in kind, his expert whistling so real that often it seemed that even the birds were fooled. Then he listened as two more notes rang out, the signal that he was needed up with the scouts. So quickly he moved forward.

"Hey, Lieutenant!" Garic whispered urgently as Ben drew nearer.

Y-Yes," Ben panted as he paused beside his scout, stooping over for a moment with his hands on his knees to get his breath.

"Lieutenant, the other side of them bushes the trail makes a split. The fork to the left goes down into that ravine yonder. The right fork ambles up that narrow ridge and looks like it might take us to our objective. What you want we should do?"

Carefully Ben considered the two alternatives. This was the hardest part of leadership, the making of decisions that would affect the very lives of others. Yet all his life he had been forced to make decisions, from the farm in Taber where his father had entrusted him with a man's work and responsibility from age ten or eleven onward, to school at Utah State where he had not only put himself through but participated in athletics and club activities and leadership, to his work as county agent in Price, Utah, where he had organized the entire 4–H program in the county. Always he had carried responsibility, and with rare exceptions he had carried it well. But now, with the lives of nearly a hundred men hinging upon his decisions . . .

There was also the feeling that Tom Dabbs had mentioned, the sense that something was out there waiting to happen, some huge, awful thing he was powerless to stop. Ben felt it too, though he hadn't wanted to frighten Dabbs by saying so. But with real anxiety he strained his eyes, trying to see through the jungle, trying to understand what had become so troubling to his spirit.

Mercilessly the sun beat down upon him, turning his helmet hot as a stoveplate. Wiping his forehead, Ben listened to the insects but could detect no change in their humming and buzzing. Nor could he see anything out of sorts, any indication the enemy might be near.

"Dabbs," he called back softly to his sergeant, "call a ten-minute halt. Tell the men to relax but not to get careless. I want to study this out."

"Yes, sir," Dabbs agreed.

Nodding approval at the position Garic had chosen, where he could both rest and guard up-trail, Ben moved up the hill a few feet and took a position in the shade of a large tree. Sitting down, however, his movements accidentally rustled the papers in another pocket, and his mind went instantly to the letter he carried there.

A letter, a woman, and, because of two radically different approaches to life, a love that now seemed irrevocably over. That's what was actually in his pocket. Ben had always wondered if things might not change after he returned home. But now, for the first time since he had received his draft notice, he found himself wondering if he might not get back at all. Because, like Tom Dabbs, he could feel something out there in the jungle, something menacing.

Taking the letter from his pocket, Ben opened it and almost without looking began to read. It was dated April 27, 1943. He had gone through it so many times that he knew it by heart. Yet still his eyes followed the words, through the first page and on to the second. There he read: "We were two young people very much in love, but there was a *problem*, a very serious problem, 'religion.' Finally, with you overseas and me here, a decision had to be made. I felt that God did not want to interfere with two young people so deeply in love. I felt that religion was important but not to the extent that it should scar people's lives. I was willing to go part way in a compromise and even more, but you were willing to sacrifice *nothing.* I had always dreamed of a beautiful church wedding, yet because of my love for you, I felt that I should be fair, and all of my family agreed. Yet you wrote in your last letter, 'It must be a Temple marriage.'

"It wasn't ever in my heart to adopt the Mormon religion. But neither did I expect you to marry in my church. I thought we could compromise and find happiness, but now I see that you will not let this happen.

"So each of us has made a decision, a decision that will end a love that might have been very beautiful . . . "

Ben's eyes continued on, but his mind drifted then, remembering picnics, dances, and other moments when he and Sherie had discussed their love. And truly he had loved her, though he had ached all the while that she either couldn't, or wouldn't, feel about things eternal as he felt. As badly as he had wanted things to work out between them, in the depths of his heart he had felt that they wouldn't.

And that was hard for Ben, who was by nature shy and taciturn. He met people easily and was socially quite graceful. But drawing close to those people and opening up to them as he had to Sherie was another matter altogether.

With Sherie he had finally managed to do so, but now it had come to nothing and he was alone again. Would his life end that way, he wondered as he sat under the tree there in the jungle? Would something happen now, the thing he and so many others of the men were feeling, that would send him hurtling from mortality before he could ever know the joys of a true and eternal love? Before he could ever feel the comfort and closeness of a wife and children of his own?

Had he made the wrong choice? Should he have been willing to compromise for a time, to patiently wait for Sherie to come around? For she had been such a good person that the truths of the Gospel should have rung loudly in her heart. Yet they hadn't, at least not in the years he and she had loved each other. So should he have waited, marrying her civilly as she had desired, and then going forth with gentleness and patience until she had finally felt the promptings of the Holy Spirit?

But no! He had been promised, in numerous blessings, that if he would strictly obey the Lord's word in all things, he would know the blessings of an eternal family and would live to fulfil his missions before the Lord. But with a war going on, and him stuck in the remote jungles of Morotai Island in the South Pacific, how would he ever find a woman who would share his ideals?

"Heavenly Father," he pleaded in his mind while he stared into the dense jungle growth up the trail, "please give me peace about this. I have tried to be obedient to Thee in this thing, and I ask now that Thou wilt let my heart rest and open the way that I might move ahead with my life, finding the fulfillment that Thou hast commanded me to find."

With a sigh Ben slowly rose to his feet and once again adjusted the pack on his back.

"Now," he went on, continuing his silent prayer, "I am having some uncomfortable feelings today, as are some of the other men, and I am worried about them. If these impressions are from Thee, then Father, wilt Thou tell me which trail I should lead the men along? Please help me know what to do so that these men and I will be protected . . . "

CHAPTER

TWO

As Ben prayed, he realized that his thinking was moving in the direction of the trail to the left, down into the ravine. In his mind, he could see the men taking that trail, could see himself directing their forward march.

Certain that he had his answer from prayer, Ben breathed a "thank you" and stood to give the order to go to the left. But as he did so, a most unusual feeling hit him, a conviction that the trail to the right, the one up the ridge, also needed to be investigated.

Stepping forward, he saw that the trail showed recent signs of usage. Grass had been crushed. and the broken ends were still moist, while footprints with the edges still crumbling showed here and there. Seeing those things, Ben realized abruptly that it would be foolish to take his men onto lower ground without first examining the ridge trail to be sure they would not be attacked from above.

Quickly the decisions came, then, almost as if they were not his own. As he gave orders, Ben wondered at that but did not have time to truly consider. There was a scout to make and a job to complete that needed badly to be done.

"Dabbs," he ordered in an undertone, "put the point

squad in position here at the forks and tell them to be ready. Then bring the second squad forward and have them scout up the ridge here for seventy-five yards. Garic and Green, both of you go with the second squad. I'm coming along with you, so keep me posted."

"Yes, sir," Dabbs said, saluting lazily. And then in his soft southern drawl, he deployed the men and they set out, Garic and Green moving silently in the lead.

Waiting, Ben looked behind him and saw that none of the men were relaxed, not even those who had no specific orders to remain alert. So they felt it still—the tension, the nervousness, the waiting for some unknown something.

He thought then of a story his father had told of a prairie fire rushing uncontrolled toward his Grandmother Bennett's tent. His grandfather had been away, and his father, a teenage boy, had wanted to rush out and begin plowing fire breaks. However, his mother had serenely told him that she feared neither fires nor anything else, for the Lord had promised her protection, and she had faith in that promise.

His father had taken the team and gone out anyway, and later the fire had jumped his hastily plowed lane as though it hadn't even been there. Still it rushed at the tent on their homestead, and all appeared lost to frightened young Alvin Bennett until, at the last possible moment, the wind shifted and the fire roared away.

The unyielding serenity of his mother had taught Ben's father much about faith that day, and that lesson had stood him in good stead as he had made his way through his own difficult life.

But now it was Ben's turn, and he found himself struggling to somehow transpose the faith of his grandmother Bennett into his own life. He knew he could do it, if only—

"Lieutenant!"

Spinning, Ben stepped forward to meet the running soldier.

"Sir," the man wheezed as he gasped for breath, "Garic . . . wants me to tell you . . . that he sees . . . clothing hanging out up on top of the ridge. Do . . . do you want to take a look?"

"I do," Ben replied. "Show me where he is but slow down a little. If it's the Japs, they won't be going anywhere, and if it isn't, then there's no need for such haste anyway. Is there?"

"No, sir," the man replied, grinning.

"I'm glad we agree. Now let's go take a look at what Garic thinks he sees."

Shortly Ben stood beside the lead scout, trying his best to make out what Garic was trying to show him.

"Up there, sir, just to the left of that biggest tree."

"I see where you mean," Ben said, straining his eyes at the lenses of his binoculars. "But I don't see anything hanging down but palm fronds, vines, and leaves."

"Sir, don't look for color. Look for shapes that don't fit. What I'm showing you looks like big leaves, but the edges ain't right."

"I still don't see anything," Ben said quietly.

"Begging your pardon, sir, but I see 'em plain. Those are clothes hanging up there, and that means we've got the enemy up there somewheres, too."

Slowly Ben lowered his binoculars. He truly could see nothing out of the ordinary, but suddenly he was buzzing all over, or tingling, he couldn't decide which to call it. But whatever it was, in that instant he felt certain that Garic was right, and so quickly he sent for Lieutenant Kempainen.

"I don't see anything either," Kempainen said after his turn at glassing the ridge top.

"But sirs, them clothes are right there, plain as day."

"We're not arguing, Garic," Ben said softly. "In fact, I believe you. I just wanted to confer with Lieutenant Kempainen. What do you think, Kemp?"

"I'm with you, Ben. Something sure has all of us spooked

today, and this just might be it. If Garic thinks he sees something, then I'm for being ready."

"Good. So am I. Go back and have Sergeant Milam set his mortar in position. Then send up four more Tommy Guns and a Browning Automatic Rifle, to reinforce my point. With the mortar behind us and four Tommys and a B.A.R. on the line, we should be able to handle whatever we might run into."

"Do you want another full squad?"

Ben shook his head. "I don't think so, Kemp. Too many men for this narrow ridge. But keep that radio cranked up, and tell Milam to be ready to give us all he has from that mortar."

"We only have eighteen shells, Ben."

"Then get all eighteen ready. We've got some rifle grenades as well as plenty of ammo for the M1's and the Tommys, so we should be okay. Wish us luck."

Lieutenant Kempainen did and then hurried back down the trail. Soon Ben and his reinforced squad were inching their way forward up the narrow ridge.

"Lieutenant." Another whispered query assailed Ben's ears as he crouched behind some thick bushes.

"Yes?"

"Green says to tell you he can see a small tent."

Ben looked ahead to where he could see his second lead scout, PFC Green. The man, one of Ben's favorite soldiers, was crouched in the dense growth, his finger pointed ahead and off to the right. Ben couldn't see what Green was pointing at, but as with Garic, he did not doubt the man's ability.

Nodding, he motioned Green forward and then turned to the remainder of the squad. "Men," he whispered, "this could be it. Use every possible precaution, keep spread out as best you can, use whatever cover you can find—sparse as it is—and keep your eyes open. Now let's go!"

Slowly, carefully, the men inched forward, a yard, two

35

yards. And then suddenly, as Lieutenant Bennett wrote suc-
cinctly shortly thereafter, "all hell broke loose!" He and his
men, in spite of their care, had walked into a carefully arranged ambush.

CHAPTER

THREE

"Hit the dirt!" Ben shouted as his own body slammed into the rocky coral of the steep ridge. Around him bullets were splatting and smacking and whining off into the distance, and even as he hugged the ground, his mind counted three Jap machine guns and several snipers, all firing at once.

In the scant seconds that he lay without moving, Ben's mind was incredibly busy. He plotted the ridge top and determined that it was only twenty feet or so across, with steep sides that would make any flanking action by the other men almost impossible. Besides that, the Japanese snipers had not only the hill covered but the steep slopes on either side as well. So he could not call up the other men.

But there was cover, of a sort. The coral ridge was uneven, and men could get into shallow pockets here and there. There was also the scattered, lush foliage behind which they could hide, and as he lifted his head for his first look, he realized that the men were already using the available cover effectively.

Still the bullets hailed around them, and with a rolling motion Ben moved toward the unlikely cover of a thick bush. But he somehow tangled in a vine he had not seen, and as he lay exposed he felt bullets slamming by the tens of dozens into the coral around his body, spewing from the muzzles of each of the three Jap "woodpeckers" at six hundred rounds per minute.

"Dear Heavenly Father," he breathed as he twisted and pulled at the entangling vines, "please help me get these men out of here . . ."

"Lieutenant," Sergeant Dabbs shouted as Ben finally rolled behind the bush, "you hit?"

"Not a scratch," Ben cried back. "How many casualties do we have?"

"Grissom, sir," Dabbs shouted back while the bullets continued to fly. "The BAR gunner. He's hit bad, in the back and in the temple."

In surprise, Ben looked at where Grissom lay, two feet to his left and maybe eight feet in front of him. So close, and yet somehow while the bullets had found others all around him, they had not hit him.

"Lieutenant," a voice gasped from the other direction. "This is Weiner, sir. They've shattered my left arm above the elbow."

"Can you move?"

"Y . . . yes, sir."

"Good. Others?"

"Two," a voice drawled from another location. "Fulton's been hit twice, in the hand and in the foot. Also Green took three hits in his left arm. Green can walk, but I don't know about Fulton."

"Is Grissom . . . dead?" Ben asked then.

"No, sir," Dabbs replied, "but he needs a medic right bad. I reckon if you folks will cover me, then I can hoist him up and pack him—"

Dabbs was interrupted by another burst of fire from an enemy machine gun, and when he stopped rolling, he was cussing mad. Bullets had torn the lapel of his fatigue jacket to shreds. Angry too were the others of the squad, and Ben was suddenly aware that American automatic weapons and M-1's were returning fire at the Japanese. Further, they were doing so with deadly accuracy.

Suddenly a mortar round from Leslie Milam's squad ripped into the Japanese position, and then a second and a third. The battle seemed to explode with even greater fury after that, and Ben found time to consider little but the enemy.

The noise of gunfire was deafening; the acrid residue of exploding gunpowder burned his eyes and nostrils; the shouts and screams of wounded Americans and wounded and dying Japanese burned obscenely into his mind. Finally the angry whining of ricocheting bullets made Ben think of the time he and Cliff, his older brother, had swatted a hornet's nest they had found in the barn on their father's irrigated farm. As the hornets had swarmed out, the two boys had been forced to run for their lives, finding safety only after they had plunged into the middle of the stock pond.

The only difference was that now there was no place to run, no place to hide.

"Men," he shouted as he kept his eyes busy trying to search out enemy positions, "ignore the snipers and hit those machine guns! We'll get the snipers later. Martin, tell Sergeant Milam to fire faster!"

In only moments, Leslie Milam and his men had expended all eighteen rounds of mortar, and seconds later they were scrambling to find more rifle grenades. Still the Japs continued to hammer the American position with machine-gun fire and snipers, seemingly unaffected by the heavy fire, and Ben wondered that his men could continue.

But continue they did, gallantly, even heroically. As Ben watched, he saw a burst of fire rip through Sergeant Harmon's fatigue jacket, blowing out four clips of ammunition the man was carrying for PFC Baylor's tommy gun, and their last two rifle grenades besides. Yet miraculously Harmon remained unhurt and quite willing to fight. So, for that matter, was PFC Baylor, who, realizing he would soon be out of ammo, suddenly leaped to his feet and sprinted forward through burst after burst of enemy fire, stopping only after he had sprayed a Jap machine gun position with his tommy gun, knocking it totally out of commission.

At that instant, another burst from a different machine gun nest hit Sergeant Dabbs, or rather it hit his tommy gun, knocking the clip out and away. Another two bullets passed through his fatigue cap, yet Dabbs himself remained untouched and more filled with the fury of battle than ever.

PFC Collins, thinking he saw a sniper, exposed himself for a moment to get a shot, and an enemy sniper in another position fired at him, his bullet striking Collins's rifle in the stock, passing through it, bending the barrel, and sending the rifle flying from his grasp.

Shocked, Collins made a grab to retrieve his rifle, and the sniper stepped from his concealed position to draw another bead on Collins. But Sergeant Dabbs was on the alert, for he had been trying for two or three minutes to locate that particular sniper. As the enemy raised his rifle, Dabbs's tommy gun spoke, and Collins's life was saved.

"Dabbs? T-Tommy Dabbs?"

In a momentary lull in the firing, Fulton's soft Virginian twang could be heard distinctly as he called his friend.

"Tommy?"

"I hear you, Fulton," Dabbs called as Ben and a medico wormed their way forward toward the wounded man.

"Tommy," the man pleaded weakly, "get me out of here! Promise me, man . . ."

"I promise," Dabbs replied fiercely. "Now you keep your head down."

"Dabbs," Ben suddenly shouted, "behind you!"

With a cry that was as primeval as any cry ever uttered by a warrior fighting to protect his loved ones, Tom Dabbs instantly leaped to his feet and swirled around. Thirty yards away, a Jap carrying an American tommy gun was sneaking around the right flank, and Dabbs's spotting him and the chattering of his .45 sub-machine gun were almost simultaneous. The burst took the enemy full in the face, and with a high-pitched scream the enemy soldier dropped the tommy gun and rolled down the steep hillside.

The firing grew more sporadic then, and in the lull Ben, Sergeant Dabbs, and the medico reached the wounded Fulton. "Lieutenant," Fulton said in his soft, mild voice as he looked up at Ben from where he lay on the ground, "my foot's gone. It will never be of any use to me again."

"Cheer up, old man," Ben said as he placed his hand on Fulton's forehead, "you're going to be all right."

Ben meant it, too, for he had every determination to get his wounded men out of the enemy fire and back to where proper medical attention could be administered.

"Heavenly Father," his mind pleaded as he wormed his way under continuing enemy fire toward Grissom, his wounded BAR gunner, "please help me know how to do this . . ."

Grissom's head was bloody, but the ghastly wound in his back was what frightened Ben and the second medico. As emergency aid was administered, still under enemy fire, Ben did his best to comfort the man.

Green and Weiner, with arm wounds, could walk, and once their wounds were dressed, Ben ordered them to the rear. Then he gave hurried directions to the remainder of the squad.

"Men, there is no way we're going to get the Japs off this ridge, at least today. They're dug in too deeply, and their position cannot be flanked. Nor would a frontal assault, without backup fire from our mortar squad, be anything but suicide. Therefore I am ordering a withdrawal."

The men said nothing, for they could see the wisdom of

Lieutenant Bennett's decision. But the pathetic looks on the faces of Grissom and Fulton told Ben of their fear, the feeling that they would be left behind because they could not keep up with the withdrawal.

"Dabbs," Ben continued, "you take charge of the wounded men. They are not, I repeat, *not* to be left behind. Pick six men to assist you. The remainder of you men are to keep up a continuing fire on the Japanese position. Garic, you direct the retreat on the left, and I will do so on the right. Any questions?"

There were none, so Ben cranked up the SCR-300 radio and told Kempainen of his situation. "Kemp," he then concluded, "get on that ridge above you and give us covering fire, plenty of it. We've got four casualties, and the Japs haven't stopped firing yet."

Kempainen acknowledged, and so shortly thereafter the squad began its slow but careful withdrawal under the umbrella of fire from Lieutenant Kempainen's squad. The Americans suffered no more casualties, but so far as Ben could tell, neither did the Japanese. Still, the Americans finally managed to retreat beyond the range of the enemy's weapons, and at that point Ben heaved a sigh of relief.

"Ben."

Looking up, Ben acknowledged Lieutenant Kempainen, who was coming down the hill above him.

"Glad you made it," Kempainen declared with sincere relief. "The boys have some stretchers here that they improvised from poles and fatigue jackets, happen you want to use them."

Grinning, Ben clapped Kempainen on the shoulder. "You'll do, old man."

"Lieutenant Bennett?"

Turning, Ben saw his friend Leslie Milam hurrying toward him, his face showing his concern.

"Leslie," he said, gripping the other's hand, "thank you for that mortar barrage. I didn't see a single wasted round."

"The boys do good work, Lieutenant. But I'm sorry we ran out of ammo. We just weren't very well prepared."

"You didn't know that, Leslie, so don't worry about it. Besides, the Lord protected us, so instead of worrying we should be giving thanks."

"I have been, Lieutenant," Leslie said quietly. "When I heard those Japs cut loose up there, I started praying even before I started dropping mortar rounds. But all along I felt certain you would be taken care of."

"And I was," Ben said quietly. "Now let's get these men back to the radar station. Harmon, have you raised the company on the radio?"

"No, sir," the man called back. "This thing isn't carrying through the jungle worth sour apples."

"Well, keep trying. We've got to have medical aid at the radar station when we get there. Give them our ETA and tell them we want Captain Gould there in person. Two of these men are in serious condition, and I don't want to lose them!"

"Yes, sir!"

"Dabbs, see that the native guides carry these litters while the men keep their eyes open for the enemy."

"The guides won't like it, sir."

Ben scowled his determination. "Neither would I, but see that they do it anyway. We simply can't afford another ambush, and I want every man-jack of this patrol armed, alert and prepared to fight. Do I make myself clear?"

"Yes, sir!

"Harmon, have you raised 'E' Company yet?"

"No, sir."

"Well, keep sending the same message. Every time we stop for a breather, I want you on that radio giving our ETA at the radar station and telling them that we have been ambushed and need Captain Gould to care for our casualties. Understood?"

"Yes, sir!"

"Lieutenant Kempainen, organize a squad for rear guard duty in case the Japs decide to come after us. Pick the best men, but leave Garic alone. I want him to scout forward and keep the trail clear for us."

"All right, Ben. Sergeant Milam, choose up a squad, and be quick about it."

"Yes, sir."

Ben then looked around. "Dabbs, you stay with the litters, and choose a squad to stay with you. Keep the natives honest and make certain they are careful. These men are already in enough pain, and I don't want our carelessness to add to it. Garic, did you hear your orders?"

Garic nodded.

"Good. Then move it out! We'll be right behind you."

On a run Garic started down the trail, and within minutes the entire patrol was spread out and moving back toward the radar station and the beach, Ben leading the way.

And as he marched, the remembered sounds of the battle continued pounding in his ears . . .

CHAPTER

FOUR

"I've got to admit it, Ben. We were protected out there by *something*! We had to be."

Ben smiled almost sadly. "Kemp, if you admit that, then why is it so difficult for you to admit that the one who protected us was God?"

Ben, Lieutenant Kempainen, Sergeant Dabbs, and Sergeant Milam were seated on the beach below the radar station. The IT boats with their four wounded comrades aboard were already almost out of sight on their way to the 106 Clearing Station where they would be hospitalized.

And the four wounded men had been true heros. During the hour and a half forced march to the radar station, none of them had moaned or complained. Once there, they had again remained silent throughout treatment. Grissom's wounds had seemed the most serious, but after they had been treated, Ben had patted him on the shoulder.

"We really gave it to them, didn't we," Grissom had said.

"Yes, Grissom," Ben had responded, "we certainly did."

Weiner had not wanted to be attended to until all the others had been treated, but the doctors had ignored his demands, for next to Grissom's, his wounds had been most serious.

45

"I think it was God who protected us, all right."

The speaker was Tom Dabbs. Burrowing at the sand with his fingers, arranging and rearranging it, he was obviously doing some very serious thinking.

"Lieutenant Kempainen, think about it. Milam here is promised by God that he will get home all right. Lieutenant Bennett prays over us and gets this good feeling about all the men in the patrol. But the trouble is, the odds are stacked against us, and protection can't possibly happen.

"Garic accidentally fires his weapon and gives the Japs the warning that we are coming, and they are really set up to wipe us out. In spite of our caution, we don't see them, and they don't open fire until we are within twenty-five yards of them.

"When they do fire, we are caught in the open with no-where but nowhere on that narrow ridge to hide, and three machine guns open up at once, pumping eighteen hundred rounds into our bunched-up group every sixty seconds. There are also anywhere from three to six snipers picking us out individually and firing as rapidly as they can, which would be another twenty to fifty rounds a minute.

"This goes on for at least five minutes, with every one of us basically exposed to the Japs the entire time. In other words, Lieutenant, as the ol' boys back home would say, we don't stand the chance of a snowball rolling uphill on a hot day in hell. Yet at that close range, with all that firing and in that length of time, not *one* of us is killed, and only four are wounded. Now you tell me, sir, who in thunder else but God could have pulled off a miracle as big as that one?"

"It does seem impossible," Lieutenant Kempainen agreed.

"That's not all," Leslie Milam added. "Think about the medical help we had waiting here. You know Harmon was on that radio constantly, but so far as we could tell, our message was never received. Yet a few moments ago Captain

Gould told me that our message had gotten through, but in a most unusual way.

"According to Gould, the company commander only got a very few of the words of our message. The words were 'ambushed,' 'radar,' 'casualties,' and 'Captain Gould.' Yet these were vital words, all of them, and they enabled the C.O. to determine the meaning of the message."

"And another 'coincidence,' " Ben added seriously, "is that Major Dees, the regimental surgeon, just happened to be visiting at the outpost today and was there when our message got through. That's why he was here with Captain Gould. I'm telling you, Kemp, there is no way our men could have had finer help."

Lieutenant Kempainen laughed. "All right, you guys, I admit it. I've seen a miracle today."

"Not just one," Ben stated quietly. "Today we saw many miracles. All the way down that trail I had worried for fear that medical aid would not be at the radar station when we arrived, and I prayed constantly to God and asked him to hear my prayers and have all in readiness.

"And He heard me, Kemp. He heard me! Everything was set up and ready when we appeared, more than I ever hoped or expected. Blood plasma was ready. Surgical instruments were all sterilized and ready for instant use. I will never forget how grateful I felt to my Heavenly Father when I walked up and saw Doctor Dees standing there—the one man on the entire island most qualified to see that my men's lives would be preserved and their health properly restored! I'm telling you, men, this is perhaps a greater miracle than the battle itself."

For a few moments the men sat in silence, each deep in his own thoughts. Up the beach a flock of sea birds squawked and screeched noisily as they circled some flotsam drifting just offshore, while high overhead an albatross hung almost motionless against the brassy sky, watching. Here and there

47

on the beach, groups of men sat huddled together, and now and then the hum of their voices grew loud enough to distinguish above the constant chugging of the generator that ran the radar. When that happened and the words of the scattered men became audible, it turned out that they were all discussing one event, the amazing escape of Lieutenant Ben Bennett's patrol from the Japanese ambush on hill #745. Nor could any explain their deliverance from certain death, not unless they, like Tom Dabbs and Lieutenant Kempainen, finally acknowledged the hand of God in it.

"So, Lieutenant," Tom Dabbs drawled as he tossed a small shell aside and turned to face the officer, "you said earlier today that you knew a way for anyone who wanted to, to get a promise of protection from God."

Ben looked up and nodded. "That's right."

"Well, I'd sure admire learning that there method."

Lieutenant Kempainen grinned and lay back in the warm sand, staring upward, while Leslie Milam rolled onto his elbow and looked at the questioning sergeant.

"Dabbs," he said, "are you a believer now?"

"A believer?"

"That's right, Dabbs," Ben cut in. "I told you I wouldn't say any more about it unless you believed enough to truly want to know."

"What does believing have to do with anything?" Dabbs asked.

"It's called exercising faith, Tom. The Lord never gives us more knowledge than we are ready to have faith in, wholeheartedly accept, and live. We may learn of more than that, but most often such knowledge will be intellectual and have very little impact on our thinking. So I ask again, are you ready to believe?"

"Lawsy," Tom Dabbs said, grinning, "after seeing what I saw today, I'd believe durn near anything. Well, unless you told me the war was over. Then I might question you a mite.

48

Other than that, you lay out the line and I'll take the bait—hook, line, and sinker with it."

"Wish I *could* tell you that the war was over," Ben said quietly.

"Just tell me how to keep my skin whole until it is," Dabbs stated flatly, "and I'll be thankfuller than somewhat and plenty satisfied."

"Very well," Ben said as he rolled over and stared out to sea, "I'll tell you. But once I do, Tom, the Lord will hold you accountable for that knowledge. You too, Kemp. You want to hear this?"

For a moment Lieutenant Kempainen was silent, but then at last he spoke. "Ben, coming from anyone else, I'd say no. But it's pretty obvious that you know some things about God that I don't know, things that right now look very attractive. Besides that, I trust you. So yes, I think I had better say that I want to hear what you have to say."

"All right. But first, let me state that Sergeant Milam here could say this just as easily as I can, and could probably say it more plainly."

"You go ahead, Lieutenant."

"Thanks, Les. Dabbs, Kemp, since early childhood I have been taught to pray. I could tell you stories about my developing faith, but now doesn't hardly seem the time. But by the time I entered the military, I had a firm knowledge that God could be communicated with through prayer, and that He would respond back to me according to my faith in Him. So, yes, I pray frequently.

"Since we have been on patrol duty, for instance, I have prayed night and morning, and often in between, that I would be guarded and directed, and that not only my own life but the lives of my men, including the three of you, would be preserved. In addition, I know that my loved ones at home, as well as my many friends, have been and are praying for my safety.

"Those combined prayers, mine and others, have great power. That is one reason I believe we were all so miraculously protected."

"And the other reasons?" Lieutenant Kempainen asked.

"A revelation that the Lord gave to a modern prophet."

"You mean some guy like Moses?" Tom Dabbs questioned in astonishment.

"Exactly," Ben told him. "This prophet's name is Joseph Smith, and he died a hundred years ago this past June."

Tom Dabbs shook his head in wonderment. "A real prophet, huh? Did he have a long beard and go around calling folks to repentance and all that other nutty stuff?"

Ben smiled. "No beard, but he did tell people they needed to repent. That does seem to be the role of prophets, both ancient and modern."

"And this revelation?" Lieutenant Kempainen asked.

"Joseph received many revelations pertaining to a host of topics, Kemp. But this one, which has always intrigued me, pertains to how a person can obtain the promise of divine protection as he goes through life. The revelation is called section 89 of the Doctrine and Covenants, which is a book of scripture we revere and use. The doctrine itself is called the Word of Wisdom."

"A word of wisdom?"

"That's correct, Dabbs. God tells man this small thing to do, or issues His word. And if man is wise enough to obey that word, then he is given some incredible promises. In other words, a word of wisdom."

Now Lieutenant Kempainen sat back up. "Interesting. So what is the word of wisdom all about?"

Reaching into his pack, Ben pulled out his worn copy of the Book of Mormon and Doctrine and Covenants. Opening it to section 89, he read it through.

"No alcohol or tobacco?" Tom Dabbs questioned in

50

astonishment. "Is that why you guys never touch that stuff, or came into town with us back in the States?"

"That's why," Leslie Milam stated softly.

"Well, I'll be doggone."

"What about those hot drinks?" Lieutenant Kempainen asked then. "I assume that means tea and coffee, for I have never seen either of you drink them. But there could be a lot of other hot drinks."

"In 1833, Kemp, tea and coffee summed it up, at least in the area of the world where Joseph Smith lived."

"So the deal is, no smoking, snuffing, or chewing; no boozing; and no tea and coffee. What the dickens do you guys do to have fun or wake up in the mornings?"

"Open our eyes," Ben said with a grin. "That's actually all it takes. But let me read this again, and this time pay attention to the positive aspects of it. The Lord didn't just tell Joseph what *not* to do. He also told him the things he should do, what he should eat and drink, and the seasons when those things would be most beneficial to his body. And, finally, God even told the prophet why he should do those things. If you will note, He says that He is giving the revelation in consequence of evils and designs which do and will exist in the hearts of conspiring men, or men who will destroy others in order to make a profit or to gain power."

"Well," Lieutenant Kempainen said thoughtfully, "I can see where alcohol can destroy people. But what harm is there in tobacco or coffee or tea?"

"I don't know, Kemp. But the Lord says that the revelation is both for the present and for the future. Therefore I assume that the day will come when we will understand the harm that those things do to our bodies."

"Couldn't he be wrong?" Tom Dabbs asked.

"Is God ever wrong?" Leslie Milam questioned right back.

Throwing a handful of sand at him, Tom Dabbs grinned.

"I didn't mean God, Milam. I meant that prophet guy, Joseph Smith. Couldn't he have made a mistake?"

"Anyone can make mistakes," Ben said quietly. "But, Tom, we have the Lord's promise in the scriptures that He won't allow His prophet to lead His people astray. Besides that, I have personally tested this revelation. In fact, I have tested it at great length. Without exception, the promises hold true, and even though I do not yet understand it all, I can bear solemn witness that the revelation called the Word of Wisdom is no mistake."

"Promises? What promises?"

Ben grinned. "And so we come at last to what you men wanted to know about in the first place, God's promise of divine protection."

"I assume it has to do with health?" Lieutenant Kempainen asked.

"Well, yes, Kemp, at least partially. The Lord does promise 'health in their navel and marrow to their bones,' and that they 'shall find wisdom and great treasures of knowledge, even hidden treasures.' He also says that they 'shall run and not be weary, and shall walk and not faint.'

"I believe these promises pertain to physical and mental health, and I will tell you that in athletics and in my college work, I have tested and proven them to my perfect satisfaction.

"But recently my attention has been centered upon verse 21, and I feel very strongly that I now know the meaning to it. Let me repeat the verse:

" 'And I, the Lord, give unto them a promise, that the destroying angel shall pass by them, as the children of Israel, and not slay them.'

"Men, today God filled that promise to the letter, both for me and for all the rest of you."

"What does it mean about the children of Israel?" Tom Dabbs asked quickly.

"It happened in Moses' time," Ben responded. "Remember the Lord's last plague upon the Egyptians, when all their first-born were killed? At that time the Lord commanded the Israelites to spread the blood of a lamb on their doorposts as a sign to Him of their willingness to be obedient. All those who did so were bypassed by the destroying angel, who went ahead and slew the first-born of everyone else in Egypt."

"Exactly," Lieutenant Kempainen stated. "Including the Israelites who refused to be obedient."

Tom Dabbs looked up. "I didn't know that."

"I didn't, either," Leslie Milam quickly added. "But it sure makes sense, now that I think about it."

"So in that Word of Wisdom revelation," Lieutenant Kempainen summarized, "God is saying that by not using alcohol, tobacco, tea, or coffee, and by eating and drinking and doing everything else as He directs, it will be making the same sort of sign before the Lord as putting the blood on the doors was for the ancient Israelites."

"I believe that's correct," Ben responded soberly. "With all my heart I know that what you have just concluded is true."

"And the two of you have lived this way?" Tom Dabbs asked.

Ben took up a handful of sand and let it trickle through his fingers. "I don't know about Les," he finally replied, "but all my life I have tried to obey the principles of that revelation. That is one of the reasons why I have very little fear of this war. No matter how many grains of this sand must trickle through the hourglass of time before the fighting ends, and no matter how many battles like this morning's I must participate in, it will not matter. I know that God is protecting me from the destroying angel, for He has so promised. Thus far, He has fulfilled that promise to the letter, and I am certain that He will continue to do so. It is my duty, and it gives me joy, to bear testimony to this. That is why I said what I did this morning."

In the silence that followed, the lapping waves of the incoming tide pushed gently at the men, unheeded, while in the background the hum of the generator went unnoticed. The men were quiet, each of them hearing again the rattle of Japanese machine guns, smelling again the odor of gunpowder, and seeing again the impossible situation from which they had all been delivered. Yet they *had* been delivered, and each of them knew, finally and without doubt, that it had been done by the hand of God.

And that was good. But when, Ben thought as he stood finally to follow after the others to their loading area, would God fulfill His other promise to Ben, the promise made in his patriarchal blessing of bringing into his life the woman who would share his eternal goals and destiny?

He didn't know, of course, but once again he vowed that he would somehow muster up the patience to wait.

CHAPTER

FIVE

"Morotai Island

"October 11, 1944, 1100 hours

"Dear Mother and Dad:"

Ben paused, watching the parrots above him in his tent. He had not written his parents in over a month, and he felt suddenly compelled to do so. The trouble was that what he wanted to tell them might worry them, and with his mother's heart condition, that could be serious.

"Well," he finally wrote, "I don't hardly know where to begin. So let me just say, dear Mother and Dad, that I am now on Morotai Island, and suppose I should tell you a little about it. First, let me say that when dawn broke on D-Day, which was September 15th, I looked across the ocean towards the Halamaheras and for the first time in my life saw an active volcano. Large clouds of smoke issued from the crater, which was hidden from view, and went spiralling and rolling upwards, upwards, and upwards.

"Secondly, I believe there are more insects on Morotai Island than any place I have been since coming overseas — every kind and description imaginable — spiders one and a half inches across, large green grasshopper-like creatures three inches long. Our bivouac areas are alive with ants, cockroaches, flies, mosquitos, wasps, sand or grass fleas, and other bugs. Scorpions and centipedes frequently hole up in our shoes or clothes. Colorful butterflies include the giant bird-winged variety. But most unpleasant of all, perhaps, are the leeches, which grab at us or drop on us from leaves in the jungle. And no matter what we wear, they seem able to get through it to our skin.

"On the bright side there are small deer, pigs, and beautifully colored parrots, which the natives use for pets. Lt. Richester has two of them in our tent at this moment. One is asleep on its perch, which is swaying gently in the breeze. Bats eighteen inches long are very common.

"This island is surrounded by coral reefs, which are serious barriers and obstacles to beach landings. Our Dukw 'duck' hung up on the coral today, and it was some time before we were able to work it loose and find another way to shore. The coral gives a beautiful green color to the water wherever it is found, and in some places the water is very shallow for several hundred yards from shore.

"These waters abound in sharks and fishes of all kinds. On D-Day a soldier from the boat company fell overboard and a shark got him. The other day I saw a large group of porpoises rolling up and over in the water, only a hundred yards or so from shore. These porpoises are supposed to be extremely fast, and clear the waters of sharks wherever they are.

"Thirdly, the natives here seem to have had a rather tough sledding for some time. Their bodies are covered with sores, but since we have been here, they are once again receiving medical attention. A number of Dutch officers and Nica Boys came in with us when we invaded the island, and are now working with the natives.

"The cold that bothered me at Aitape for a month after our Aitape Campaign has almost entirely left me. The excessive perspiration associated with our activity of the past week has done the trick and I feel better now than I have for some time.

"Enemy bombers have been over us almost every day, but have done very little damage. Their motors have a characteristic off-tune sound, which has caused the men to dub them 'Windmill Charlie,' or 'Washingmachine Charlie.' On D-Day a Jap bomber attacked the Liberty ship on which our kitchen and kitchen force was loaded. The bomber came in very fast out of the sun but swerved just before reaching the ship, and its bombs missed by thirty feet. Our anti-aircraft fire was terrific but, although the tracer bullets could be seen to pass through the wings and fuselage, a vital spot was not hit and the plane was not knocked down. A good number of enemy planes have been downed since D-Day, however.

"Well, folks, mostly I spend my time here in administrative tasks and in censoring the mail of my men. But yesterday some promises were fulfilled in my behalf. I will write all the details later, but out on patrol I was involved in a rather nasty little skirmish with the enemy that should have seen me, and many others of my men, killed. As it turned out, only four were wounded, and I wasn't even scratched.

"Uncle Archie promised me in a blessing that if I would live the Word of Wisdom I would be protected just as much as he had been in the First World War, and yesterday I saw that promise fulfilled. I also saw the Lord's promise fulfilled, to those of us who live the Word of Wisdom, wherein the destroying angel passed by my men and me and did not slay us. So yes, I am seeing the hand of the Lord in this war, and I do not want you to worry about me.

"I've not made many converts to the Word of Wisdom, however. The officers in the battalion received some whiskey and rum today, but of course I had no use or desire for any of it. They paid ten pounds for two quarts of whiskey and two pints of rum. What a waste.

"I did have a long chat yesterday with some of the men who were in the skirmish with me, concerning the Lord's protection. I felt greatly honored to be able to bear my testimony concerning the Lord's Law of Health.

"I have collected some seashells, which I will be sending you as quickly as I can package them. I find them quite attractive, and hope you like them.

"Well, I have little left to report. I told you that the girl back in Price has decided to go her separate way. I miss her, for I thought a great deal of her. But she would not examine Mormonism, and so could never go to the Temple with me. Thus her decision is most likely for the best, for I will never marry except in the Lord's Temple. It is a very lonely thing, though, when all the men around me have girls or wives back home, and I have no one. Even Leslie Milam believes that he is in love, with a girl named Dorothy, who is a real peach. Of course I wonder if I will ever be fortunate enough to find another girl that I can learn to love. My blessing says that I will, but when I am way over here, I do not see how that can possibly happen.

"Please take care of yourselves. Give my love to all the family, and I will be writing them as I have the opportunity . . . "

PART TWO

CHRISTMAS AT THE FRONT

October 12, 1944–December 24, 1944

THE WAR

By the end of 1944, the Allies in Europe were slowly advancing on virtually all fronts but Belgium and the Netherlands. There the Germans had launched a V-weapon campaign in retaliation for the port at Antwerp being opened to the Allies. In the next five months, 1,213 V-1s and V-2s were launched, killing about 3,000, mostly civilians, and wounding 15,000 more.

In Arnhem, after terribly bitter fighting that resulted in victory for neither side, Allied forces were finally evacuated. And Rommel, Africa's "Desert Fox" and once Hitler's "favorite" general, was convicted of association in the anti-Hitler plot and was given his choice of suicide or execution by the desperate Fuhrer. He took the poison capsule, thoughtfully provided by Hitler's representatives. Berlin then claimed that he had died of wounds suffered in combat.

On October 20, after two and a half years, U.S. troops returned to the Philippines. The Sixth Army went ashore on the east coast of Leyte and within a day's time had landed 132,400 men and 200,000 tons of supplies. Four hours after the first men stepped ashore, General MacArthur waded in and broadcast his famous "I have returned" address to the Filipinos.

Three days later, the Battle of Leyte Gulf began, and after four days of fighting it had become the greatest battle in the history of naval warfare. Japanese Imperial Navy losses were staggering. They lost three battleships, four carriers, ten cruisers, thirteen destroyers, five submarines, and thousands upon thousands of seamen. U.S. losses included one carrier, two escort carriers, two destroyers, and a destroyer escort.

Shortly thereafter the first kamikaze attacks occurred, and the first hit by a kamikaze was made on October 28, inflicting slight damage on the U.S. cruiser *Denver* off the Leyte coast.

In November, the Japanese launched their explosive balloon campaign, sending over 9,000 large balloons carrying incendiary material and bombs toward the United States on the prevailing westerly winds. Eventually about 285 of the balloons reached North America, but the only casualties ever reported from the balloons were a minister's wife and five young children who were killed when a balloon-carried bomb exploded on a church outing just south of Klamath Falls, Oregon.

On November 7, 1944, F. D. Roosevelt was elected for an unprecedented fourth term as president, and U.S. forces on Leyte began their push against heavy resistance toward Ormoc. For over a month the battle raged in the Philippine jungles, ending finally on December 11 with the securance of Ormoc Bay. In the fighting, U.S. forces captured vast stockpiles of Japanese munitions, and the Japanese force in Leyte was reduced to 35,000 men.

On December 15, Mindoro in the Philippines was invaded by U.S. forces, who encountered heavy resistance from Japanese suicide planes. A day later, in Europe, the Germans launched a major counteroffensive against the U.S. First and Ninth Armies along a forty-mile front in the Ardennes Forest in Luxembourg. This encounter became famous as the Battle of the Bulge.

The 300,000 Germans in the Ardennes Forest caught the Americans by surprise. By the next day, the U.S. 82nd and 101st Airborne divisions were rushed in as reinforcements, but it was too little and too late for about ninety Americans captured in Malmedy. On a farm field, after they had been captured and stripped of their weapons, they were massacred by German troops.

That same day, about five hundred miles from the Philippines, a mighty typhoon hit the U.S. Third Fleet, inflicting greater losses on the U.S. Navy than they were to suffer in any single battle in the entire Pacific war.

By December 22, American forces in Luxembourg and Belgium were either retreating or desperately shifting positions to avoid a fatal entrapment. Besieged and facing the German ultimatum to surrender or be annihilated, Brigadier General Anthony C. McAuliffe replied, "Nuts." And then Patton, in a brilliant shift of position, launched an attack from the Ardennes salient to the south, and the Americans began to feel hope.

The day after Christmas, the U.S. 4th Armored Division broke through the German siege with their tanks, and the Battle of the Bulge was over. While it was a tactical victory for the Germans, it was so costly for them that they were never able to recover. They lost 220,000 men, half of them prisoners, and more than 1,400 tanks and heavy assault guns. The net effect upon the Allies, meanwhile, was to delay their final victory in Europe by six weeks.

And by New Year's Eve in the South Pacific, Americans were celebrating almost total victory on Leyte. The U.S. 77th Division had killed 5,779 Japanese while losing just 17 Americans, a remarkable victory.

But on Morotai Island in the Moluccas Islands the fighting continued unabated.

THE MAN

Until October 24, Ben and his men continued patrol duty from their bivouac area near the Morotai Radar Station. Then they were transferred to the area of the airstrip, on the beach, where they went into perimeter defense and also assisted in dock work, unloading cargo from landing craft, LCTs and LCMs. This activity continued through Christmas and into the new year.

Air alerts occurred daily and often several times a day, the primary Japanese target being the airfield and supporting areas. Often no planes were seen, and just as often they were seen but no bombs were dropped. But when they were dropped, the experience was horrendous. Yet still Ben and his men continued, living from day to day in the midst of the dangerousness of war. He wrote: "How tired I am of all this. I long to get away from it all—a long way away. I'd like to relax and forget it all. I am listening to a radio program which seems to be coming from a station somewhere in China. There is a woman announcer and she has the most interesting and pleasing voice. My, but I am a long ways from home."

Every two or three weeks, Ben and "E" Company changed bivouac areas, either to the outer edge of the perimeter or back toward the beach away from it. On most Sundays, Ben found time to get with Leslie Milam and other LDS men and hold church services, occasionally even enjoying the sacrament when time permitted it.

But still the war continued. Even when they were not on patrol and were not experiencing air raids, Ben and his men were in constant danger. He wrote: "Last night some Japs got through the perimeter and . . . set up a booby trap in a tent occupied by an anti-aircraft crew. When those men returned they set the booby trap off, and five of our boys became casualties. The Japs then went and blew up part of the gas dump. It was a hectic night. About 0330 hours a Jap plane dropped an incendiary bomb along our line. It hit about 27 yards in front of Sergeant Higgins' pillbox. This plane also did some strafing, but then one of our night fighters, a 'Black Widow' P-61, shot him down."

But more often than not, Ben's thoughts reflected his deepened understanding of, and commitment to, his religion: "Last Sunday at our LDS service, many of the men testified that living the Word of Wisdom and obeying the Gospel had resulted in many blessings to them while overseas. A large percentage of soldiers suffer from 'Jungle-rot' and other skin infections, but we LDS are quite free from such things. I have worn my garments and know that I have been richly blessed with health and strength. I have been almost entirely free from tropical ulcers, skin infections, jungle-rot, etc. For this I am grateful."

And like all the men, Ben worried that his absence from his home and work would have a negative impact on his life and career. In December, he received word that his brother Jim had been appointed Assistant Professor of Animal Husbandry at Utah State Agricultural College. While immensely proud of his brother, the news caused him to reconsider the course of his own life and to worry that he was not advancing professionally as he would liked to have been doing.

"But," he wrote that night, "I am not complaining. Who am I to question the lot that is mine? There is wisdom always in God's purposes, and I always want to be able to say, 'Thy will be done.' Yes, I am marking time professionally, but I am gaining much in other ways. In the long run perhaps it will all be for the best. I think so. In the meantime this is my life, and I want to make the best of it."

CHAPTER

SIX

"Stag? Hey, Stagliano, where are you?"

In almost total frustration Ben peered through the lush tropical growth, searching for his company clerk. Coconut palms loomed everywhere, a stately grove that with recent shelling now looked like a tumbled pile of matchsticks. The trees were huge, too, the ones still standing reaching a hundred feet and more into the air. But now, to Ben's mind, it looked like some weird land of desolation, a place where humans should not feel welcome.

"Stag?" he shouted again. "Sergeant Stagliano?"

"Hey, Lieutenant," a man called from a couple of dozen yards away, "I saw him and Sergeant Dabbs heading for the supply dump."

"The supply dump? But . . . " Suddenly Ben smiled, remembering. The night before, men all up and down the line out on their perimeter had opened fire, and the staccato bursts from tommy guns and BARs had gone on for the next two or three hours. This morning there had been two dead rats and one dead pig, but no Japanese.

Sergeant Stagliano, a man who loved his sleep, had made up his mind that he could rig better trip wires than were up, stringing them in such a way that rats and pigs could be distinguished from any of the enemy that might be sneaking in.

"Getting more trip wire?" Leslie Milam asked as he leaned on his shovel."

Ben grinned. "He is, and to tell the truth, I hope his idea works. I'm just about exhausted. And the fact that this happens to be Sunday doesn't help a bit."

"You're right about that. But the war goes on whether it's the Sabbath or not."

Ben sighed. "I know, and we did have a fine service this morning, for which I am thankful. The boost I feel from the Holy Ghost is not only welcome but essential in circumstances such as these. Les, you have no idea how much I hate war!"

"Maybe as much as I hate it?" Leslie Milam replied, grinning.

"Probably," Ben said softly, grinning back. "Now if I can just get my men to hate it enough so that they will stop their crazy firing all night long . . . "

"Well, you can't blame them for being jumpy, Lieutenant."

"Maybe not, but I've told them time and time again to use their carbines instead of the automatic weapons. Happen there *are* Japs out there, those automatic weapons will be dead giveaways to our positions."

"That's true enough. You think this bunker is deep enough?"

Ben surveyed the huge pit. "It ought to be. If the powers that be would just decide now whether they wanted it walled and covered or banked and open, it would surely help. To tell you the truth, Les, I'm fed up with bureaucratic bumbling and idiotic non-decision making."

"Ditto again, old man. But as far as our bunkers go, I thought we knew what the brass wanted."

"For today, we do. Captain Dismukes wants them

covered. But you just watch. Tomorrow Colonel Starr will come along and tell us to leave them open."

Leslie grinned. "So which do we do?"

Ben lifted and threw another shovel of sand out of the pit, and then a third. "We cover it, Les. And mark my words: We will barely get it finished, either covered or open, and we will be wrong. Then, the minute we get it changed, we will be moved out, leaving it for a bunch of Joes who'll never appreciate it in a million years."

"Is that a prophecy, Lieutenant?"

Again Ben grinned. "It might as well be, Les. I've been in the army long enough to know the laws by which it operates, and one of them is that no matter what you build, somebody else will get to use it."

"Is that the same law that says all foxholes will be muddy?"

"Exactly, unless you want water, in which case they will be dry. Another part of the law is that all equipment will operate perfectly unless it is needed."

"Yeah, and that my squad will always have too much mortar ammo unless we get hit by the Japs, in which case we will have about one fourth of what we need."

"Same law, all right."

"You just watch, Les. We cover this, they'll make us uncover it. We leave it open, they'll make us cover it. And either way, we'll be gone as soon as we're finished. And that's a true prophecy, according to the spirit of the war. Tell me, wouldn't you prefer having it covered?"

Leslie lifted his cap and scratched his head. "Well, it isn't really my pillbox, Ben. I'm only here temporarily. But if it was mine, I'd say to cover it."

"Then since Lieutenants Jordan and Kempainen are out on patrol, and since the top brass can't seem to get their heads together, it's unanimous. Further, we won't change it again unless the order for an open pillbox is made definite by *both* Dismukes and Starr."

"Hip, hip . . . " Leslie cheered, grinning.

"And hooray!" Ben added. "So let's move this sand back from the lip, then take some measurements and build the walls up with some of these thick palm logs that the artillery boys have so conveniently blown to kindling wood for us, then—"

"Hey, Ben, you didn't get the mail yesterday."

Looking up, Ben saw Lieutenant Kastanas standing on the pile of sand, grinning down at him.

"Hey, Kas," Ben said, sweeping off his fatigue cap in an exaggerated salute, "I hear you're a hero!"

The man grinned even wider. "I've been telling you I was, all along."

"Well, now I'm a believer. Les, meet Lieutenant Kastanas. Lieutenant, this is Sergeant Leslie Milam."

The two men nodded a greeting. "All right, Kastanas," Ben continued, "tell us about it."

The man grew serious. "There isn't a whole lot to tell, Ben. The Japs hit our patrol, and we were just better prepared than they were. We had one casualty, but we got twelve or thirteen of them. Unless they have time to set up, the Japanese don't seem very organized."

"I don't know, Kas. The ones who hit us a few weeks ago were surely set up. But on the other hand, I've heard the same. The Japs are rushing their men into the field so fast that they don't have time to train them adequately. And they're just kids, too. I tell you, I can hardly bear to think that we're firing out there against small children."

"I know, Ben. Trouble is, those kids are armed, and given half a chance, they'll be nailing you good. Or me."

Ben nodded. "Say, how are your wife and baby daughter?"

"Fantastic," Kastanas replied instantly. "Penny is lonely,

but in her letter today she told me how busy the war is keeping her. She's a welder now, you know, working on an aircraft assembly line. And little Andrea is growing like a weed. Penny says she talks about me all the time, and she pretends to read all my letters, over and over and over. Boy, but I miss those two."

"I'll bet you do."

"Penny asked about you, Ben. She was remembering the dinner we had together just before we all shipped out, and she was wondering if you had found yourself a girl yet."

Leaning on his shovel, Ben shook his head. "Not yet, Kas."

"Well, I'll write Penny and tell her. She said something about a girl who was working with her at the factory, some cute little number that you might want to write to. Interested?"

"He's interested," Leslie Milam stated categorically. "He'd better be, the age he's getting to be."

Lieutenant Kastanas chuckled. "Amen, Sergeant. If we don't get him married off, my little three-year-old girl will grow up and Ben will fall for her. And I can tell you right now, I don't want Ben Bennett for a son-in-law!"

All three men laughed at that, and then Lieutenant Kastanas pulled something from his pocket. "Speaking of letters, Ben, I found this one down at the post. It's addressed to you, but the return address says Bennett, so I don't think it's from a girl."

Taking the letter, Ben looked at it. "You're wrong, Kas. This is from the greatest girl in the world—my mother."

"Hear, hear," Lieutenant Kastanas agreed softly. "Sure do wish I could hear from mine. Oh, yes, Ben, I have something else for you."

Removing his pack, Lieutenant Kastanas reached inside and withdrew a solid brass ball that was between four and five inches wide. Then he held it up.

"Ben, some of the boys found this on patrol some time back and thought of you. It looks like it was part of a ball and chain arrangement that the Japs used on their prisoners, but the boys thought you could use it to practice your shot-putting. They said it would beat coconuts all hollow."

Scrambling up the bank, Ben put the letter from his mother in his pocket and took the shot. "How much does it weigh?" he asked almost reverently as he turned it in his hands.

"Just under fourteen pounds. I weighed it myself."

Slowly Ben turned the shot this way and that, hefting it, positioning it, and then positioning his body to hold it properly for a heave. "Thanks, Kas," he said finally. "You have no idea how badly I have missed working out with the shot."

"Yeah, I heard you won first in the All-Canada games before the war."

"More than that," Leslie stated quietly. "Ben has set all sorts of Canadian records in the shot, and has done just about as well with the discus and the javelin."

"Are you serious?"

"Absolutely. He likely won't talk about this much, but in the 1936 Olympic Trials in Montreal, he won gold medals in the shot and the discus and got a silver medal for the javelin. I'm telling you, sir, Lieutenant Bennett is a real champion."

"I had no idea," Lieutenant Kastanas stated. "You must have quite a string of medals, Ben."

"I have a few sitting around."

"Come on, Ben, don't be modest. How many have you earned?"

"Uh . . . " Ben replied, squirming uncomfortably, "I don't exactly . . . "

"Ben, this is me, Kastanas. Your buddy, remember? You've shared a table with my wife and me. You've heard us brag about our little girl. So remember, I know the difference, and I'm asking — you're not boasting. I know how modest you are, and I admire you for it. But for pete's sake, man, you can still tell me. I'd really like to know."

Gently fondling the shot, Ben looked off through the trees, remembering events, places, moments of glory and moments of failure, but remembering most of all the glorious feeling of training his body to respond to his will. And in his mind he could see his trophies, medals, plates, and ribbons, all lined up by his mother so she could look at them and think of her son. Actually, he could not remember how many of them there were. But the medals, he could easily remember the medals.

"All right, Kas," he finally replied, "I have, let's see, six, no . . . seven golds in the shot and the discus, some of them All-Canada and others just from the Alberta Games. Two of the golds, in fact, came from the Olympic Trials in Montreal. Then I have five silvers, three of them for the javelin. Only one of them was All-Canada, but one of them was from Utah State, too. It is called the Cardon Medal. Finally, I have four bronzes, one for the discus and three for the running high jump. All four of them were from the Alberta Games. That makes, let's see . . . sixteen medals altogether."

"Good heavens, Ben, you're the hero around here, not me!"

Ben shook his head. "Not hardly, Kas. I was just blessed to be in the right place at the right time, and the Lord gave me strength—"

"Lieutenant! Lieutenant Bennett!"

"Oh, no," Ben groaned as he lowered his shot and turned to peer toward the distant voice. "Have you ever noticed, men, how you can tell by the tone of a man's voice that trouble is in the air? That's Stagliano, and by the way he's shouting I'll bet you a dollar against a hole in a donut that there will be trouble somewhere."

"You're right," Leslie Milam replied as he resumed shoveling. "I've also noticed that the more rank a fellow gets, the more other people's troubles get dumped on him."

"Me, too. And that's why I'm getting out of here," Lieutenant Kastanas stated as he started away through the trees.

"And its also why I'm staying a sergeant," Leslie Milam said as he tossed out another shovel of sand and coral.

"Until I recommend you for a field promotion," Ben stated flatly while he watched Kastanas' fleeing back.

"Say, you wouldn't do that . . ."

Leslie was interrupted by another call for Ben, and then Sergeant Stagliano appeared, running and jumping as he made his way through the errantly destroyed palm grove.

"I'm here, Stag."

"You . . . you won't be in fifteen . . . minutes," the man panted as he stopped to catch his breath. "Lieutenant Jordan's platoon retreated after some little skirmish with the Japs, and Major Fowler is hopping mad!"

"You mean Colonel Fowler?" Ben corrected him softly.

"Yeah, I forgot that promotion. Anyway, Lieutenant, Fowler sent Dabbs and me on the double to rustle up a platoon and to tell you you're in charge of it."

"What? But Stag, I just got off a patrol yesterday."

"Can't help it, Lieutenant. Jordan muffed it up bad. He's been relieved of duty, and now you're it. Lieutenants Shavers and MacNamire from 'H' Company and Powell from 'F' Company will be with you, but you're in charge. You're also to take a 60-mm mortar and an 8-mm mortar under Sergeant Milam here, and Dabbs is out rounding up the rest of the men."

"Does Colonel Fowler mind if I ask what our objective is?" Ben asked with resignation.

Stagliano grinned. "Sure. Just be on your way by 15:30 hours and knock out before nightfall the Japs who hit Jordan's men. That's all. Oh, yeah, there is one more thing. Spend the night there, and in the morning proceed up the river far enough so you can be back here by 16:30 hours. Don't sustain any casualties, take all the prisoners you can, and make good Japs out of the rest."

"What a way to spend a Sunday afternoon," Leslie Milam grumbled as he grabbed his pack and struggled into it. "First it's digging bunkers and now it's killing Japs. Can't the army ever do *anything* on Monday?"

"To survive this war, Les, you'll need to learn to look on the bright side," Ben said as he struggled into his own fatigue jacket and pack. "For instance, at least we had the sacrament with Lieutenant Calder this morning."

"Yes," Leslie sighed, "at least we did that. So we take the sacrament and then go out and shoot people. This is a crazy world, Ben. You know that?"

"Do I ever! Les, sometime I'd like to meet a Jap and just visit with him. No guns, nothing but him and me and some friendly conversation. Christian or not, I'll bet that most of them are good people. Wouldn't that be great?"

"I don't know, Lieutenant. The Nips seem pretty set against us Americans."

"But the Holy Ghost could change that, Les. So could a little trust and kindness and compassion. I'll tell you what — maybe if I pray about it, the Lord will let me get to know these people a little better someday and maybe understand why they do the things they do. After all, they're God's children just like we are, and the gospel will be just as important to them as it is to you and me."

"You mean there will be Mormon Japs?" Leslie Milam asked incredulously.

Ben laughed outright at his friend's surprised expression. "Of course there will, Les. In fact, there probably already are. If the gospel goes to all the world, won't that include Japan?"

"I . . . I suppose so, but I never thought . . . "

"None of us do think, Les, at least not often enough. But it won't surprise me if the Lord is allowing this horrible war

72

to continue for that very reason—to open Japan for the preaching of the gospel. You ready to go now?"

Leslie Milam grinned. "As ever, Elder Bennett."

Ben grinned in response. "Thank you, Les. I'd love to be a missionary to the Japanese people. Now we'd better get after it, don't you think? Stag, keep shoveling in this pillbox of ours."

"But Lieutenant, I've got my own—"

Ben looked up, his brow smooth and his voice low. "Sergeant Stagliano, you will dig here. Three feet deep with straight sides and level bottom, the pit twelve feet to the square. And keep the lip cleared, so we can go from here with log walls. Am I clear?"

"Yes, sir!"

"Good. And Stag?"

"Yes, sir?"

"Thanks."

Both Ben and Leslie grinned, and after a moment, so did Sergeant Stagliano. Still chuckling, Leslie climbed the pit, and then he and Ben were gone, and Sergeant Stagliano began shoveling sand and bits of coral. Twenty minutes later, as he paused to wipe his brow, he was still grinning. "Doggone," he muttered to himself as he bent back to his work, "if only all the officers in this army were like Ben Bennett . . . "

CHAPTER

SEVEN

"So how is your mother?"

"What?" Ben asked as he turned in surprise. It was dark, and the patrol had established an uneasy perimeter. Already they had encountered two of the enemy, one of whom had been killed. But the other had escaped into the river, and they had no idea how soon he might be back with reinforcements. They had also captured important Japanese documents and maps, and Ben was certain they would be helpful as soon as they could be returned to HQ and interpreted.

In the darkness the insects sounded louder, huge bats fluttered overhead, and nightbirds in the jungle sounded almost like people crying. Night in the tropics, Ben had long ago concluded, was the noisiest experience a Canadian country boy should ever have to endure—especially when one didn't know what sort of surprise the enemy might conjure up next.

"I asked how your mother was," Leslie Milam repeated. "You got a letter from her. Remember?"

Turning around, Ben abruptly reached for his pocket. "My goodness, Les, I completely forgot my mother's letter. How embarrassing! I just hope she never finds out."

Sliding under a poncho, Ben turned on his flashlight, and then he opened and read the letter. Finished, he read the short news article she had enclosed. Then he read the letter again, and then one particular portion of it he read for a third and then a fourth time, unintentionally committing his mother's words to memory. Finally, he scanned the news article again quickly, and only then did he turn out his light and re-emerge into the jungle night.

"So how is she?"

"Pretty good, Les. She had an attack a week or so ago and is in the hospital recovering from what she calls minor surgery, so her heart is still giving her problems. But she isn't a complainer—never has been. In fact, she wants me to know that whatever I may have heard from other family members, she is doing fine and doesn't want me to worry."

"She sounds like quite a woman, Lieutenant."

"That she is, Les. She isn't much on size, but she can back any of us down any time she wants, or anyone else, for that matter. I remember when my brother Den was little, I used to pick on him something fierce, tormenting him until he would run to Mother for protection. She would get mad as a wet hen at me, but I could always outrun her and usually did. One time, though, she caught me, and I got *my* mouth washed out with soap for the angry words Den had said. I don't remember ever picking on Den again.

"Then there was the time that our school bullies, the Gallately brothers, started picking on my brother Cliff and me, locking us in a cellar after school and not letting us out until they were good and ready. When Mother got word of what they were doing, she marched to their home and told Mister Gallately just what his sons were doing and what she would do if they continued. Needless to say, we never got locked in the cellar again."

Leslie Milam chuckled, and Ben grinned into the darkness, remembering. "But you know," he continued, "she's a dainty woman, too, and loves beautiful things. She treasures her pretty dishes, her gleaming white damask 'best' table-cloth, and the bright floral oilcloth on her kitchen table. On her kitchen floor she has a Navajo rug I sent her, as well as a rug my brother Ray sent her from Eastern Canada. And you know these seashells I've been collecting and sending home? Well, they will be priceless to her; they'll take their place alongside the childlike pictures and pieces of ceramics we have given her over the years. To her, the value of those things is in the memories they provide, and so she never even sees the cracks, the chips, and the blotched paint.

"You know, Les, I can see her now, as clearly as if she were here. She has a high-backed black rocking chair that sits by the dining room window, and there she sits doing her mending out of the fabric-covered 'grape' mending basket. But what she is really doing is watching for the postman, who will surely bring her word from one or another of her family members. She holds court from that chair, too, dispensing justice and wisdom and counsel with equal ability. In fact, if this letter hadn't been written from the hospital, it would have come straight from that chair, where she spends so much of her time."

"Then . . . is your mother an invalid?" Leslie Milam asked.

Laughing, Ben shook his head. "Heavens, no. Did I give you that idea? I surely didn't mean to. She has health problems, but they have been with her ever since she had rheumatic fever as a young girl. But that doesn't slow her down, Les, not at all. She never stops working, and she's always cleaning the house, beating the rugs, or working in the kitchen.

"In fact, let me tell you about our breakfasts, which of course she always prepared. In our home they were big meals, beginning with some sort of porridge or another, followed by bacon and eggs, and then toast, pancakes, or baking-powder biscuits. If there were any potatoes left over from the night before, they were served with the bacon and eggs. Then there was always cream for our cereal and all the milk we could drink.

"In the summers, though, the biggest meals of the day were served at noon, when we had spent all morning in the fields. After breakfast had been cleaned up, Mother would start in immediately on the noon meals, which were really something. But I'll tell you, Les, what I remember best about those meals is the desserts. My favorite was something Mother called Rhubarb Betty, which was sort of an upside-down cake with the rhubarb on the bottom. Even now my mouth starts watering, just thinking about Rhubarb Betty.

"Mother loved music and athletics, too. Most of my family are quite musical, but I must have been given the short end of that stick—about all I could ever play was my mouth organ. But I was good enough that our dog Tip wanted to howl along with me. In fact, the only way we could ever shut Tip up was to put him in the coal shed.

"It was in athletics, though, where Mother really shined. It wasn't exactly that she was good at sports, though she was. But she had the ability to make us boys really want to perform to the best of our abilities, and all of us have. Between her and the coaching of my uncle Archie, Archibald F. Bennett, we've done pretty well. Cliff is a first-rate high jumper and sprinter, and I have never seen him beaten in a hundred-yard dash. In fact, my brothers and I had our own relay team, which was pretty good, if I may say so. We also had our own family basketball team, with me as center, Cliff and Ray as forwards, and Den and Jim as the guards. We could beat any team we ever played, and if I remember right, we usually did. But Mother was always there, cheering us on.

"She was a doctor, too, Les, though that was more out of necessity than anything else. And a good part of her skill came from a neighbor of ours, Grandma Engleson, who had a real gift for doctoring. I remember one day I was cutting hay, and the mower clogged. As I bent to unclog it the horses moved, and the blade nearly severed my right forefinger.

"Well, there was blood everywhere, so I hurried home for help. But Mother was busy in the kitchen, so I simply asked where the turpentine was, figuring that should do the trick. Mother told me without even looking up, and I poured a bunch of it on my finger.

"The next thing I knew, I was on my back and Mother was trying to bring me back to consciousness. I had never felt such pain! Then here came Grandma Engleson with her famous black salve, and she told Mother to swab me real good with it, wrap me up, and not undo the wrapping for two weeks.

"Mother did as she was told, but that two weeks nearly did her in. The bandage got filthy, and she fretted for days that she could smell decaying flesh. However, when we took the bandage off, I was healed completely, with just a thin white line to show where my wound had been. Since then, that black salve has been very prominent in our home.

"She also uses creosote sheep dip on occasion, one time being when I stabbed my foot with a pitchfork while Cliff and I were cleaning the barn."

"And it worked?" Leslie Milam asked incredulously.

"Well, my foot's still with me," Ben replied, and then both men laughed.

"She certainly sounds like a wonderful mother, Lieutenant."

"Yes, Les, she is. And she is very much like yours. Though they look nothing alike, when I met your mother back in Louisiana, I thought immediately how much she seemed like mine. I think we've both been very blessed."

"We certainly have. My mother's health has been good, so I'm glad your mother is doing better."

"She is. In her letter she tells me all about a Relief Society social she attended recently, where the sisters displayed what vegetables or handicrafts they had grown or made, and so on. So her spirits surely seem up."

"That's great, Lieutenant."

"Yes," Ben said thoughtfully as he stared off into the night. "I don't know what I'd do if . . . if she were to sicken and die . . ."

"The Red Cross would help you get home . . ."

Ben looked away. "That isn't what I mean, Les. I need my mother—I need her alive. There are things I want to ask her, to discuss with her, to learn from her. As I said, she has an amazing store of wisdom, and she is so close to the Spirit of God. I want to spend time with her, to learn how she does what she does when she is so ridden with pain."

"Maybe that's how she does it."

Ben looked at his companion. "What do you mean?"

Leslie Milam shrugged. "I-I don't know all about this, Lieutenant, but I know a little. From what I have observed, and from what my folks have taught me, there seems to be a correlation between suffering and wisdom, between pain and a closeness to the Holy Spirit. I don't remember the quote exactly, but in the second volume of the Journal of Discourses, page 7, I think, Brigham Young said that if Joseph Smith had not undergone the sufferings and persecutions he had been forced to endure, he could have lived a thousand years and not been able to accomplish the spiritual objectives that he reached during his brief lifetime."

"I don't think I've ever considered that idea, Les. But now that you mention it, I can think immediately of two or three scriptures that seem to bear the idea out. For instance, the Lord says that He chastens those whom He loves, and in another place He says that all Saints who will not endure chastening but deny Him cannot be sanctified."

"Yes," Leslie Milam agreed, "those seem to say it, all right."

"So you're postulating," Ben continued thoughtfully, "that my mother's suffering might be a blessing to her even while she is going through it . . . "

"Perhaps many blessings, Lieutenant, for herself and even for her family. One of those blessings might be that she is able to be as close to the Holy Spirit as you say she is."

Ben smiled. "I must write her as soon as we get back tomorrow and tell her about this idea of yours. Perhaps it will give her a bit of comfort. One thing I know, Les. When she says she is inspired about something, my brothers and sisters and I always listen. I don't think I've ever seen her wrong."

For a few moments the two men sat in silence, the darkness a living thing around them. Behind them the river gurgled quietly as it drifted past, and here and there the reddish glow of a cigarette marked the position of one or another of Ben's men.

But Ben thought only of his mother, of her closeness to the Spirit. Was she right this time, he wondered? Could it possibly be true, what she had written? There was also the news article, the small clipping from the *Salt Lake Tribune* that she had sent him. How did he feel about that? How should he feel? For crying out loud, he wondered, what was wrong with him that he couldn't seem to pull things together in his life?

"You want to talk about it, Lieutenant?"

Ben turned in surprise to look at Sergeant Milam. "What's that, Les?"

"The letter from your mother. Something in it is sure enough bothering you. Happen you'd like, we can talk about it a little."

Sighing, Ben picked up a piece of tree bark and flicked it into the darkness. "I didn't think I was that transparent. Mostly I try to do all my crying on the inside, where my dad always told me that real men did their crying."

"I know you do that, Lieutenant, and I admire you for it. But there are also times when crying on the outside is good, even if the crying is only done through talking out a fellow's troubles. If this is one of those times, then I'd sure admire being able to help you out."

Ben took a deep breath and then stretched back on his sleeping bag. "All right, Les. Let's talk, and see what comes of it. I . . . uh . . . Well, I might as well start right now. You know I'm a little older than you or most of the other fellows in the outfit?"

"I know."

"By my age, most fellows are married and raising their families. I'm not married and never have been. Not that I wouldn't like to have been. I just . . . well, it isn't easy for me to meet girls and make much of an impression on them — too serious, I guess. Or I get too busy with schooling, athletics, or work and simply forget to notice that they are around and perhaps showing some interest in me.

"In fact, Les, I got a Valentine card after I moved to Price, and I kept it to remind me I had some changes to make. The card had a lovely woman all tangled in a fishing line as she tried to reel in a huge fish. The caption read, "The Daddy of them all, and I thought he was mine. But he wrapped me up in my own fishing line."

"That's kind of funny."

"It would be, Les, except for what she wrote on the back. She said, 'Wake up before you are too old to appreciate life, and find me, a girl who likes you a lot.' There was no signature."

"So who sent it, Lieutenant?"

"I have absolutely no idea. Strange, isn't it? And she apparently gave up after that, for I never heard from her again. But my unknown admirer had a point, which I thought of often after that. I needed to wake up and appreciate life before I got too old to do so."

"But you never could pull it off?"

Ben smiled. "On the contrary, Les. I did pull it off, as you put it. I fell madly in love with my secretary, a girl named Sherie, and she fell just as deeply in love with me. I had never been so happy, and she seemed equally so. But there was a problem, and the longer our relationship lasted, the worse the problem grew. She was not a Mormon, nor did she wish to become one. I gave her a copy of the Book of Mormon, and she read a bit in it but never prayed about it. I talked to her at great length about the Church and Joseph Smith and the true priesthood, and she never argued with me. She just didn't believe me. And I would imagine that we had a thousand conversations about the temple and about how I could never be married anywhere else.

"She never understood my position regarding the temple at all, and I suppose that was the straw that broke the camel's back, so to speak. She wanted a church wedding, I wanted a temple marriage, and 'never the twain did meet.' I received a letter from her a few weeks ago, telling me that with my selfishness I had blown it and that whatever we might have had was now lost forever."

"Did you write her back, Lieutenant?"

"Of course. I don't remember all I said, but I did recommend that she burn all my letters and cards, and possibly hers as well. I also told her that since I might not be coming home anyway, the life expectancy of a soldier being what it is just now—which was a ploy to get her sympathy, obviously—that she needn't worry about having caused me pain. Finally I told her to go forward in her life to find as much happiness as she possibly could.

"Apparently she has done just that, Les, for today my mother sent me her wedding announcement. It was printed in the *Salt Lake Tribune,* and my Aunt Margaret sent it to Mother. I guess she was married October 28."

Leslie Milam took a deep breath. "And you feel now that you made a mistake?"

Ben laughed. "Certainly not! I know that a worthy temple marriage is an absolute requirement for entrance into the celestial kingdom, and I want to go nowhere else. Funny thing, though. In Mother's letter today she wrote that she once had to make the same decision."

"Is that right?"

"Apparently so. She says that at one time she was keeping company with a fellow by the name of Jack Hamilton, a fine man who wasn't a Mormon. She had some very deep feelings for him, but when he asked her to marry him, she had to turn him down. He couldn't give her a temple marriage or walk beside her into the celestial kingdom, and so she stepped back and waited for another, a man who could do as she wanted. Shortly thereafter my father appeared on the scene, and now we are all part of an eternal family."

"So I gather that you think you will also be able to love another woman?"

"Absolutely. You see, I meant what I told Sherie about the temple. I know that the Lord wants me to be married in His holy house. If Sherie doesn't want to be a part of that, then despite the intense pain such a decision makes me feel, I truly don't want to be a part of her life. And since I have loved her so deeply, I assume that the Lord will grant me the ability to love another as well."

"Or more so, Lieutenant."

Ben nodded. "Yes, if I understand the concept of eternal marriage, that will surely be so."

For a moment the silence closed around the two men again, each alone with his thoughts. But finally Leslie Milam pushed the conversation ahead.

"So where does all this lead, Lieutenant?"

In the darkness Ben grinned. "Back to my mother's letter, of course. Les, do you believe in prophecy?"

"Of course I do."

"From your mother?"

"The scripture says, Lieutenant, that the testimony of Jesus is the spirit of prophecy. My mother sure enough has the testimony of Jesus, so if she decides to prophesy to me, why, I'll sit right up and listen. I assume that your mother is the same."

"Exactly. And now you know why I am so pensive. My dear mother prophesied to me in her letter today, and ever since I read it, I've been sitting right up and listening."

"And she said?"

"She said," Ben replied as he tossed another hunk of bark into the darkness, "that she felt impressed to tell me that I was about to . . . become acquainted with my wife."

"Whoowee!"

"Quiet, sergeant! We're on perimeter, you might remember."

"Lawsy, Lieutenant, I plumb forgot. But that's wondrous news, uh . . . happen you were home in Utah or somewhere. Since you aren't, who you going to meet out here? One of the natives, maybe?"

Leslie Milam dissolved into laughter, and though Ben did not find the humor so fine, nevertheless he said nothing, waiting for his friend to wind down.

"Whew, Lieutenant," Leslie Milam gasped at length, "but that there is funny!"

"I suppose it could be, Les, if this wasn't such a serious thing to me."

Leslie Milam finally read the tone of his friend's voice and immediately apologized. "Lieutenant, I . . . I was only joshing you a bit. I hope you know that."

Ben reached out and patted his shoulder. "I do, Les. I just wish I knew where this woman is to come from that my mother tells me I'm to meet. However, it will surely be interesting to see it happen. Perhaps when it does —"

Blaaattt!

"What in thunder was that?"

Instantly on the ground with his carbine before him, Ben stared into the darkness. Soon the sound was repeated, and then a similar sound came from another direction.

"Lieutenant," Sergeant Dabbs called from several yards away, "you want we should open fire?"

"No, Sergeant," Ben called back softly. "But find out if anyone knows what the dickens that noise is."

"Yes, sir."

There was silence along the line, broken only by the occasional blatting of the strange noise. Finally Dabbs slid to the ground next to Ben and reported.

"Sir, one of the men says it's Jap signaling horns. He heard 'em down in New Guinea."

"So how many of the enemy do we think are out there."

"Well, sir, we can't be sure, but I've been listening close, and I reckon there are three — at least three with horns. I'm also fairly certain that there are only three Japs out there, too."

"Three? Why's that, Dabbs?"

"Two of 'em put me in mind of my hounds back home, Lieutenant. Their baying is like a man's voice, easy to tell apart. Same with these horns, or two of 'em, at least. The third one is off a ways, and though it sounds the same as one of the others, I know it ain't. There's distance between 'em."

"Interesting."

"Yeah, but there's more. You listen careful, Lieutenant, you can tell those Nips are blowing and then moving a few yards and then blowing again. I've listened to coon hounds enough in my life to be able to spot the location of sound right fair. They ain't signaling, sir, at least not to themselves. That's why I reckon there's only three men. They're trying to make us think there's a whole herd of 'em out there, and maybe scare us into doing something foolish."

"Such as?"

"Using up our ammo, maybe. Or cutting and running from 'em in the dark and slamming into some sort of bobby trap."

Thoughtfully Ben nodded. "Thank you, Sergeant. Tell the men on guard to keep their eyes open extra sharp but not to fire unless they are absolutely certain of a target. Then tell the others to get some sleep. We've got a long hike tomorrow, and they're going to need their rest."

"Yes, sir."

"And Dabbs?"

"Yes, sir?"

"I've heard you howling like your old coon dogs back home can howl. Can any of the other men do that?"

In the darkness Tom Dabbs sounded confused. "Yes, sir, Lieutenant, I reckon so. Fact is, there's maybe twenty of the men that can howl down an ol' racoon even better than I can. But I don't—"

"Good," Ben said, interrupting him. "Maybe if you passed the word and asked the men to do a bit of baying and howling, we could give these Japs a taste of their own medicine.

"Yes, sir!" Tom Dabbs replied, grinning with sudden understanding. And then with a chuckle he disappeared into the darkness along the line.

Ben and Leslie Milam waited, anticipating, and not many minutes later the mournful howling of a southern hound dog suddenly pierced the jungle night. The howl was joined by another, louder and more sorrowful but from some distance away, and the blatting that was going on at that instant came to a squeaking, mid-blatt stop. Within another sixty seconds a whole pack of 'hound dogs' had begun to yip and bray and carry on as though they had discovered a giant tree filled with raccoons right above them. The howling men continued their chorus unabated, and when they finally quieted down after perhaps another five minutes, they did so to a totally silent jungle.

All waited, their breaths held and their weapons at the ready, but no more horns sounded. Nor could any of the Americans hear the sound of anything moving out in the jungle night. Every living creature had been howled into silence.

"Now that's more like it," Ben breathed as he closed his eyes.

"It certainly did the job, Lieutenant."

"That it did. Now for a change there is only us and the stars. You know, Les, I used to wish on the stars when I was a kid. Since it's almost Christmas and since you and I have been discussing eternal matrimony, I think I will do the same tonight. With all my heart I wish that all the nations of the earth would take 'Miss Peace' by the hand, lead her to the altar, and be sealed to her for time and all eternity. She has been courted long enough and by now should have made up her mind. But like all women, she is an evasive thing, and so it is time for the nations of the earth to force the issue and make her marry all of them at once. Just a bit of polyandry in a polygamous age, you understand. But wouldn't it be wonderful if it could really happen?"

Leslie Milam quietly agreed, and no further words passed between the two friends. Finally the insects tentatively resumed their chirruping, the men relaxed even more, and soon the jungle returned to normal. And if there were any other horns blown that night, Ben never heard them. Nor, for that matter, was a single round of U.S. Army ammunition wasted that night, either.

Ben slept peacefully, his dreams filled with shadowy feminine images that seemed always just out of his reach but getting closer, definitely getting closer . . .

CHAPTER

EIGHT

"All right, men," Ben grunted, "on three everybody push again! One . . . two . . . three!"

To the tune of groans and grunts from Ben and two other men, the huge coconut palm log inched up the incline, teetered for an instant on the top, and then slid and rolled down and into place. With a little more effort the log was secured, and the three men plodded down the hill to where the next log waited in place.

"How many more of these do we have to push up there?" Sergeant William "Tiff" Tiffin asked as he plopped onto the log.

"Twenty," Ben replied listlessly.

"Twenty-two," Sergeant Tom Dabbs corrected with even less enthusiasm. "My gosh, Lieutenant, how come so doggone many?"

"We have to finish the walls," Ben answered, "and then cover the roof. Unless, Dabbs, you would prefer living and sleeping in an open-air bunker."

Tom Dabbs groaned. "At this point, I'd welcome the stars."

"So would I," agreed William Tiffin. "Lieutenant, Dabbs

and I ain't supermen like you, with muscles busting out everywhere like flowers on a June day. We're just poor southern boys with only enough muscle to hold body and soul together and no more. All this hauling logs is killing us for fair."

"And look at you, Lieutenant," Tom Dabbs added. "You ain't hardly even worked up a sweat. How can you expect Tiff and me to ever keep up with you on work like this?"

Ben looked at the two men carefully. "You fellows are nuts. Why, compared to you, I'm an old man. Both of you ought to be able to work circles around me."

"You old?" William Tiffin scoffed. "Lieutenant, I'm nearly twenty-five years old, and Dabbs here is almost twenty-four. Ten bucks says we're both older than you."

"For your sakes, it's a good thing I don't bet," Ben replied easily. "According to my driver's license, I'm well past thirty, and if you want to press it, I'll prove it to you."

"Thirty? Naw, sir, that can't be so."

"But it is, and though I don't want to hurt your feelings, I'm going to tell you why I look so much younger and more fit than you do. And again, I'm telling you this for your sakes. You say this hard work will kill you off?"

"Yes, sir," Sergeant Tiffin nodded, "it very easily could do just that, sir."

"Is that what causes your bleary, bloodshot eyes?" Ben asked, grinning. "Or gives you the yellow nicotine stains on your teeth or fingers? You men have plenty of muscle for your bodies and souls, only you're destroying it with poison. Dabbs, weren't you and McQuirt drunk last night?"

Tom Dabbs dropped his eyes. "Yes, sir, I reckon we were, at that."

"And look at you, Tiff. We hardly take a breather and you practically break your own arms trying to get another cigarette into your mouth."

"But I get the shakes, Lieutenant."

"Of course you do, Tiff. That stuff you smoke is pure

poison, and you've gotten yourself hooked on it. Just like these poor souls that are called dope fiends, you're addicted. Same with you, Dabbs, on that and alcohol. Now I've told you fellows about the Word of Wisdom—"

"But that's religious stuff, Lieutenant! Just puffy words. This here is the only way us boys can keep going in this real war."

Ben laughed outright. "That, men, is absolute nonsense. If religion is to be real, and it is, it must be more than spiritual ideas. Now the two of you have been complaining that I have been working you too hard, and on the other hand you have been accusing me of being unsympathetic because I am stronger than you. Is that correct?"

"Yeah."

"What's that, Sergeant Tiffin?"

"Yeah, sir!"

"Thank you. Now you don't want to listen to me, either one of you, so I intend to change the subject. I saw some rat poison down at the supply dump yesterday and brought a bunch of it back with me."

"Great," Tom Dabbs stated, relieved that Ben was off his back. "One way or another we'll get rid of those filthy little beasts."

"Uh . . . Dabbs, that isn't exactly what I had in mind for the poison."

"What? But we've got all those rats . . . "

"Listen to me, men, for this is an order. Since our rations have been running low, starting today the cook will be mixing a little of that poison in with our food. It will give us more to eat, you understand. There won't be enough in any one serving to hurt anyone, and all the men will finally feel satisfied."

"What?" William Tiffin screeched. "Lieutenant, that's plain crazy! You can't order us to eat poison! Why, I wouldn't touch that stuff."

Ben smiled thinly. "You won't need to, Tiff. I was only kidding. But it would be no worse than drinking alcohol, or smoking, or taking anything else into our bodies that is harmful. If my body is stronger than yours, it is only because I treat it the way God has suggested that I treat it — with respect. There's nothing religious about that, or spiritual, either one. If I avoid tobacco, alcohol, and other harmful substances because they are poisonous, then my body will respond by being more healthy, and I will be stronger. You would experience the same renewed vigor if you did the same."

"Lieutenant," Sergeant Tiffin groused, "you just don't understand."

"Oh, I think I do." Now Ben grinned. "I even understand tired muscles and exhausted bodies. That's why I went out an hour ago and called for a caterpillar to come and finish this job up for us."

"A caterpillar? What . . . "

"In fact, I believe I hear our tractor coming now, right on time. They'll move the logs for us, and it will give us plenty of time to get ready to celebrate Christmas together tomorrow morning."

Now the two men were truly stunned. "Celebrate Christmas . . . together?" Tom Dabbs squeaked. "But . . . but . . . "

"Lieutenant," Sergeant Tiffin whined, "you . . . you can't do that! We've got plans, big plans, and . . . well, if you was there we couldn't . . . couldn't . . . "

"Yes, Sergeant Tiffin?"

"Uh . . . what I mean to say, is . . . uh . . . well, you don't hardly do . . . uh . . . the things . . . "

"Oh," Ben stated sincerely, "but I *do!* And the things we will do are *fun,* too. We'll have races, volleyball matches, contests in throwing my new brass shot, a singalong . . . "

"Lieutenant . . . " William Tiffin wailed.

"And best of all, we'll do a surprise Christmas for the native kids in the village down on the Dixie Highway."

Ben almost laughed at the startled looks on the faces of the two men. Crusty as they were, and tough as they acted, Ben had never seen two men who loved children more than did Tom Dabbs and William Tiffin. Both came from large families, both were older children themselves, and both had been used extensively by their mothers in caring for their younger siblings. Consequently neither feared children, and time and again as they had passed through native villages there on Morotai and earlier, on Goodenough Island and in New Guinea, Ben had seen one or the other of his "tough" sergeants kneeling in the road surrounded by kids, having the time of their lives.

So now he watched with great anticipation as his suggestion of giving Christmas to the native kids slowly sunk in. Tom Dabbs was the first to respond.

"By jings," he breathed, "that there is a fine idea, Lieutenant. I thought on that idea a mite myself, one day, but I reckon I forgot about it in the mess of this here war."

"Well, I never thought of it at all," William Tiffin stated, "but I sure enough wish I had. I'm with you in this, Lieutenant, booze or no booze. What do we do to start?"

Quickly Ben gave instructions to the two excited sergeants, and three hours later, as the sun dropped toward the smoky, volcanic horizon of the Halamaheras, he watched with satisfaction as the caterpillar tractor scooped the last blade of sand and coral onto the top of his completed bunker.

"Sergeant Stagliano," he then called to his company clerk, "what's the latest on Dabbs and Tiffin?"

Stagliano looked up from the table where he was working. "Last I heard from Lykes, they had hit up the guys at Supply. From what I can figure out, Lieutenant, those two have really made a haul."

"I thought they might. Come over here and tell me what you think of this bunker."

"You need a door on it," the clerk said as he drew nearer.

"Tomorrow, Stag. That'll be your department. We'll also need some gun emplacements out here in front, but I'll let Lieutenant Jordan take care of them."

"You sleeping in there tonight, Lieutenant?"

Ben shook his head. "Not on your life. Without a good, solid door, this thing could be a death-trap. No, I'll take my chances in my tent for another night."

"You think we'll have another air alert tonight?"

"Probably so. The Japs don't seem happy to have us in the neighborhood, and air raids must seem to them like a good way to discourage us from staying."

"Why do you think they are always false alarms?"

Again Ben shook his head. "I don't know, Stag, unless they are out of aircraft and send out single planes just to keep us nervous."

Stagliano laughed. "Well, if that is their objective, Lieutenant, it sure does do the job."

"On me, too. Stag, call down to Supply and round up Dabbs and Tiffin, will you? And if they need a hand with their haul, get some of the boys to help them. I want everything they've managed to round up stacked here right outside my tent. And if possible I want it done before dark. I have some mail to censor now, but tell the men I will conduct an ordinance inspection in the morning at 0800 hours."

"Yes, sir."

Stagliano didn't move, and after a moment Ben looked up. "Yes, Stag? Is there something else?"

"Well, yes, sir, there is. I . . . I just wanted to tell you what a fine thing I think you are doing for those little native kids. I . . . I mean, well, I have three kids of my own, and so I know how much Christmas means to them. But you, sir, unmarried and all, well, the men and I agree that . . . that this is a fine gesture and we . . . we surely support you . . . "

Startled at the man's surprise, Ben cut him short. "Thanks, Stag. If I had kids, I would want them taken care of. In fact, some day I hope that I do, if I can just get past this blamed war."

"By golly, sir," Staglio declared, interrupting Ben's reverie, "I completely forgot. You got a letter yesterday, and I've been carrying it around in my pocket ever since. The name on the return address says 'Miss,' so I imagine you will want to read it alone."

And grinning, Sergeant Stagliano handed the letter to Ben. Quizzically Ben took it and was just reading the envelope when the air-raid sirens went off again, the shrieks blasting furiously against his eardrums.

"Hit the dirt, Stag!" he shouted as he tumbled into the nearest foxhole with his chubby supply sergeant directly behind and suddenly on top of him.

CHAPTER

NINE

There was something hideously obscene about the tiny silver planes buzzing around high against the blue, cloudless sky. They were so small that it looked like they might all be put in a matchbox. Yet they were absolutely lethal, and every man on the ground understood that.

From his foxhole, Ben watched as the first load of bombs was dropped some distance off, down toward the airstrip, and then he listened to the explosions. In the interval of silence, then, that occurred while the planes were out of the range of the anti-aircraft guns and were circling for their next run, Ben could hear their motors plainly. That sound, still uneven and chugging, suddenly seemed deadly vicious. Ben thought of being tied down to slimy tree roots in a muddy jungle and having a rattlesnake weave its ugly head just a few inches from his throat, waiting and picking its place to strike. Then he thought of all the other evil nightmares he had ever had, and none of them could compare with the helpless nightmare feeling he experienced every time the Japs circled above him.

Everybody on Morotai knew when the planes were coming, or at least they could make a pretty good guess. First, about seven-thirty or eight in the morning, when the sun was still hidden behind the mountains to the east, would come the observation plane, "Washingmachine Charlie," in his high-wing monoplane. Charlie would circle over the compound and the partially constructed airstrip, and the .30 and .50 caliber machine guns would shoot golden tracers all around him. The three-inch guns had orders not to open up because Charlie had a camera and would photograph their flashes and get their locations. So they remained silent, and Charlie remained airborne.

Charlie would circle deliberately and then would release a silver balloon and watch the wind carry it up into the sky. That was to test the wind currents. It filled Ben with bitter anger to see the way Charlie got the stage set for the daily carnage and destruction, and many times he wondered that humans could be so calloused.

Charlie would then putt-putt away, flying straight over Morotai to wherever his airfield was. And then the wait would begin, as the Japs prepared their planes, loaded their bombs, and examined the photographs Charlie had brought back to them. "Fine weather. Good hunting," they would probably be told, and then the planes would take off.

Later the sirens would sound on Morotai, and crews would run to their posts on the three-inch anti-aircraft guns and the .50 caliber machine guns, and everybody else would try to get under cover.

Then the planes would come over — one, two, half a dozen of them, and sometimes many more. They would criss-cross Morotai without dropping, taking their time, deliberately getting their targets lined up. The anti-aircraft guns would open up and burst in them and around them, but if one of the planes was shot out of the sky, the others just reformed and kept coming.

Having picked their targets, they would usually come back in low, flying straight in from over the channel toward the Halamaheras. But sometimes they would come in from the north, sometimes from the south, and sometimes from all directions at once, making it impossible to know for sure where to best hide from their metal-encased death.

Now the planes were coming back again, and as Ben lay helplessly in his foxhole with Sergeant Stagliano, he counted the seconds to determine their distance. Suddenly came the noise of the bombs falling, and Ben knew—they were close!

The falling bombs didn't screech or whistle or whine. Rather they sounded to Ben like a pile of wooden planks being whirled around in the air by a terrific wind and then being driven straight down to the ground. They took thirty years to hit, or longer, and while they were falling, they seemed to change the dimensions of the world.

Their noise stripped the eagles from the colonel's shoulders and the bar from the lieutenant's and left them both little boys, naked and afraid. It drove all the intelligence from the eyes of the nurses and medicos, all the courage from the hearts of the enlisted men, and left them all vacant and staring. It seemed to wrap a steel tourniquet of fear around a person's head, until his skull felt like bursting. In fact, it made the men realize why mankind had found he needed God.

Suddenly there was a terrific sort of "swish" through the air, but before Ben could do more than realize he had heard it, a tremendous concussion and flash of light filled his world.

As Ben did his best to steel himself against the concussion driving against his ears, he wondered where the bomb had hit, which of his men had been killed, how much damage it had done to the bivouac area, and why it had not been followed instantly by a second, third, and so on. And even though his mind was filled with all those questions, he still somehow found time to consider what a relief it was to hear the explosions rather than the freight-train roar and deadly swish of the falling bombs.

Finally came the silence as the planes drifted off and

banked for another turn, and into the void came the sound of fires, fires and heroism. Men dashed about picking up wounded and dead and beating down fires even as more bombs were falling from the last and final run of the bombers.

Scrambling from his foxhole, Ben began giving orders, trying to bring order out of the chaos created by the Japanese. As stretcher bearers gently lifted from other foxholes the bloody remnants of what had been American soldiers a few minutes before, Ben steeled his mind against the horror before him. Down the line, the casualty was a handsome captain whose legs were now only bloody stumps, back near an anti-aircraft gun emplacement it was an eighteen-year-old American boy who would never again remember his name, or his mother's name, or anything else, but would spend the remainder of his life staring at people blankly when they spoke to him. One "bomb-proof" bunker had been hit directly, and the several bodies inside, while not blown apart, had suffocated from the dust and smoke. Now their families would need to be notified, and Ben knew that would ultimately be his task, or the task of some other officer like himself.

"Lieutenant, I . . . I think they're gone."

Ben nodded. "I think so, too. But look at those fires down at the airstrip, Stag. The Japs did some damage this time."

Standing, surveying his men, Ben was once again astounded to see that none of them in "E" Company had been hit. Of course, he didn't know about Sergeants Dabbs and Tiffin, but he wasn't too worried about them, either. Somehow they always seemed to be in the safest place, and at the most opportune moment possible.

"Stag," he called softly as he set to work clearing up some debris, "get the men together, and let's see what we're going to need to do before dark."

CHAPTER

TEN

Slowly Ben walked to his tent and stepped inside, where he spent a moment just breathing deeply. It had been two hours since the air raid, and he was exhausted. But things were back in shape, and for the moment he could breathe more easily.

Walking slowly to his bunk, he reached into his pocket and pulled out the letter he had been given, and for a long moment he did nothing more than look at it.

Curious, he thought, how he felt. First, throughout the air raid he had not stopped thinking of this letter, wondering about it, almost aching to read it. Second, and almost contrary to his other feelings, he got mail all the time, from family and from a great host of friends. But never, until now, had he felt a reluctance to open a letter. Yet now he did, and for the life of him he could not understand why.

In the sweltering heat of the tent he sat on his bunk, where again he examined the front of the letter. The postmark was Ephraim, Utah, a community in Sanpete County not far from Price, where he had lived. But a mountain lay between Price and Ephraim, and he had rarely gone there. And so far as he knew, he had never met a young woman while he had been there, either.

And this letter had definitely been written by a young woman, in fact, a Miss Patricia Christensen, he discovered as he turned the envelope over to examine the back.

So—a Miss Patricia Christensen from Ephraim, Utah, had written him a letter. But he didn't know her, could not place her name at all. And that being the case, why was he feeling such a crazy reluctance to open her letter?

Grinning, he thought of his mother's probably prophetic statement that he would soon meet his wife, and then he knew the source of his reluctance.

"Ben Bennett," he chided himself softly, "you're *afraid*. All along you've told yourself how anxious you were to find your wife and settle down, and now that you might be holding your first letter from her in your hands, you're afraid to open it.

"A girl from Sanpete County, huh? Funny, but I never thought . . . "

Suddenly Bill's grin grew even wider, for he remembered an old joke he had heard years earlier back in Price—about it being a wise move for a fellow to marry a girl from Sanpete, for then no matter where he took her to live, she would always have had things worse.

Chuckling, Ben tore open the letter, and even while he was unfolding the contents he was telling himself how ludicrous his fanciful dreams had suddenly become. But still his heart was pounding in an unusual way, and like it or not, he knew that he was feeling a strange sense of excitement.

Glancing down, he read:

"Dear Mister Bennett:

"Now that I write that, it seems terribly formal, and since we have already been properly introduced, perhaps I shall change it to 'Mister Bill.'

"I am sure this letter comes as a surprise to you, but let me reacquaint you with who I am. My name is Patricia 'Pat' Christensen, and for two years I was a roommate to your

100

sister Lila, when we were all attending Utah State University up in Logan. In fact, that is where I met you. As I remember, you were on your way to the army, and you stopped in to visit with Lila and to tell her good-bye. Now do you remember?

"You don't? Very well, I will tell you more. I am the tall, not-thin-enough girl with the blonde hair that is almost dishwater blonde and may even have been almost bleached blonde when you met me because I had been out in the sun so much. I am also the one who stumbled (how embarrassing) when I reached to shake your hand, very nearly forcing myself into your arms. There! Now I am certain that you will remember me."

Pausing, Ben looked out the tent door, his mind years and thousands of miles away. Could he remember this young woman? Actually, he did have a faint recollection of one of Lila's roommates stumbling, but to put that memory to a face? So far at least, it wasn't happening. But maybe if he kept reading—

"If Lila were to describe me (and she has, to my face, many times), she would say that I was a friendly, happy, outgoing person who is very sociable. She would say (I hope this doesn't sound boastful, but it probably does) that I am informal and put on no airs. She would say that I find it easy to be myself and have no false pretenses. What I think she is really saying is that I am a country hick, and that there is no hope that I will ever change.

"I come from a large and wonderful family. My father is Oscar O. Christensen, my mother is Mary Lund Christensen, and my brothers and sisters are Walton J., Hazel M. Christensen Mortensen, Dean C., TreVor L., Kathrine A. Christensen Foulger, myself, Eugene O., Ronald D., and Jerry M. Christensen. We are all from Ephraim, in SanPete County.

"Besides my family, I have two real loves in my life. I love music, and I cherish my testimony of the Gospel of Jesus

Christ. I love very much to sing, and I have been in many chorus groups, cantatas, operettas, girls quartets, and Relief Society choruses. While at Snow College I sang in the Messiah, and at Snow and Utah State I was active in musical and drama productions. And all my life I have served in church organizations, for I believe that service is necessary if one is to keep her testimony secure."

Well, even if he couldn't remember her, Ben was impressed with the things she was saying. In his mind, he could see his own family gathered around the old pump organ, singing all the old favorites, and he could see himself singing in men's quartets and at church functions. Wasn't it strange that this girl should enjoy the same things?

And what she said about testimony and service — that was a profound thought. He would need to consider that more deeply later on. Looking down, he continued reading.

"Now that is far and away enough about me. Lila wrote me recently and suggested that you might be in need of some letters from home, 'Mister Bill,' and so I decided to send you one.

"It is beautiful here today, Sunday morning in the country. Rain has fallen during the night, but the sun is out and everything is shining with freshness and new life — something very unusual for October. Birds are chirping merrily — it is a beautiful morning, and gives one a thrill to be alive.

"Most of the folk here in Ephraim are off to Church, and I find myself wondering if 'Mister' Bill has the chance to attend church in the far-off Pacific. I certainly hope so. I enjoy Sundays filled with Church activities, and that's the way they were intended, isn't it? So that we could all be filled with enough of the Spirit to carry us through the next week? I would imagine that 'Mister' Bill would have even greater need of the Spirit because he is where he is, and so I sincerely pray that you have the chance to attend church at least every now and then."

Pausing, Ben thought again, considering the things that this girl was saying. To the best of his knowledge, he really couldn't remember her. Nevertheless, thus far he was impressed with her thinking. Her handwriting had an artistic flair that was borne out by her description of a Sanpete County morning, and that he liked. But more important, here was a young lady who understood the importance of weekly worship exactly as he had come to understand it. Further, she was not afraid to express herself regarding spiritual matters. Truly he had not made the acquaintance of many like her.

"Deer hunting is in full swing in these parts right now. Do you enjoy deer hunting, 'Mister Bill?' I imagine from what Lila has told me of you, that you do, and that now you will be wishing that you were here to go hunting. My brothers would take you if you were. The weather has been beautiful for hunting, too. We had snow for a week, but then it warmed up and melted off, and yesterday for opening day it was lovely. As I said, it rained last night, but today the sky is fresh and blue, and I think we will be in for another gorgeous week.

"All my brothers went hunting with my father, all six of them, as well as my two brothers-in-law, while my sisters Hazel and Kay and I stayed home with Mother. I don't know exactly which canyon the boys hunted in, but they had good luck, for my brother Jerry caught one. We will be having roast venison this afternoon."

Dropping the letter again, Ben grinned. "Caught one." What an interesting phrase. Of course one didn't "catch" a deer when one went hunting—that was the domain of the fisherman. But all her life, Ben's mother had used the same phrase, and no amount of laughter or coaching from her sons had ever been able to wean her from it. Thus the phrase seemed especially nice to Ben, who read it through twice more, a wide grin still on his face.

But there was more that impressed him, too. First, this

young lady had come from a large family who were still close to each other. Because he had done the same, he knew what an impact for good that would have on her life. Second, she was interested enough in the things her brothers did that even though she did not participate except as a spectator, she could describe them with interest and excitement. To him, that meant that she was not self-centered or selfish. These were great qualities, he thought, grinning again. Truly would he enjoy getting better acquainted with this Miss Patricia Christensen.

"Lila told me, 'Mister Bill,' that you had recently been forced to make a very hard decision in your life, and that perhaps you were still struggling with it. I don't know what your difficult decision pertained to, and without meaning to pry or preach, either one, may I just tell you how I feel about such things?

"I know how hard it is to make decisions, but somehow I have always been happy in the decisions I have made — thanks to prayer.

"Let me give you a 'for instance.' Not long ago I was dating a very fine fellow. He did not smoke or drink, he had exceptionally high standards, and I liked him very much. But when I tried to get him interested in the Gospel, my efforts were to no avail. He asked me to take his engagement ring, but I prayed and prayed, and when it came right down to it, I just couldn't take the ring. My feeling was that I could not deny myself an eternal marriage.

"That decision, 'Mister Bill,' was made through prayer, and though hard, I feel good about the decision. I believe prayer is the greatest guide we have at a time of indecision, or any other time! Here is a verse from "If I But Pray."

> "And when life's trials
> pass my way
> They grow much lighter

when I pray.
I've many blessings in reserve,
God gives me more than I deserve.
R.N. Gibson

"From what Lila has told me, I know you are a man of prayer, and so I know that God will help you to make the right decision and to feel good about it once it has been made.

"Well, I must get ready to catch the bus back to Salt Lake City, where I work as a secretary at Fort Douglas. Maybe I will see you there when you are discharged. If you would like to write me, I am enclosing my Salt Lake City address on 1st Avenue. I would very much enjoy hearing from you. Hope everything turns out for you just the way it should. Knowing what Lila says about you, I'm sure it will.

"Sincerely,

" 'Miss' Pat Christensen

"P.S. I have not mailed this for several weeks—I have been afraid of what you might think of me for being so bold. But I have decided that is not showing much confidence in friendship, so today I mail it. I hope you have a wonderful day.

" 'Pat' "

Dropping the letter, Ben lay back on his bunk, his eyes open but unseeing. What an interesting—no, *unusual* would be a better word—girl! How clearly she seemed to see things! And her description of herself, or at least Lila's description, was accurate, too. She was certainly outgoing and informal, with no false airs or false pretenses or prideful sophistication. How refreshing it was to discover that a girl like her actually existed.

Yet she exhibited great maturity, wisdom, and an abiding faith in God. What an ideal combination of qualities to find in a woman! And it was very interesting that she would have had an experience in romance so similar to his own.

105

Yes, whether or not this was the girl his mother had felt impressed was coming into his life, he would most definitely write her back. This was a young lady he would very much enjoy getting to know better. In fact—

"Lieutenant! Lieutenant Bennett!"

Sitting up and looking out through the tent flaps, Ben saw sergeants Dabbs and Tiffin barreling toward him in a jeep, Dabbs driving and Tiffin standing and waving frantically. Behind them came another jeep, driven by Sergeant Lykes and carrying Lieutenant Richester, and the second jeep was pulling a tarp-covered trailer.

Well, Ben thought as he rose to his feet, refolded the letter and slipped it into his pocket, *back to this grand and glorious war.*

CHAPTER

ELEVEN

"Lieutenant," Sergeant Tiffin shouted as they drew nearer and as Stagliano returned to his table-desk, "would you take a gander at all this loot? I never had no idea this would be so easy."

Grinning, Ben watched the two jeeps pull to a stop near his tent. Quickly the men scrambled out, and while Lieutenant Richester came toward him carrying his pack and duffle, the two sergeants pulled the tarp away from the heaped-full trailer that Supply Sergeant Lykes had willingly lent them.

"Hi, Ben," Lieutenant Richester said amiably, "you got an extra bunk I could borrow for a night or so? That air raid wiped me out, and I need a place to crash."

"We do," Ben responded, "if you don't mind ants or rats or air alerts or itchy trigger fingers by the men on guard. How are you, Rich? I haven't seen you since New Guinea."

"I'm doing fine, Ben, and any bunk you have will beat sleeping near that confounded airfield. Every Jap pilot in the whole war wants to bomb airfields. You should see what they did today."

"Bad?"

"Worse than that. Fifty-two of our planes were damaged

or destroyed, with seventeen completely gone. Five B-24s, one P-61, three C-47s, and several B-25s and A-20s. Of course, we have hundreds of planes left, so they won't stop us, you can bet on that."

"I'm glad you weren't hurt, Rich."

"It's been crazy, Ben. I saw at least a dozen casualties." Ben shook his head sadly.

"Anyway, Ben, when these two crazy yahoos told me what you and your men had going for the natives, I decided to take a couple of days off and visit the easy side of the war."

Ben laughed. "Well, I hope we don't disappoint you. Looks like the boys did real well, though, gathering presents."

Lieutenant Richester nodded. "I'll say. When the word got around, every Joe in the army wanted to give something. I wager there's never been such a pile of chocolate for the kids and cigarettes for their parents in all the south Pacific."

"The Lieutenant's right, sir," Tom Dabbs said as he stepped up. "Why, there must be enough there for every kid on Morotai, let alone the village down on the Dixie Highway."

"The Dixie Highway?" Lieutenant Richester asked, sounding confused.

"The road around this end of the island," Ben explained. "Most of my men are from the south, Rich, and when the caterpillars cut that road, it just seemed natural to call it the Dixie Highway.

"Dabbs, did you get any toys, or anything that might pass for toys?"

Tom Dabbs nodded. "We got a few knives, three or four whistles made from shell casings, something else made from a shell casing that I ain't got the foggiest notion what it is, and one guy gave us a dozen dolls he's been making from coconut husks and seashells. They're ugly things, but you never know. Kids like crazy things."

"That's what I hear. Anything else?"

"Yeah. The fellows down at Ordinance are making up a

hundred toy trucks. They'll be real simple, but I looked at one a man was sending home to his kid, and it's solid and the wheels all turn. I think the native kids will like them."

"And they can get us a hundred of them by morning?"

Tom Dabbs nodded. "They've set up an assembly line, sir. One of the men used to work for Ford in Detroit, they say, and he's got the whole dang platoon working on those trucks. I guarantee it, we'll have a hundred of them here by first light."

"Even with that raid?"

"It didn't even slow them down, sir. In fact, the CO down there excused them from duty *and* clean-up, just so they could get the toys done. They're all pretty excited, sir."

"Wonderful. Hey, Sergeant Tiffin, park that trailer here by my tent."

"Yes, sir."

"And Tiff? Put the booze you collected for you and Dabbs and McQuirt inside my tent. All of it."

The sergeant looked shocked, and then his face slowly fell with discouragement. "Aw, Lieutenant, how did you know?"

Ben tapped his head with his finger. "Smarts, Tiff. Comes from keeping my body free from that poison we talked about. I told you it paid off. Now hop to it, and I'll hear no more about partying until after we've been to the native village tomorrow. "Rich, come in and make yourself at home. I've got some letters to censor before it gets full dark, and that means I've got to hurry."

"Do you enjoy censoring, Ben?" Lieutenant Richester asked once they were in the tent.

"I'll say not!"

"I wouldn't, either. It doesn't seem fair, cutting out things men say in private."

"No," Ben agreed, "it doesn't. But this is war, and security is a real issue. The thing that bothers me most, though, isn't the censoring but the contents of these letters. I'm constantly being shocked at obscene stories, lewd and obscene pictures, and so on. Besides being unhealthy for me personally, I worry about the men, and I wonder how the Lord can possibly answer the prayers of their loved ones back home to protect them when they are so grossly disobedient to His commandments."

"Interesting thought. You're Mormon, aren't you?"

"I am."

"Why aren't you a chaplain, Ben? You have the perfect disposition for it, and your religious nature would make you a natural."

"Well, Rich," Ben responded slowly, "you aren't the first to suggest the idea. Lieutenant Proska said the same thing the other day when I wrote a letter to the wife of one of my men, trying to help her sort out her marriage problems with him. And Sergeant Stagliano hinted something about it recently. But I don't want to be a chaplain. I'm not a very good speaker, and besides, somebody has to keep an eye on these wonderful 'gentile' reprobates the Lord has entrusted to my care."

Lieutenant Richester nodded. "You really believe in Him, don't you, Ben."

"More than you or anyone else will ever know, Rich. I know the Lord is there because I have found Him, and He has responded to me with His Holy Spirit throughout my life. So yes, more even than believe, I *know* He is there."

"Do . . . do you think I could know? I . . . I mean . . . well . . . "

Ben grinned. "Absolutely, Rich. He's there for every person who wants to find Him. Just seek Him out with diligence, and you will know of Him as well as I do."

For a moment Lieutenant Richester was silent, but finally he spoke again. "Could you tell me how to begin to find Him, Ben?"

Ben did not respond immediately but gave his friend a searching look. Finally, however, he spoke. "Sure, Rich. At least I can tell you one way—the way that I found Him. I have a book of scripture here, the Book of Mormon. Read it, Rich, and as you read, pray about it. The Holy Ghost will give you a witness that it is true, and when that happens, you will have made the first significant step in finding the Lord."

"The Book of Mormon, huh?" Lieutenant Richester asked as he reached over and took the book from Ben's outstretched hand. "What's it about?"

Ben settled back with his uncensored letters before him. "Actually, Rich, it's a religious history of the ancient inhabitants of America. But more than that, it's another witness for Jesus Christ, that He is the divinely resurrected Son of God. You see, it tells of the Savior's visit to America shortly after He had been crucified and resurrected in Palestine. A gathering of 2,500 men and women saw him descend from the sky, and they all bore record . . ."

An hour later, with no letters censored and with Ben and his slowly gathering tentmates in bed but still talking religion, the air alert siren pierced the air once again. Groaning, Ben and the six other men in the tent started to roll out of their cots. Suddenly, only a few yards behind their perimeter, a newly placed battery of 90 mm. anti-aircraft guns opened up.

"Bombs!" somebody shrieked, and as one the seven men dove for the single foxhole near the tent, located just outside the door from Lieutenant Richester's cot.

Ben came out of his bunk like a shot, skinned both of his knees on his foot-locker, and, still in his long drawers, crabbed on his hands and knees through the tent flaps to the foxhole and rolled in. Others did the same, and within seconds all seven were crammed into the hole, Lieutenant Richester on the bottom.

Ten minutes later, the raid over with no bombs having

fallen, seven unclothed and snickering officers crawled from their foxhole to the jeers and laughter of the men on the line.

"Hey, Lieutenant Bennett," called a voice that Ben recognized as belonging to Sergeant Tiffin, "want a drink? It'll sure enough steady the nerves."

He may not," Lieutenant Richester shouted back, "but I do! I like to have been squashed by these guys!"

"Who's that in the captain's foxhole?" another voice called.

"Sergeant Lykes, blast his eyes!" responded the voice of the captain, who was also undressed. "Both he and Corporal Smith beat me to it, and I like to have not been able to get in. Lykes, don't you have a foxhole of your own?"

"I didn't," another voice responded, "but by gadfry I'm digging one now, four feet deep! Where did all those bombs hit, anyway?"

"Those weren't bombs," Tom Dabbs shouted down the line from his pillbox. "All you fellers were running from our own anti-aircraft guns, and they were shooting into the air, not at us."

There was another smattering of laughter, and as Ben listened to it, he suddenly felt good, better than he had felt in a long, long time. Pulling on his trousers and buttoning his shirt, he stepped down to where Lykes was digging his foxhole.

"Good job, Lykes," he said conversationally. "Dig it deep enough, and next time I'll be joining you. That last hole was too crowded for me."

"You're welcome anytime, Lieutenant," Lykes growled as he dug. "Just make sure you get on the bottom so I don't get smashed to death like poor Richester did."

Ben laughed. "It's a deal. Did you see where Lieutenant Richester went, by the way?"

"I didn't, sir. I—"

"Who wants me?"

"I do, Rich," Ben replied. "You still sing like you did in New Guinea?"

"A little," the man replied as he appeared out of the darkness. "Why?"

"I got a letter today," Ben grinned. "Somehow it really put me in the mood to sing, and I hoped that maybe you would join me."

Lieutenant Richester threw his arm around Ben's shoulder. "Well, then, old man, let's do it. Where's Young? He's got a great baritone."

"Does he?" Ben questioned. "Hey, Lieutenant Young, where are you?"

"I'm over here. Why?"

"Give an ear and you'll know," Lieutenant Richester called. Then, after giving a pitch, he and Ben broke forth with "I Dream of Jeannie with the Light Brown Hair."

By the end of the song, perhaps fifteen men had gathered in from the darkness, including Lieutenant Young, and for the next thirty minutes they joked and swayed and crooned such favorites as "My Grandfather's Clock," "Take You Home Again, Kathleen," and "The Letter Edged in Black."

From there the group started in on Christmas songs, including the newest hit by Bing Crosby, "I'm Dreaming of a White Christmas." Written specifically for the men serving in the Pacific, the song had a great impact on the moods of the men, and when the song ended, they stood together in silence, united as rarely before in camaraderie and a desire for peace.

"Ben," Lieutenant Richester suddenly said, "it's Christmas Eve. We may not get another chance, and I'd surely like to hear a Christmas message. Would you mind sharing with us some of your feelings about Christmas?"

"Oh, Rich, I don't know . . . "

"Please, Lieutenant Bennett," pleaded the voice of Sergeant Stagliano.

"But I haven't prepared . . . "

"It doesn't have to be a sermon, sir," Tom Dabbs stated quietly. "The whole outfit knows how you feel about the Lord Jesus, and since it's His birthday tomorrow, well, coming from you, sir, just about anything would be right."

The others agreed, so slowly Ben stepped to the front of the group and turned to face them.

"Well, mostly," he began, "what I feel tonight are memories, and maybe I could share them with you. Do you remember the day when you first heard the story of Santa Claus and understood it? Do you remember how that jolly old man with his long white beard and snow-trimmed red suit enchanted you? And helped you to do especially well those little routine jobs your mother had given you? Do you remember how you always made sure that your stocking, the largest one you had that was without holes, was hung by the chimney with care? You always made sure that the fireplace was checked and that the chimney was safe before you went to bed on Christmas Eve. Then you closed your eyes and made believe that you were asleep, but all the while you were listening intently for the sound of sleigh bells and the clattering of reindeer hooves on your roof.

"Ah, those Christmas Eves! Do you remember how you would all gather around the table in the living room, after the supper dishes were done? 'Twas the night before Christmas . . . ' You can still hear the sound of Dad's voice as he recited that to you. Then Mom would read Dickens' *A Christmas Carol,* and you would think about that horrible man Scrooge, who still gives you occasional nightmares. Then you would all gather around the old pump organ and sing Christmas carols—just as we did tonight.

"It was hard to stop your singing, then as now, but you did because it was Christmas Eve, and Santa was due to arrive soon. Up bright and early the next morning, you bounded down the stairs—you could hardly wait to see your presents!

Wasn't it a grand feeling to find that you had received just what you wanted? Of course you made merry, and of course this woke Dad up. He grumbled because his sleep had been disturbed, and Mom cautioned you that you shouldn't eat any candy before breakfast. But out of the corner of your eye you saw Dad wink at Mom, and you knew that everything was all right.

"And those Christmas dinners! What scrumptious feasts they were—turkey, dressing, cranberry sauce, plumb pudding, cake, ice cream, candy, and nuts. Dad said grace, and sometimes he would pray so long that you would fidget and squirm, for you were anxious to be on with the eating, the glorious eating of that Christmas dinner.

"Now, men, tomorrow will be another Christmas Day. It will find us on the front lines here on Morotai Island in the Netherlands East Indies, surrounded by the beautiful waters of the South Pacific. It will also find us thousands of miles from home and the things we love so much. There will be no snow and no mistletoe, and no dear loved ones to surround us. But we can still keep alive the spirit of Christmas.

"Though far away, we can, with Bing Crosby, be home for Christmas, if only in our dreams. We can relive in memory the days of yesteryear. In our mind's eye, we can once again light the fire in the fireplace, decorate the tree, fill the stockings, and even enjoy a kiss under the mistletoe. We can relive the past, and, while we are at it, we can plan those same things again for the future. As the song says, those things will be 'so nice to go home to.'

"And there are other things we can do as always. We can sing those beloved Christmas carols—with more than usual feeling now. And we can read that grand Christmas story in the New Testament with a deeper appreciation than ever before. For more than ever, now, we understand the real meaning of Christmas, for we have seen and experienced what happens when peace on earth and good-will toward men disappear from the face of the earth. Truly, men, we have seen the works of the Anti-Christ, and we have learned that the best way to fight him is with love, not hate.

"So tomorrow, men, let us do something about this war. The Wise Men of the East, when they brought their gifts to the newborn Christ child on that first Christmas nearly two thousand years ago, established a custom that has been carried on through the centuries—the giving of Christmas presents to friends and loved ones, and the exchange of greetings and good wishes one to another.

"Christ Himself continued that custom with the giving of Himself, His very life, which was the greatest gift ever given to mankind.

"When the true spirit of Christmas is uppermost in our minds and prompts our giving, then the observance of this custom is a wonderful demonstration of love and affection and can only be smiled upon by our Lord. But if that spirit is absent or lacking, the practice becomes commercialized and cheap and is a form of hypocrisy.

"As Christians, men, each of us knows the why of these things, for they hearken back to our Lord and Savior, Jesus Christ, who bought our souls with His suffering that we all might live. The true spirit of Christmas is within us, for we know that our Redeemer lives. As we take Christmas to the children in the village, may we remember this and keep it uppermost in our hearts.

"May the world accept Christ and His gospel. May the forces of righteousness triumph speedily in the present conflict, and may victory soon be ours is my prayer tonight and every other day of my life.

"In Christ's name I pray it. Amen."

There was a subdued chorus of amens from the group, which had grown in the darkness to quite a crowd. As Ben grew still, Lieutenant Richester began to softly sing "Silent Night," and almost instantly he was joined by dozens and dozens of voices. They were battle-hardened, these voices, used to shouting orders and screaming death-threats at mortal enemies. But now with softness and tenderness these same gruff voices sang with great feeling of the silent, wondrous night that saw the birth of their Lord and Savior, Jesus Christ.

And Lieutenant Ben Bennett, who tried at all times to keep his crying silent and on the inside, gave in with no struggle as his tears mingled with the tears of dozens of other men who were just as tough as he, men who truly yearned that peace might come to earth and that there would finally be good-will toward all people.

CHAPTER

TWELVE

Three more times that night, air alerts sounded. The anti-aircraft barrage was terrific, searchlights played across the sky constantly, and Ben and the others on perimeter were treated to an unusual show—90 mm. guns, 40 mm. Bofors, 50 caliber machine guns, and 20 mm. Oerlingens laced the sky with shells and ack-ack, while high overhead, Japanese bombers and fighters criss-crossed the sky, their incendiary bombs and high explosives wreaking havoc on the ground. Several more B-24 Liberators were destroyed, an ammunition dump was hit, and fires raged everywhere.

Yet through it all, Ben's soul beamed, and the sound of dropping bombs no longer seemed so frighteningly horrible. What a glorious day he had had, working with good men, helping a few who seemed troubled and downtrodden, sharing the joy of song and fellowship with others, receiving a letter from an unknown girl who seemed to feel in so many ways exactly as he did, and finally being able to bear his testimony to the men of the truthfulness of the gospel of Jesus Christ and to the divinity of his Savior's mission.

And now the dawn of Christmas was showing in the sky to the east. This day he could celebrate the birth of his Savior by taking his men and giving Christmas to the native children whose lives had been so torn apart by the war. But first there was something else he needed to do.

"Morotai Island," he wrote in the dim light of a new Christmas morning.

"December 25, 1944, 0700 hours

"Dearest Mother and Dad:

"On this Christmas morning, may I be the first to wish each of you a very Merry Christmas! I also wanted to present you with a gift—my heartfelt thanks to you for being the wonderful parents you have always been. No man could have been blessed with better examples of righteousness, and daily I thank Heavenly Father for you—and for the wonderful brothers and sisters you brought into the world to be my best friends throughout life.

"I am also thankful today for the preservation of my life and the lives of my men—protection from harm, danger, evil, sickness, and disease—for the privilege of being born in these the last days when the fullness of the Gospel has been restored, for the Gospel and for the testimony I have of its truthfulness. I am thankful that I have been born in the New and Everlasting Covenant and for my membership in the Church of Jesus Christ of Latter-day Saints, for the Priesthood which I hold, for my lineage in the House of Israel, for my college education. Oh, there are so many things I am thankful for, that I can't begin to enumerate them.

"The other night as I was on guard, my mind began to reflect on the miraculous way in which my life and the lives of my men have been preserved. As I did so, three things were indelibly impressed on my mind. First, let me tell you about prayer. I know beyond all doubt that my prayers and those of you loved ones at home have been answered. Secondly, the Word of Wisdom has a greater meaning for me now. It says: 'And I the Lord give unto them a promise that the destroying angel shall pass by them even as the children of Israel and not slay them.' I have always tried to keep the Word of Wisdom. In some ways I have perhaps failed to keep it completely, but I have never used tea, coffee, tobacco or liquor, or other harmful substances. I have tried to eat very little meat and to eat proper foods. I have endeavored to avoid overeating, oversleeping, and overworking. Thus the destroying angel has passed by me — time and time again — and in amazing ways. I know more than ever before that the Word of Wisdom is of God, and that its observance brings protection as well as health, strength, wisdom, and great treasures of knowledge.

"The Bible also has something to say about protection. It is in Psalms: 'The Lord is my shepherd; I shall not want . . . Yea, tho I walk through the valley of the shadow of death, I fear no evil, for thou art with me.' Patrol work in enemy territory in tropical mountainous jungles — along jungle paths and stream channels — is the closest thing to walking through the valley and shadow of death that I know of. It means a lot to a patrol leader to feel that God is with him.

"Mother and Dad, I feel within my heart that I will be preserved throughout this conflict and that I will return afterwards to perform a mission in life, which is still very much unfinished. If it be God's will, then that is the desire of my heart, and I want to have the chance to do that. But if God wishes it to be otherwise, or if he has a more important work for me to do elsewhere, then I always want to say — 'Thy Will Be Done.'

"Now please know again that I love you, and that I wish you the very merriest of Christmases!"

Though physically exhausted, Ben put down his pen and smiled into the dawn. He was happy, truly happy, and he knew it. For besides all else, he thought as he beamed toward the heavens that were now filled with God's light rather than enemy aircraft, he might very possibly have "become acquainted," as his mother had put it, with the girl of his dreams, the woman he would lovingly walk beside into the rest of eternity.

Now if he could just hang onto his peace and sanity until they could get together.

PART THREE

DUCKS AND BUFFALOS

January 1, 1945 — April 17, 1945

THE WAR

As 1945 began in Europe, Hitler's forces were reeling from Allied blows almost too numerous to chronicle. Among other problems, serious fuel shortages were affecting armored units everywhere. Allied bombing of transport had cut supplies drastically, the Panzer Lehr division alone abandoning fifty-three tanks the first four days of January from lack of gasoline.

On the frigid and snow-covered battlegrounds of Northern Europe, the U.S. First and Third armies hooked up at Houffalize and eliminated the German Ardennes salient. The German "bulge" had inflicted 75,000 casualties on twenty-nine U.S. and four British divisions, while the Germans themselves had suffered 100,000 dead and wounded, losing 800 tanks and about 1,000 planes.

Meanwhile, British 7th Armored Division units drove northeast, capturing Dieteren in the Netherlands, while Russian troops reached the Auschwitz concentration camp, freeing 2,819 inmates. Berlin itself was subjected to heavy Allied bombing, which continued almost around the clock. Yet Hitler remained defiant, and on January 30, the twelfth anniversary of his rise to power, he delivered a fiery speech designed to arouse his people but destined instead to be his last radio broadcast.

Still German strength spiraled downward. By February, the Colmar pocket was closed, eliminating the German 19th Army, which had lost 25,000 men in the Alsace fighting. Eisenhower then announced that the Allies were holding over 900,000 German prisoners. Also, U.S. and British RAF planes flew against Dresden in the most intense incendiary bombing of the war. In these "terror bombings" or "firestorms," at least 35,000 people perished, and in the wake of the human tragedy, Allied leaders paused to rethink their strategy.

In March, German fifteen–year-olds were ordered to frontline duty. At the same time, U.S. Ninth Army and First Canadian Army troops continued their swift pursuit through Germany and Holland, capturing twenty towns and villages and taking 66,000 German soldiers prisoner. Meanwhile, First Army troops advanced toward Cologne after crossing the Erft River, the 2nd and 3rd Canadian divisions cleared the Hochwald and Balberger forests, the U.S. 10th Mountain division made broad advances in Italy, and the Rhine River was crossed at Remagen by the U.S. 9th Armored and the U.S. 78th divisions. When this final natural barrier to the German heartland was breached, all German resistance began collapsing.

In desperation, Hitler decreed: "Anyone captured without being wounded or without having fought to the limit of his powers has forfeited his honor. He is expelled from the fellowship of decent and brave soldiers. His dependents will be held responsible." Then, a few days later, he added, "We know what the fate of Germany would be otherwise. Our enemies, drunk with victory, have made it clearly known; extermination of the German nation."

Desperately Germany fought on. While the Luftwaffe lost eighty planes attacking Allied positions along the Rhine River, massive new air attacks involving thousands of planes were launched by the Allies against Berlin and Frankfurt. After leaflets were dropped warning civilians to flee, the bombs followed, further reducing these cities to rubble. Finally, for the first time, Hitler directed that Allied aircraft be attacked by his new jets, the ME-262s. Also, he issued his infamous "Nero Decree," ordering destruction of Germany's own industrial, communications and transportation facilities, all of which were threatened by Allied capture.

While Hitler's jets achieved minimal success by downing twenty-four planes, his ground forces continued to crumble under Allied pressure. In what was the largest airborne operation of the war, involving 5,051 aircraft and 40,000 men, British 6th and U.S. 17th Airborne division paratroopers were dropped northeast of Wesel and soon made contact with British units advancing from the west. Then U.S. Third Army units attacked across the Rhine, the 6th Armored division breaking through and moving along the Autobahn toward Frankfurt.

As Frankfurt was occupied, British Second Army forces drove toward the Elbe. Mannheim's burgomaster sought to surrender the city to the Allies, and Eisenhower determined to knock Germany out of the war by attacking Leipzig rather than Berlin, a decision that had wide-ranging political implications. Churchill futilely tried to change Eisenhower's plans, fearing Russia's long-range political desires. But Eisenhower remained adamant, ultimately Berlin fell to the Russians, and the Berlin Wall became a reality.

While Adolf Eichman declared that he could go to his grave happy, knowing that he had helped kill six million Jews, the U.S. 4th Armored division, under General Patton, liberated the concentration camp outside Ohrdruf. Patton, who vomited on visiting the site, rounded up townspeople to witness the horrors that had been perpetrated in their immediate area. Many victims were still lying where they had been shot by the retreating Nazis. Ohrdruf's burgomaster and his wife were among those brought to the camp by Patton. When they returned home, they hanged themselves.

As the Allied Fifteenth Army group, composed of troops from Britain, the U.S., France, New Zealand, South Africa, Poland, India, Sengal, Brazil, Italy, Greece, Morocco, Algeria, and the Jewish Brigade began its final offensive in Italy, U.S. Ninth Army units captured 300,000 German soldiers, bringing the total of captured Germans for the month of April alone to 755,573. Shortly thereafter, even as Hitler was giving the order that all who ordered retreat were to be shot, another 325,000 German troops in the Ruhr pocket surrendered, making it the single largest capitulation of the war.

Meanwhile, in the South Pacific, the war with Japan continued unabated. As U.S. forces pushed across the Philippines and other islands, the Japanese government directed the military to "concentrate converting all armament production to special attack weapons of a few major types." This meant Japan's limited facilities were to be concentrated on suicide planes, human torpedoes, and small, high-speed suicide attack boats.

The U.S. 11th Airborne Division landed at the south entrance to Manila Bay, the U.S. 6th Army drove west toward Manila, and U.S. Eighth Army units pushed toward Manila from the south.

As 4,000 Americans were released from Manila prisons, where they had suffered brutality and starvation much as had the Jews in Europe, a severe earthquake rocked Tokyo, followed almost immediately by a devastating raid by ninety B-29 bombers. Much of the world concluded that God had sided with the Allies, and subsequent events made the conclusion seem a fact.

Not only was there further destruction in Japan from earthquakes, typhoons, and hurricanes, but days after the first quake, the 6th Army had pushed through Japanese forces to the Bataan Peninsula. And then U.S. paratroopers landed on Corregidor. They were followed two hours later by boat-born 34th Division Infantrymen, and the completely surprised Japanese lost 4,215 men, while the Americans lost 136.

On February 19, following the deaths of 170 U.S. Navy frogmen who attempted to clear the beaches of Iwo Jima, U.S. Marines invaded the island, Japan's "unsinkable airfield," 775 miles from the main Japanese home island of Honshu. Over the next thirty days, progress by American forces was measured in yards, paid for dearly by both men and equipment. On February 23, Mount Suribachi was taken by the Marines, and Associated Press photographer Joe Rosenthal took what is probably the best-known photo of the war, the marines raising the flag on that volcanic cone.

U.S. B-29s then began night-time fire raids on Tokyo. In the first raid, 334 planes dropped 1,667 tons of incendiaries from 7,000 feet, destroying fifteen square miles of the Japanese capital. In the thirty minutes of that single raid, an inferno was created that killed 83,793 Japanese, while another 41,000 were injured. In terms of death, this raid was far more severe than the two atomic bomb raids that were to come the following August. It also brought about leaflet dropping – warnings to Japanese civilians to get out of key industrial areas before the bombs came a few hours later.

By March, Japanese forces in Manila were overcome, and while the 8th Army began its invasion of the southern Philippines, the central Pacific was effectively cleared of all Japanese submarines. As the month wore on, B-29s bombed Osaka and Kobe, and a small U.S. force landed on the Zamboanga Peninsula, the westernmost part of Mindanao, the Philippines.

As Japanese piloted suicide bombs made a futile attack against the U.S. naval fast carrier task force, Iwo Jima finally fell to American forces. When the Kerama Islands were taken shortly thereafter, U.S. forces discovered 350 suicide boats that had been positioned for attacks against Allied shipping during the expected invasion of Okinawa.

On April 1, in what was to be the last — and the bloodiest — major amphibious operation of the Pacific war, the U.S. 10th Army invaded Okinawa, 360 miles south of Japan. Two army and two marine divisions, a force of 60,000 men, came ashore after intensive naval and air bombardment. At first there was little resistance, but then Japanese opposition stiffened to a level probably unmatched in the Pacific war. It was there, on April 18, that American war correspondent Ernie Pyle was killed by a Japanese sniper.

In early April, the Japanese Imperial Navy gave its remaining men-of-war an unmistakable order for mass suicide. Their orders: "Second Fleet is to charge the enemy anchorage of Kadena off Okinawa Island at daybreak of 8 April. Fuel for only a one-way passage will be supplied."

As the engagement began, the first of the concentrated kamikaze (divine wind) attacks sank two U.S. destroyers and four auxiliaries. Only 24 of the 355 suicide planes from Kyushu actually hit targets, but they caused great damage and destruction.

A day later, in the Battle of the East China Sea, 900 Task Force Fifty-eight planes intercepted the Japanese Second Fleet heading for Okinawa. In three hours of fighting, the Japanese lost the super battleship *Yamato*, the cruiser *Yahagi*, four destroyers, and fifty-four aircraft. American losses were ten U.S. planes.

On April 17, the U.S. X Corps of the 8th Army, containing units of the 24th and 31st divisions, landed on the largely primitive southwest coast of Mindanao and met little initial resistance. Moving inland on the first leg of the hundred-mile march to Davao Gulf and the unsuspecting Japanese, they found the roads so destroyed and the terrain so difficult that the decision was made to use ocean-going landing craft to carry the 31st Infantry regiment up the Mindanao River, while the 24th continued overland.

THE MAN

As a New Year's celebration, men along Ben's perimeter on Morotai spent three hours firing into the darkness. The Navy boys joined in from their ships, their tracer bullets forming a "V" for victory sign in the sky. Then in the morning, Ben got together with Leslie Milam, and they sent an order to Deseret Book Company in Salt Lake City for a package of new LDS books.

On January 7, 1945, just as the rainy season was beginning, Ben was reassigned as commanding officer of the 31st Division LVT and Dukw company (LVT stands for "landing vehicle, tracked"—affectionatly called a "water buffalo'; and Dukw is a code name for a 2 1/2 ton, six-wheel drive, watertight truck equipped with a propeller for operation in water—also known as a "duck").

Ben was told in frank language that his new company was a mess, and that he was being assigned there to clean it up. He began immediately by meeting the personnel, and within two days he was in the midst of court proceedings against several of the men for unauthorized leaves and attempted rape of native women. He also inspected the equipment and found that many of the vehicles were inoperable, so within days he began an extensive clean-up and vehicle repair operation. As he wrote after undergoing his first inspection of the area, "If they will just give me three weeks, this area will knock their eyes out."

He didn't get three weeks, for the pressures never let up. Nevertheless, on February 8, in a surprise inspection by General Martin, his company received at least a "satisfactory" rating. Then, on February 13, the rating was upgraded to "excellent."

On February 22, Ben and his company began intensive

training with the 124th Infantry in landing procedures, starting with the first battalion. He also sat in meetings to discuss the problems being encountered by the Marines on Iwo Jima.

Daily the rain continued to fall, making life miserable and the entire operation on Morotai a muddy mess. Yet still Ben and his company trained with the 124th in amphibious landing operations. All knew that soon they would be making an amphibious landing on another island, but none knew the exact location or date. So they worked, trained, and endured the thirty-ninth straight day of rain, and waited.

Throughout March, this same regimen continued without let-up, the only relief being LDS Church services with Leslie Milam, Tom Doxey, Parley P. Pratt, and a few other LDS men. The brethren were also visited regularly by Lieutenant Kempainen, Tom Dabbs, and Nick Kastanas, who all expressed continuing interest in the gospel message.

Yet Ben's mind was not always consumed with the war. For instance, one day he wrote: "The scriptures, in presenting the story of creation, state that one day to the Lord is as a thousand years to man (Pearl of Great Price, Book of Abraham; and the Bible, Book of Genesis). Applying this to the story of the creation, man has concluded that the earth was created in six thousand years. A careful perusal of Genesis and the Book of Moses (Pearl of Great Price) will indicate, however, that such reference to the element of time pertains to the creation of things spiritually, and does not have reference to the temporal creation. Have we been told how long it took God to effect the creation of things temporally? I think not."

On April 13, Ben received news of the death of President Roosevelt, and that afternoon he began loading men and machines aboard ship for their journey north to the Philippines. For four days they loaded, and then, incredibly, as the LVTs attempted to pull away from shore to join the convoy, three of the vessels were stuck on the coral bottom.

For two days they fought that before breaking loose, and

then in convoy Ben and the others sailed north, landing on Mindanao April 22. Shortly thereafter, he and his company were assisting the 124th Infantry up the Mindanao River, using the buffaloes and ducks in the unusual river convoy.

CHAPTER

THIRTEEN

The hill where the U.S. troops were encamped was about three hundred yards long and a hundred yards wide, grass covered, and almost treeless. The men were dug down in the sides of the hill, and the mortar platoon was at the foot, on a bluff above the Mindanao river, all set up to throw mortars in any direction.

The men, already yellow from taking atabrine to prevent malaria, looked even more yellow in the light from dozens of small, flickering fires. Lieutenant Bennett, his wavy hair close-cropped even shorter than usual, shared a fire near the upper perimeter with Lieutenant Nick Kastanas, who by chance had ended up in the LVT that Ben was commanding.

"This is quite an outfit you've got here," Kastanas said as they waited for their K rations to heat in the fire. "How many of these LVTs do you have?"

Ben poked at his rations with his foot. "Twenty-seven, six of them armed. I also have twenty-seven dukws, though the word is that they will be going to the Marines in the next few days. My armed buffalos have crews of six, but the open buffs can be run by two men. Normally I don't get to leave our bivouac area, but one of my crewmen is sick, and I was the only one available to replace him."

"I'm glad you were, Ben. It's great to see you again. Why isn't Milam up here with us? I thought you guys were always together."

"He's down with his squad," Ben replied. "We spent a good portion of yesterday together, holding Sunday services and so forth. Tonight he told me he thought somebody ought to be there to protect his men, so I suppose that is what he is doing."

Kastanas laughed and then looked out over the beached convoy of LVTs. "Lot of money tied up there in your equipment, don't you think?"

"You bet I think it," Ben replied soberly. "The regular buffs cost just under $30,000 each, while the ones armed with the 75 mm. howitzers and the .5-inch and .3-inch Browning Machine Guns run about $35,000. Then the ducks run a little over $8,000 each. The way I figure it, that makes me responsible for about one and a half million dollars worth of equipment. Needless to say, Nick, I would rather be back with 'E' company of the 31st and responsible for a few hundred dollars worth of infantry weapons. Besides which, I miss the men."

"They miss you, too, Ben. There was some real grumbling when you were reassigned."

"It's easy to be an officer over men like them, Nick."

Lieutenant Kastanas pulled his rations from the fire and carefully peeled back the top of the can. "It may be, but there was more to it than that. The men felt a real sense of security when you were leading them. Or maybe I should call it a sense of safety. You may not know this, but people from all over the 31st wanted to get into 'E' Company because the word was out that your men didn't get killed."

"What?"

"That's right. Your Mormon law of health has turned into some real scuttlebutt."

"I don't see too many of them throwing away their cigarettes or pushing aside the jungle juice," Ben responded, grinning. "So our beliefs can't have made that much of an impact."

"Maybe not that way, but they sure talk about it. I've even given some serious thought to getting rid of my smoking habit. I think—hey, these rations are moldy!"

Ben scraped his own rations a little, flipped his scrapings into the grass, and continued eating. "Mine, too," he said between mouthfuls. "But these are the old kind, manufactured in 1942 and stored in Australia until now. Bad as they are, though, you must admit that they beat the alternative."

With a sigh, Kastanas nodded. Both men ate silently then, and when Ben had finished, he looked again at his friend. "I'm tickled that you're going to stop smoking, Nick. It's a wise choice."

"Why?" Kastanas asked, grinning. "So I'll live to get back to work as a furrier in St. Louis? I know you, Ben. All you really want is that fur coat I promised to make for the future Mrs. Ben Bennett."

Ben grinned back. "Aw, Nick, I thought I hid it better than that."

Suddenly, from a few yards downhill, a man jumped to his feet with a wild burst of cussing and yelling. There was instant quiet, and then a ripple of laughter spread across the long hill.

"What happened?" somebody yelled.

"It's Jasper Harmon again," another voice responded, chuckling. "He forgot to release the pressure on the lid, so his ration can of hot egg yolks sprayed him."

There was another round of laughter, and after Ben and Lieutenant Kastanas had enjoyed the moment's humor, they carefully burned their ration boxes.

"Poor Harmon," Kastanas said then. "That's the third time this week. You'd think he'd learn."

Ben nodded. "I know Jasper pretty well. He's very artistic, a real dreamer, and I think that's why he has such a hard time concentrating on these mundane acts of survival. But put that brain of his to work on a new or better way to get something built, and you would be amazed at how his ideas flow."

"Could be. But if we run into the Jap forces that HQ thinks we will, he'd better start concentrating on the mundane facts of war in a hurry."

Ben looked at his friend. "You expect it to be rough, then?"

Kastanas nodded. "We sure do. Intelligence tells us that the entire Jap 30th division is spread out along the Sayre highway—25,000 men! And we're supposed to simply walk over them."

"That's going to be a rough assignment, Nick."

"Don't I know it! Did you read that article in Maptalk a couple of weeks ago? The interview with that Jap general?"

Thoughtfully Ben shook his head.

"Well, you ought to hear what he said. Here, I saved it. I'll read it to you. It's . . . yeah, his name is Lieutenant General Masaharu Homma, the same guy who's supposed to be in charge of all the Nips here in the Philippines. Listen to this. He says: 'I think I understand your American psychology very well. I think that every American believes that he can handle any two Japanese soldiers. Is that not true?' "

"Who was he talking to?" Ben asked.

"A fellow named Clark Lee, an American correspondent who interviewed him just before Pearl Harbor. Anyway, Homma goes on. He says: 'I think I am right in my analysis. At any rate, we are proceeding with this in mind and are prepared to lose ten million men in our war with America. How many are you Americans prepared to lose?

"'We will fight inch by inch. We will fight to the last man. We will make the cost in blood, ships, and planes so frighteningly great that, we believe, America will eventually become discouraged. The American people will decide that the cost is not worth the gains. They will say that, after all, the Orient is a long way off and perhaps Japan is the logical nation to govern it. Then our war will be won.' "

"Oh, Nick," Ben said as he stared at his friend, "that's tragic."

"I'll say. It's no wonder that MacArthur and Admiral Halsey believe that our only hope of winning the war is by killing Japs and more Japs until finally their price is unacceptable. The trouble is, so many of us have to give up our lives to reach that goal. Did you read that article in "Maptalk" about how the Japs plan to deal with America once they win the war?"

Ben shook his head.

"I saved it, too. I'm telling you, Ben, this stuff scares me to death. Listen to this, and remember, these are ten-year rules. First, they will confiscate all naval vessels and charge the U.S. all expenses for taking them over and transporting them to Japan. Ocean liners will be dealt with in the same way. Naval arms and ammunition will also be confiscated, and all naval facilities, including stations, yards, and schools, will be done away with. Private shipbuilding facilities will be done away with, except for coastal and river craft. All aircraft will be disposed of and all airfields and facilities will be destroyed except those to be used by Japan. American steel and oil production will be allowed only with restrictions. Also, currency and government bonds will be purely financial instruments but will not be marketed domestically. Private banking organs will be abolished, monopolistic trusts and cartels will be abolished, monopolistic industries will be dissolved and capitalistic agriculture banned, stock market speculation will be prohibited, and labor unions will be dissolved as workers are given a definite social status. Can you believe all that, Ben?

"If the Japs, by some dark miracle, win this Pacific conflict and then try to enforce rules like these, why, we'll be in the middle of another war in two shakes of a lamb's tail."

"Yes," Ben breathed, "and just like now, it will be at the expense of more good, innocent men—on both sides. Oh, somebody will have to pay dearly for this war some day!"

"I hope they do," Kastanas stated flatly. "Ben, you've been in on a few prisoner interrogations, haven't you? What are the Japs like? I mean, who are we fighting out here?"

Ben sighed. "They're just loyal, good men, Nick. Their culture is different than ours, so they don't laugh at the same things. Nor do they feel the same about death and life. Whereas Christ taught that this is our one single experience in a mortal probation, they are convinced that we will come back again and again, in increasingly better positions, depending upon the way we lived and met death in the life previously. At least that's how I understand it.

"But it's the common soldiers I feel sorry for, Nick. They're just victims of circumstances and hardly know what this war is even about. A patrol recently brought in a Jap prisoner, Matsayama Shikoshi. He was a private, in very poor physical condition, who had been subsisting on tree leaves, grass, and other vegetation for some time.

"He indicated that some five hundred men of his force had become ill and died, no doubt from malaria. We gave him a few K rations, and he was very thankful, bowing and saying 'Thank you' in English, as though he was getting the best treatment he had ever received. I was told he even had a chance to escape, but the men doubted that he would try, even if forced."

Nick Kastanas shook his head. "I don't know if I would have taken him prisoner, Ben. I don't like those guys very much right now."

Ben nodded. "I understand. In fact, many of the men who brought him in felt the same way you do. But all of them have lost good, close friends in the war. 'A' Company, for instance, has suffered 75 percent casualties, and so they would rather have killed him there.

"But personally, Nick, in spite of all the horror and treachery I have encountered in combat, and I have encountered a great deal, I don't agree with you. I still feel that if a man has a choice between bringing in an enemy prisoner or taking his life, that he should be brought in a prisoner. And it's not only that I think these poor fellows are innocent dupes of higher authority. If they were the actual decision makers, I would feel the same, for God has clearly stated that human life is precious and ought to be respected."

"I know that, Ben," Kastanas stated emphatically, "but most of the time the Japs don't even act human."

"Unfortunately, you're right, Nick. As meek and docile as they seem when captured, they are vicious and cruel when they have the upper hand. We've had bodies of Americans brought in that had been hung in trees and then systematically bayoneted in the back and buttocks until loss of blood brought unconsciousness and death. Then, at least we hope it was after they died, their arms and legs had been hacked off. Our men also found a group of thirty-five Filipino scouts lying face down in a stream. Their hands had been tied behind them, and they had been bayoneted in the back and left to drown. So we aren't seeing very much of the milk of human kindness in their hearts.

"Captured, though, they seem weak and small, and those I have met seem very glad to still be alive. Most officers commit suicide rather than be captured, and the infantrymen we have captured tell us they do that because they find it too fearful expending their last bullets at us and then awaiting the suspense of us killing them at our leisure."

"I didn't know that," Kastanas stated. "I thought it was some sort of religious thing that made them do it."

"Well, partially maybe it is, for I've heard the same story. But the common soldiers don't seem to share that belief.

Certainly they will fight to the death, but you don't see many suicides among them that are not ordered and enforced by ranking superiors.

"From what I understand of their history, Nick, Japan is probably the closest thing we have to a barbarian nation in the world today. For centuries she was closed to the outside world, until Perry opened the door to her in 1853. Immediately she began to adopt the civilization of the West; but she took it ready made and did not have to go through an adolescent period of growth. She became a great imitator of the West scientifically, but she still retained her mystic, barbarous, fanatical ways. The code of the Samurai was reinstituted, and the Black Legion was established, which murdered, laid waste, and so forth, and was a secret society or combination exactly like the evil societies that existed anciently.

"They considered the poor peasant class to be no-accounts, ignorant and stupid, and they were little more than the property of the rulers. Through the ages, these ordinary people have been treated this way, and they know no other way of life. They accept their subjugation to leadership as a natural thing.

"And that, my friend, is why I have never had it in my heart to hate these enemy soldiers, even when they have caused so much pain, bloodshed, and destruction. We Americans cannot understand the fanaticism behind a 'Banzai' attack unless we know the background and way of life of the Japanese people, who have behind them centuries of training in non-thinking submissiveness."

Lieutenant Kastanas nodded thoughtfully. "Well, like the men in 'E' Company say, Ben, you are liberal in your views and do not put yourself above others. I hope one day when the war is over, the Japs will recognize you for the friend you are."

"I hope so, too, Nick. But whatever their beliefs and circumstances, they are still well drilled in the tricks of jungle fighting, and I respect and fear them thoroughly. One of their favorite stunts here on Mindanao is to toss firecrackers into the trees some yards from one of their machine-gun nests. Our men, thinking they are Jap rifles, move to investigate and are cut down by the hidden machine gun. They also use firecrackers at night to create confusion and the illusion of strong forces. And I've seen two captured sets of knee and hand pads that they use to creep silently behind our lines after dark."

"Yeah, I heard about that."

"They also like to shriek what they imagine to be blood-curdling yells when they attack, and they intersperse their war crys with such English words as *assault* and *attack!* But from all I've heard, in spite of their fanatical fighting, most of them don't quite manage to sound ferocious."

Kastanas grinned. "Well, the ones I fought didn't. But it isn't their yelling that kills, Ben. It's their bullets, and I am afraid of them."

"I don't blame you. They will infiltrate our lines at every opportunity, they will strip dead soldiers of uniforms, especially the Filipinos, and try to pass our sentries at night, where they can toss grenades and in general create mass confusion. Also, they are very clever at lying in the brush until they learn our passwords, which they can then imitate. That worked very well until our officers discovered that the Japs can't pronounce the letter L. Since then, all our pass-words have been liquid with Ls—words such as *hula-hula.* The Japs invariably pronounce this as 'hura-hura.' It's a dead giveaway, and when one of them tries it, that's how he ends up, too."

"I'll remember that, Ben.

"You should. I'm telling you, Nick, in the field we can't afford to ignore them or consider them a lesser foe. The man who does that, usually ends up dead."

CHAPTER

FOURTEEN

For a time, Ben and Lieutenant Kastanas sat in silence, thinking. Around them the early night was alive with the soft sound of human voices, groups of men scattered here and there, smoking and talking about hundreds of different things. The men talked about past experiences, shared scuttlebutt about the coming campaign, and repeated the latest news from Europe. They told jokes, they cussed a lot, they laughed that they were not fighting in the cold and snows of Europe, and at the same time they cursed the heat, the mosquitoes, and the malaria-preventing atabrine that came with fighting in the Pacific. They spoke gravely about what would happen to them when they finally got home. And while the voices around them droned on, Ben sat silently next to his friend Lieutenant Nick Kastanas, each man feeling as alone as he had ever felt in his life.

With full dark, the order to douse the fires was passed along the hillside, and then began one of the longest nights Ben had ever spent. It was too early to sleep, so the men lay awake on their ponchos and packs, staring skyward at the southern stars that even yet were not familiar to the majority of the men.

Nobody undressed, for that wasn't done in the field. Ben took off his boots, but since Kastanas had to watch the field telephones from midnight until one, he left his boots on.

Around them, men smoked one cigarette after another, not hiding them under their blankets and ponchos because they were in a protected position where glowing cigarettes couldn't be seen very far away. And then, while Ben wondered how in the world so many men could be caught up in the same terrible habit, the mosquitoes started buzzing around their heads.

"Aahhhh, noooo," Kastanas groaned as he slapped at his face. "Ben, do you have any mosquito lotion?"

"I do," Ben replied softly. "It's here in my pocket, if you really want it. But I don't think it will do you much good."

"I know," Kastanas breathed. "But doggone it all, Ben, I've got to feel like I'm doing something!"

Reaching, Ben handed the lotion to Kastanas. "You know," he said thoughtfully, "these Filipino mosquitos sound like flame throwers. The ones we had in Alberta used to be bad, but you can't drive these little beasties away."

"So, why don't you put lotion on?"

"It doesn't do any good. But I was bitten so many times as a kid that I can just about ignore them."

"Just about?"

"Yeah," Ben said as he slapped himself again, "just about."

Again the two grew still, and after a while so did the entire hillside. The hours passed slowly, but from occasional slaps at the mosquitoes, each of the men knew that the others weren't asleep. Suddenly Ben sat up and pulled down his socks and started scratching.

"What now?" Kastanas asked, trying not to grin.

"Dad-blasted grass fleas," Ben muttered. "I'll bet I have a thousand red welts on my legs from them, and every one of the thousand has its own separate little itchy brand of misery. Oh, lawsy, as Dabbs would say. This is awful!"

"I've never had a flea bite," Kastanas said thoughtfully.

"Poor fellow."

"Don't feel too bad about what I might be missing, Ben. The mosquitoes more than make up for what the fleas don't get. I'll tell you, there hasn't been a morning since I came to the Pacific that I didn't wake up with at least one eye swollen closed. My blood must be grade 'A' prime, at least to the mosquitos."

"And my legs to the fleas," Ben stated. "Almost makes me wish the Japs would attack."

"Do you think they get eaten alive the way we do?"

Ben thought for a moment. "Probably, though you never know. We had Indians up in Alberta that never did get bitten, or at least that's what the story was. Maybe the Japs are the same. I doubt it, though. They die of malaria, and they wear mosquito nets over their helmets, so they must be protecting themselves from something."

"Yeah, I guess you're right. But if so, then why the dickens do they want these islands?"

"Since when was greed sensible, Kas?"

"Good point. Well, to tell you the truth, Ben, I'd rather get eaten alive by the mosquitoes than face the Japs in the dark, any day."

Ben grinned. "Well, since we're telling the truth, so would I. In fact, the theme song of the American soldier in the South Pacific ought to be 'I Hate to See that Evening Sun Go Down.'"

"Is that a real song?"

"Well, it's a real sentiment, at least. But I composed the title. Unlike us Americans, the Jap prefers to do his fighting at night. He isn't so hot on etiquette and sometimes doesn't even knock when he enters our foxhole homes. And he's even less agreeable once he's there.

143

"A night spent in the deep, mountainous jungles of New Guinea or the Philippines, with the enemy all around and about, is something never to be forgotten. A man's nerves become his best friend. The queer noises, the weird sounds, and the ruses and tactics of the Jap keep these overwrought nerves always at their best. The sound of a falling tree, and even the patter of raindrops on the leaves, are treated with the greatest of respect and suspicion. So yes, 'We Hate to See that Evening Sun Go Down.' "

"Boy," Kastanas said, chuckling, "you've got that one down. You could turn it into a heck of a sermon."

Ben nodded in agreement. "I could, I guess. Actually I already wrote those very words to my girl the other day, and in the writing I memorized them."

"Your girl?" Kastanas cried, sitting up. "For crying out loud, Ben, I didn't know you had a girl! Come on. Give me the scoop."

"There's no scoop," Ben said, scratching at his legs again. "As I remember, you brought me her first letter, back on Morotai. So you see, you already do know about her."

"I did?" Kastanas asked, incredulously. "And now she's your girl?"

Lying back down, Ben nodded. "As far as I'm concerned, she is. Of course I haven't announced that fact to her yet, but . . . "

Kastanas laughed quietly. "Well, you old son-of-a-gun. Still shy old Ben Bennett. But you truly have a real-live, honest-to-goodness girl! Wow! Maybe I really will have to make you a fur coat. Just wait until I write Penny about this. She'll be so excited that she'll call Edward R. Murrough and have it broadcast worldwide on the six o'clock news. Tell me about this girl, Ben. Who is she? What's she like? What are your plans? Come on, man, spill it, so I can send all the juicy details home to Penny."

Closing his eyes, Ben pictured in his mind the photograph

that lay in his trunk back at the base on Polloc Harbor. "She's a peach, Nick. That's all."

"The heck it is. Now give, Ben."

Chuckling, Ben turned onto his stomach and lay looking down across the river. "What do you want to hear? She's blonde, willowy, pretty. She sings, I guess, almost professionally. She works as a secretary at Fort Douglas, back in Utah. She comes from a big family and wants to have the same when she gets married. Her letters indicate that she is not only intelligent but insightful. In fact, her insight and her spirituality have been the things that have impressed me most about her. As I said, Nick, she's a peach, one in a million, and that's why I've decided to make her my girl."

Kastanas grinned. "So when are you going to tell her what a lucky girl you've made her?"

Ben smiled, rolled back over, and stared up into the darkness. "I . . . I don't know."

"Ben! Come on . . . "

"Well, I don't, Nick. I don't want to foul things up by pushing myself at her. She's too fine a girl for that, and I would probably hurt her if I became overly bold."

"Nonsense! If she's half the girl you say she is, she would probably welcome some terms of endearment from a man such as yourself."

"Well, I've read so much garbage in the letters I've spent the past year censoring that maybe I have pulled back a little."

"That's not what I'm talking about, Ben, and you know it! But if she's as fine a girl as you say she is, and she's still unattached, then she's probably just dying for you to make some sort of move."

"But why?"

"Because women like security, Ben, the security that a good man can provide. Penny has told me a hundred times her feelings about that. It's funny, too. Women, or at least the good ones, don't really care about money or automobiles or fancy houses. What they care about is being loved and accepted. And if it happens to be a good man who provides that emotional support for a woman, a good man like you, I might add, then her happiness is simply increased."

"You learned all that from Penny?" Ben asked.

"I did. Penny's a sharp girl, Ben. Of course you know that already, because you've met her."

Ben nodded. "I did, both at Thanksgiving and at Christmas dinners. And I thought then, Nick, that if I could ever meet a girl like Penny, I would be happy being married to her."

"Well, it sounds like wedding bells are in your future, all right."

In the darkness, Ben looked at his friend. "You think so, Nick? Seriously?"

"If your description is accurate, and I suspect that it is, for you are not one to exaggerate, then I am dead serious. Talk to her, Ben, and not just about foxholes and creepy Japs. Discuss your feelings with her and see how she responds."

"But . . . what if she stops writing?"

"She might. But if that happens, then she isn't who you think she is, and you wouldn't be interested anyway. And besides, the odds are just as good that she will fire a letter right back telling you that she feels the same as you do and has just been dying to hear you say the words. Do you have a picture with you?"

"No, just at the base."

"When this is all over, Ben, and if I get home, I want to meet her. You remember that."

"Well, if it works out . . . "

"Doggone it, Ben, it will work out. Just you write her like I told you."

Suddenly there was a terrific outburst just down the hill, and a soldier came jumping out into the moonlight, swearing and jerking at his clothes. "I can't stand these blankety-blank fleas any longer," he cried. "I've got to take my clothes off and scratch!"

Ben and Nick Kastanas laughed with the others while the poor man stood in the moonlight stripping off every article of clothing and shaking them violently. Then he scratched himself thoroughly, dusted himself and his clothing with insect powder, and, batting at mosquitoes who were zeroing in like kamikazes on the new and unexplored territory of his body, hastily put them back on. Then the hillside grew quiet again.

At a quarter to midnight, one of the men on guard came to awaken Kastanas. He wasn't asleep, though, and as Ben watched him rise and walk away, he thought that perhaps he might finally get some sleep himself. But it didn't come, for the grass fleas were nearly crucifying him, and so for a time Ben simply lay in the darkness alone, suffering.

But the air was sweet and cool, with a plant smell to it, and Ben liked that very much. The moon made the leaves of the nearby shrubs all shiny, and the rays of light shown through them like light through the church windows back in Canada.

There were also plenty of jungle sounds to keep him company. Every hour on the hour and every half hour on the half hour, as regularly as if they had clocks in them, the Kalow birds would start up their kalow-kalow, kalaw-kalawing. One would start, just to sort of give the pitch, and then all would join in from every direction for about fifteen seconds; then they would all shut off at once. It was as good as a cuckoo clock, only not so strident but more rumbling, and Ben could hear the sound of the jungle clocks kalowing-kalowing over the hills and down toward the sea and up along the river as far as his ears could carry. Then silence. The birds usually shut off before midnight, but as long as it lasted he could mark the half-hours by it.

There were also owls, which had a very plaintive hoot. It was low and sad, like a mother regretting her tiny child's sorrow. The sound carried a long distance, and Ben could never tell if the owls were near or far, nor even the direction they were crying from.

Also, Ben could hear the white cockatoos with their squawking, shrewish screams at everything that disturbed them, even their own dreams. Some nights they screamed themselves purple over nothing at all, and the sound grew tiresome indeed.

He also heard the bojong birds occasionally, and once the mating bark of the red deer, not a real dog bark but rather the sort of bark a dog makes after it has been hit and has run away and wants to come back but is afraid to for fear of being hit again.

So there was plenty to listen to and to see, as long as he couldn't sleep. But mostly Ben neither saw nor heard, except on the outer edge of his thoughts. Instead, his mind swirled inwardly, for he could not get his mind off what Kastanas had said about Pat Christensen, the girl he was already thinking of as "his own."

Was it possible that his Greek friend was right? Kastanas was a good man, a solid man, and Ben respected his opinions. Besides, he truly had been impressed with Kastanas's wife, Penny. Both of them were very stable people.

Perhaps they were both right, then, and Pat was sitting back in Utah anxiously awaiting some expression from him concerning his feelings for her.

But how could he do that? For goodness sake, he had never even seen the girl, let alone talked to her. All he had were an even dozen letters, penned words that could just as easily be painting a false picture of her as a true one.

But no, that wasn't right, and he knew it. For he also had something else, something that allowed him to have much greater confidence in his impressions of her than others might have had. And that was the Holy Ghost, whose assignment was to bear witness to the truth of all things.

Well, whether or not Pat Christensen was as sweet, pure, and true as she seemed to be was certainly one of those things. Ben needed to know the truth of the matter concerning Patricia Christensen, and since he was doing his best to be worthy of having the Spirit with him, surely the Lord would allow the Holy Ghost to bear witness of it to him.

All along he had had good feelings about the young woman, and he couldn't believe how much he looked forward to her letters. But strangely, he had never prayed about her. He had never asked that he might receive or sought that he might find or knocked that an understanding might be opened unto him.

Briefly he remembered a two-and-a-half-minute talk he had once given in Sunday School, when he had been perhaps thirteen. His topic had concerned the Lord not giving information until people had put forth the effort to ask for it.

Now, he suddenly realized, that child's talk he had prepared and given applied perfectly to himself as an adult. He had not yet put forth the effort to ask, and so he was still fighting the situation, still fearful, still unsure. And so, with a sudden, firm resolution to put it off no longer, Ben rolled onto his stomach and closed his eyes.

"Heavenly Father," he prayed mentally in the darkness, "I need to know about Sister Patricia Christensen. Is she the one that Mother was telling me about in her letter? Thou knowest Sister Christensen, and I would ask thee if she is as she seems in her letters. Wilt thou grant unto me the companionship of the Holy Spirit? Wilt thou allow him to fill my heart and my soul with his presence and power, that I might know the truthfulness of the image I have drawn from her letters? I truly feel good about her, but I want very badly to have thy witness as well.

"If I am right, Father, then let my bosom burn within me.

Grant me peace concerning her. And if thou wilt, dear Father, I would also be interested in knowing if she is the girl that my dear mother felt inspired to tell me of—the girl who will one day become my wife . . . ''

CHAPTER

FIFTEEN

Just before dawn, long after Kastanas had returned and begun snoring softly beside him, Ben finally fell into a fitful sleep, giving the mosquitoes and fleas a clear field of fire. He dreamed, then, a nonsensical situation where he was running along a line of Jap POWs trying to find his wife. But the Japs kept reaching out and piercing his skin with needles; and besides, he could see no women anywhere. But he knew he had to keep looking until he found her, so despite the pain he ran on — and on —

The "whump" of mortar fire brought him groggily to his feet, and as he tried to clear his mind and his vision, a brilliant flare exploded high overhead, bathing the hill with light. Instantly small-arms fire opened up, and as Ben grabbed his boots and turned to race down the hill toward his LVTs, a ripple of laughter spread up the hill toward him, stopping him.

With a sigh of exhaustion he sank back onto his pack, and slowly Lieutenant Kastanas lifted himself out of the shallow foxhole he and Ben had dug earlier.

"Now what's going on?" Kastanas grumbled.

"I don't know for certain," Ben replied as he stifled a

yawn. "But all the activity is down near the bank of the river. That means one of two things: Japs sneaking through the water, or crocodiles. My bet would be crocs."

Lieutenant Kastanas looked down at him in shock. "Crocodiles? Here?"

Silently Ben nodded.

"Oh, no! I thought we left them behind in New Guinea."

"We didn't, Nick. Take my word for it. And they're every bit as mean as the New Guinea crocs, too. I was told by a fellow at HQ that 35,000 of them were killed in one year on this river alone. So not only are they here and real, but they can create some very real problems, too."

As the flare slowly died overhead, word came up the hill that the firing had indeed been at a crocodile, which had apparently wanted nothing more than to share a foxhole with a couple of men from Leslie Milam's mortar squad, and perhaps also to have one of them for an early breakfast.

Slowly the hillside grew quiet again, and then from way off to the south, flashes from the big guns from a part of the American fleet suddenly lit up the sky. For some reason, they were shelling the island of Basilan and shooting flares to light up the front lines and beaches there. Sometimes Ben and Kastanas could actually see the red-hot shells, at least ten miles away, traveling horizontally the whole length of their flight. They could also see them explode, but the sound from the explosions never did reach the hillside where Ben and the others watched.

Later, just as the first touch of pink was tingeing the sky to the east, a rustle in some bushes down the slope and just beyond the American perimeter brought a flurry of activity again, and more firing.

"Can you hardly imagine this night?" Kastanas asked as two men finally dragged a dead carabao, a Filipino water buffalo, out into the opening where the men waited with ready weapons.

"It's been a long one," Ben agreed as he watched the men attack the carabao carcass and begin butchering it for use by the troops. "That poor carabao surely needed backup support before he began his attack; mortar if not artillery. What happened to your eyes?"

"Dagnab mosquitoes," Kastanas replied as he tried to rub his swollen left eye back open. "I told you, every morning it's like this. I've got a sign on my forehead written in mosquito-ese, telling all comers that I am grade A prime on the hoof. And I don't know how to erase the blasted sign."

Both men chuckled without mirth, and then they sank back to await the all-clear command to build their breakfast fire and begin the new day.

"You know, Ben," Lieutenant Kastanas said after a brief interval, "I thought morning would cheer me up."

Ben looked at his friend. "I didn't know that you needed cheering, Nick. You having problems at home or something?"

"Not that I know of," Kastanas replied. "Its just that . . . well, I have this . . . this terribly lonely feeling. It's as though I'm the last man left alive, and all the time I feel like bawling because I can't talk to Penny or hold her and my little girl and smother them with kisses and tell them how much they mean to me. Ben, what's wrong with me? Other guys handle this war. What's suddenly going on that I can't seem to hold it together?"

"Maybe it's battle fatigue," Ben replied gently.

"You mean I'm a psycho? I don't think so, Ben. Everything's too clear—I can make decisions easily, good decisions. No, I don't think that's it. Besides, don't you ever feel lonely?"

Ben looked off into the graying morning. "I do," he said simply.

"See? And you're not psycho. So what do you miss most, Ben? Tell me about it, please."

"Nick, I don't think—"

"Please, Ben. Maybe you can get my mind going in another direction. Just talk to me, let me see the things you think about and miss most."

Ben sighed deeply. "I . . . I don't have a family like you do, Nick, so I can't miss them the way you do."

"I know that, Ben."

"But I do miss my own family, my four brothers and two sisters."

"What are their names?"

Ben grinned. "My sisters are named Ruth and Lila, Lila being the eldest. My brothers are Cliff, who is the only one in the family older than me, and then Den, Jim, and Ray. My mother's name is Mary Walker, and my dad's name is William Alvin, William Alvin Bennett."

"So is he called William or Bill?"

"Neither," Ben replied with a grin. "He's called Alvin."

Kastanas grinned back. "Is he a big man, like you?"

Shaking his head, Ben responded. "Not exactly. I'm the biggest in the family. But Dad is about six feet tall, with a big chest and slender waist and hips. I would say he weighs about 170 pounds. He's a very dignified looking man, and he's strong as can be. In fact, before he started to stiffen up a little, he used to be very athletic. The other thing I can tell you about him is that his movements are planned and deliberate, and he is naturally quite shy and reserved."

Kastanas laughed. "Ben, except for the height and the stiffness, I would say that you have just described yourself."

"In some ways," Ben replied, "other people have said the same thing. Especially, I think, with the shyness."

"So how did your dad ever get together with your mother?"

"It took him a while," Ben replied. "I guess the first time he ever saw her, she was shaking a scatter rug outside her father's home in Taber, Alberta, and he liked everything that he saw. But Mother was quite popular, so Dad went after her the roundabout way, by making friends with her brothers, especially Will, who was just older than her.

"Finally the Walker boys took Dad home, and that was when he was formally introduced to the lovely Mary Walker. But he was too shy to do anything about it, so he just bided his time and hoped that she would get used to having him around her."

"Smart move, if you have the patience."

"It took that, all right. And effort, too. Mother and her sisters were considered some of the best dancers in Taber, and Dad had never danced more than a step or two in his entire life. So at home he got his own sisters to teach him how to dance, and finally he was ready to make his first move.

"The trouble was, Dad could never get Mother alone long enough to ask her out. So one night he decided to wait her family out—to stay up longer than they could. As he and Mother sat together, first one and then another of Mother's family went to bed. Finally it was just the two of them and Will. But Will had somehow figured out what Dad was up to, and he had determined to outstay Dad. The contest of determination went on into the wee hours of the morning, and whoever gave in, I don't know. But it worked out just fine, for Dad and Mother's courtship began."

"Is that it?" Kastanas asked quickly.

"Well, they dated—"

"Tell me about that, their first date, I mean. Do you know what they did?"

"I think so, Nick. As I remember it, Dad took her to a traveling show in the Taber Opera House." Suddenly Ben laughed. "In fact, Nick, I do remember something funny that happened. On their way home afterward they had to walk across a plank that crossed a ditch or puddle or something. Anyway, it was slippery underfoot, and Mother's feet slipped out from under her and she fell in a heap, her flailing feet kicking Dad's feet out from under him as she fell. As Dad went down beside her, he saw her petticoats, which he always afterward claimed were plaid. Of course, Mother claimed that she never owned a plaid petticoat in her life, so instead of seeing stars, Dad was seeing plaids."

Quietly both men chuckled. "Anyway," Ben concluded, "on that first date, as they like to say even yet, they both sort of fell for each other."

"Ouch!" Kastanas chuckled.

"Yes, I know it's a bad joke."

"But funny," Kastanas said, still chuckling. "So it led to marriage?"

"Over a sometimes rocky road," Ben responded. "But they did get married, in the LDS temple down in Salt Lake City. Once back in Canada, Dad began his life's work in agriculture. And that, Nick, is where I experience some of my worst loneliness."

"For the farm?" Kastanas asked, surprised.

"Well, not exactly for the farm, for we had several of them. More, Nick, I miss the soil, the land, and that's a hard thing to explain. Even after all these years, it seems I won't ever be weaned away from it. Sometimes I feel sorry for my men, for I don't believe a person has ever really lived who did not spend his boyhood days on a farm. The old saddle pony, the collie dog, the smell of new-mown hay or freshly turned sod, the old swimming hole, and even the coyote's howl at night—well, they do something to a youngster on a farm. He learns to meditate when he becomes lonesome. As he looks at the stars in the unbroken quiet of a prairie night, he begins to get a look at life that so many people never see."

"Yeah, I looked at these southern stars and thought a lot last night," Kastanas stated softly.

"So did I, Nick. So did I. And you know, besides thinking a lot about what we talked about last night, I also thought about our farm. How I would like to be in Canada for the wheat harvest this coming fall! How I long to see those miles upon miles of waving, ripening fields of grain, fields that are so characteristic of Manitoba, Saskatchewan, and parts of Alberta.

"The hum of the combine would be sweet music to my ears, and pitching bundles into the old threshing machine would be the greatest activity in the world for me.

"But instead, Nick, here I sit on a hillside on Mindanao, surrounded by palm trees, of all things. The dense jungles also extend for miles and miles, but what a contrast to Canada's fields of grain! I listen to the weird jungle noises and long for my boyhood paradise, for you see, I have heard the call of the land."

CHAPTER

SIXTEEN

As Ben grew silent, sudden tears started in Kastanas' eyes, and quickly he looked away.

Sensing something, Ben reached over and placed his hand on his friend's knee. "Nick, old man, what is it? What's troubling you?"

"I . . . I've heard a call, too," the man replied softly, wiping his eyes with the back of his arm. "But it's not the land, Ben. I . . . I keep dreaming that I am . . . dead . . . Oh, confound it all, what's wrong with me? Why am I so scared . . . so lonely?"

"Maybe that's all it is, Nick—a dream."

"No, Ben," Kastanas replied, shaking his head. "I can feel it, way down in here. Somewhere up ahead of us in the jungles some Jap is going to kill me, and I know it. Only I'm so doggone scared that I can hardly sleep. Oh, confound it, why didn't I listen to you back on Morotai? If I had just stopped smoking, then this wouldn't be happening . . . "

Ben squeezed his friend's knee. "Nick, it takes a little more than that, so don't be so hard on yourself. Besides, even if you do die, you've no need to be frightened."

"But what about Penny and the baby?" the man cried.

"Yes," Ben agreed, "it would be very hard for them, for they love you very much. I know, for I saw it in Penny's face both times I was in your home."

"But I . . . I don't want to leave them," Kastanas declared as more tears fell. "Ben, my life's finally getting good! It . . . it isn't fair . . . to die . . . to have the whole thing between Penny and me, end forever . . . She's the best thing that ever happened . . . in my whole miserable life . . . her and our little girl . . . "

"And it doesn't have to end," Ben said softly.

"Wh-what?"

"I said, my friend, that it doesn't have to end, even with death."

"But . . . but I don't understand . . . "

Ben smiled gently. "Nick, the Word of Wisdom that you were so worried about is only a tiny part of a glorious host of eternal truths that the scriptures call the gospel of Jesus Christ. You see, whether we live the Word of Wisdom or not, all of us are going to die sometime or other. So the Word of Wisdom isn't really designed to prevent us from dying."

"But . . . I thought . . . "

"Don't worry, Nick. I likely didn't explain it well enough back on Morotai, and that's my fault. You see, as I understand it, the Word of Wisdom is one of a number of commandments given by God to His children because He loves us, and because He wants us to learn obedience. The purpose of these commandments is to enable us to enjoy mortality a little more, and to live a little longer in this probationary state, than we otherwise would."

"Enjoy?"

"That's right. We enjoy better health, we have greater stamina, and so forth. But the real blessing, Nick, is one that isn't so easily measured. It is a spiritual blessing, a promise of wisdom and understanding of the things of God. In other words, we grow spiritually and become closer to God by

159

becoming more like He is. And, interestingly, all of His commandments accomplish that same purpose—to help us become more like He and Jesus are."

"I . . . I hadn't ever thought of it like that," Kastanas said thoughtfully. "But . . . what does that have to do with Penny and me?"

"Everything. Do you remember in the New Testament, when Christ gave to Peter and others what he called the keys of the kingdom?"

"I . . . I don't think so."

"Try to remember," Ben urged. "He told Peter that whatsoever he bound on earth would be bound in heaven, and whatsoever he loosed on earth would be loosed in heaven."

"Yeah," Kastanas breathed, "I do remember reading that. But I don't think I ever understood what it meant."

"It's simple, Nick. What Christ meant was that Peter's authority to perform ordinances went beyond the grave. Binding and loosing, here and in heaven. Do you understand?"

"Well, I'll be doggone . . . "

"Let's give you an example. You and Penny were married until death do you part. Right?"

"That's right."

"Well, suppose Peter had been there to marry you. If he truly had power to bind on earth as well as in heaven, and the scriptures say that he did, would he have married you until death do you part?"

Slowly Kastanas shook his head.

"That's right, my friend. He wouldn't have."

"But Peter wasn't there! So what does that have to do—"

"I'll tell you," Ben replied, interrupting him. "The same authority that Peter and Christ's other apostles held anciently is on the earth today. Twelve apostles, men who are alive right now, in April 1945, have been called to that position by Christ through modern revelation and have the power to bind on earth and in heaven."

"Are . . . are you serious?" Kastanas asked in a whisper.

"Absolutely. These marriages are performed in sacred buildings called temples—"

"Yeah, you said your parents were married in a temple."

"That's correct, Nick. And one day, I too will kneel in a temple with my sweetheart and be married for time . . . and for all eternity, as well."

Slowly Kastanas shook his head. "Amazing. Ben, I had no idea . . . My gosh, why don't you tell people about this?"

"We do," Ben replied, grinning. "Thousands of missionaries have searched the world, and will yet search it further, seeking out those who truly desire to hear this great message of eternal hope and joy. I've even tried to tell you about it a time or two. But you weren't ready to hear me."

"I . . . I'm sorry. I didn't realize . . . "

"I know that, Nick, and so does God."

"So, what happens when people are found who are ready?"

"Once found," Ben responded, "they are baptized, again by proper authority, and then they too can begin the process of growing, until ultimately they have done as Jesus commanded, becoming like Him and His Father."

"But . . . Ben, how do I do it? I mean, I never even knew! And if I . . . go out there and get . . . killed . . . "

"God is a just God, Nick, and He is not partial to the living or the dead. Therefore he has provided a way whereby you and Penny can enjoy these eternal blessings just as much as I can, or as anyone else, for that matter. And it doesn't matter if one or both of you are alive or dead."

Kastanas slowly shook his head. "But how—"

"Through vicarious work, Nick, a living person standing in as proxy for one who has passed away, as the marriage ceremony is performed again in the holy temple."

"You mean . . . "

"I mean that if you should die, if Penny accepts the gospel and is baptized, then she can go to the temple . . . "

"This vicarious stuff happens there, too? In the temple, I mean?"

"That's what I said. That's why God's temples are so sacred. So Penny can go to the temple and kneel at the alter with some other man who is there to represent you, a person who is acting as your proxy. Then an apostle, or one of their representatives, using their God-given authority or priesthood, seals your marriage to Penny for eternity as well as time. Then, Nick, even though death has parted you for a brief period, you will have God's promise of being together as a family, forever."

"With our daughter, too?" Kastanas asked hopefully.

"Of course."

Slowly Kastanas shook his head. "Ben, I have never heard anything like this in my entire life. If only it can be true . . . "

"It is, Nick. I know it is true, for the Holy Spirit has borne witness to me that it is. I also bear that witness to you, and do it in the name of Jesus Christ!"

Kastanas looked up. "I . . . I believe you, Ben. I . . . You know, all of a sudden I'm shaking like I am cold. But I'm not. I'm hot, down here in my chest. And I feel so good . . . "

"Your witness," Ben said, smiling. "All things from God make His children feel good, and the Holy Ghost is now telling you that what I have said is from God, and is true."

"Well, I'll be doggone . . . "

As Kastanas pondered, the order came up the hill to light fires and eat, and so in silence he and Ben did exactly that. Later, as they hoisted their packs and started down the hill toward the LVTs, Kastanas suddenly handed Ben a brown envelope.

"Ben, this is my last will and testament. If . . . anything happens, will you see that Penny gets it?"

"Of course, but—"

"Ben," Kastanas said seriously, stopping him, "not now. I know what I feel, and thanks to you, I'm not so bothered as I was. But I have another request."

Silently Ben looked at his friend.

"Will you . . . will you go see Penny, I mean, if I am killed, and tell her what you have told me?"

"I'll do that. Certainly."

"Tell her, Ben, that I believed you . . . No, tell her that I believed God, for He had told me that she and I really could be together forever. Persuade her, Ben. Please persuade her. She can be real stubborn, but she's a good woman, the best I ever knew."

"Why don't you write her, Nick?"

"I will if I have time. I wish I could get baptized, too. Could you do that, Ben? I mean, do you personally have that authority?"

Ben nodded. "I do, and next time we get together—"

"Ben," Kastanas chided gently, "there won't be a next time, at least here. I really feel that. Do . . . do you do baptisms . . . in the temples, I mean?"

"We do."

"Then do it for me there, Ben. Promise me that, please?"

"I promise, Nick."

"And one other thing. If Penny goes along with this, and I think she will, then will . . . will you kneel beside her . . . for me . . . in your temple, and be my proxy?"

With sudden tears in his eyes, Ben silently nodded.

Suddenly Lieutenant Kastanas spun and threw his arms around Ben, and for a moment the two battle-hardened friends stood holding each other closely, their tears falling freely.

"Thanks, Ben," Kastanas muttered as he patted Ben's back fiercely, "this has helped more than you'll ever know. I . . . I don't feel scared anymore, or lonely, either one."

"You're welcome, Nick. I sure do love you."

"Yeah, I know. I can tell. And I feel the same about you, you big, muscle-bound galoot. Outside of Penny, you're the greatest friend I ever had."

"And you're a great man, Nick. It's easy to be a friend to a fellow like you."

"Confound it all," Kastanas said gruffly as they broke apart a moment later and started again for the LVTs, "I still wish you were leading this outfit, Ben."

"You'll do fine, Nick."

"Maybe," Lieutenant Kastanas replied, grinning. "But it's you that has God's promise of protection for you and your men, Ben. Not me. I only quit smoking maybe fifteen minutes ago, and I don't think that'll be long enough to do the trick. And to tell you the truth," Nick Kastanas concluded with a wry smile, "I'd really rather live than do otherwise."

PART FOUR

THE DEPARTURE OF A FRIEND

April 18, 1945 — April 30, 1945

THE WAR

After fierce fighting in Germany itself, Nuremberg was taken by the Allies, and then Rothenburg, while units of the First White Russian Army reached the suburbs of Berlin. Refusing to leave the city, on April 27, 1945, Hitler sent what turned out to be his final message to Mussolini: "The struggle for our survival is at its height. Employing great masses and materials, Bolshevism and the armies of Jewry allied themselves to join their malignant forces in Europe in order to precipitate chaos in our continent." One day later, Benito Mussolini was shot and killed by Italian partisans as he and his mistress, Clara Petacci, attempted to flee Italy.

The day thereafter, April 29, in his Berlin Bunker, Hitler designated Karl Donitz as his successor and then married his mistress, Eva Braun. The next day, April 30, 1945, dressed in a new Nazi uniform and modestly bemedaled, Hitler took a cyanide capsule while seated on a couch in the Reich Chancellery in Berlin. So ended the "Thousand Year Reich." Hitler's bride also took poison. Their bodies were then doused in gasoline and burned, and as only the Russians saw their remains, it is still not known what became of the final evidence of Hitler's death. Joseph Goebbels and his wife also killed themselves and their six children the same day.

Most of the world rejoiced at the news of Hitler's death, but it was by no means a universal sentiment. Neutral Portugal, for example, declared two days of national mourning, and flags were flown at half-staff.

And in the South Pacific, the war continued unabated. While land and sea battles raged in and around Okinawa, U.S. bombers from various island bases made run after run against the Japanese homeland. In these raids, tens of thousands of tons of bombs were dropped, and the human-caused devastation was unimaginable.

On Mindanao, the Americans pushed their way into Digos on the Davao Gulf, meeting only scattered resistance from the 3,350 Japanese stationed there. Then the Japanese retreated into the mountains seventeen miles northward, where they dug in. The Americans had crossed the entire island in just ten days, beating the rainy season as they did it.

As the 24th Division headed north toward Davao along the costal road, fighting burned bridges, roadblocks, hundreds of buried mines, machine-gun nests, and artillery pillboxes and caves along the road manned with thousands of enemy troops, Japanese General Harada finally realized that he was facing the main American attack rather than a diversionary force. With Davao already in shambles from weeks of American bombing, he retreated westward some three miles to a mountainous area where his men had earlier constructed an extensive series of defense works, complete with heavy artillery. There he prepared to make his last stand against the oncoming Americans.

Meanwhile, to the northwest along the Sayre Highway, the 31st Division got the word to move out from General Sibert, and the 124th Regimental Combat Team, including Company "E," Ben Bennett's old outfit, began its advance northward from Kabacan. Sergeant Leslie Milam still led his mortar squad; Tom Dabbs, now decorated with a Silver Star, still served as platoon sergeant; and Lieutenant Nick Kastanas commanded the company.

Nine miles north of the Pulangi River crossing, at 10:00 P.M., as the 31st was searching in the dark for a suitable place to bivouac, they ran into a Japanese battalion who were on their way to retake the crossing.

The unsuspecting Americans were weary, sullen, and interested mainly in where they would bivouac. On the other hand, the Japanese were alert and aggressive — and their automatic weapon fire almost annihilated the American advance patrol.

What followed was a confused battle that raged on and around the highway. Somehow the Americans managed to hold their ground through attack after Banzai attack. In the morning, the Japanese battalion commander was found dead within American lines, one of fifty killed to the Americans' ten. The rest of the Japanese battalion, its morale apparently shattered, vanished into the underbrush and jungle.

While the battle was small, its significance was great, for it deprived the Japanese of precious time to establish defenses. For several days after that, all that delayed the American advance to and through Kibawe was the lengthening of their supply lines and the condition of the highway, which was atrocious. In the first twenty-five miles north of Kabacan, there were seventy bridges along the Sayre Highway, none of them intact, and all of them defended bitterly by sniper fire. There were also bogs and swamps, and a thirty-mile stretch of roadway that had never been paved at all. It had been corduroyed, but the logs had rotted, and the first truck on them bogged down of its own weight.

Despite the difficult terrain and scattered opposition, the 31st moved northward, traveling so fast that it was soon out of range of supporting artillery and supplies. After a strike by Marine dive-bombers, the Americans crossed the Mulita

River and secured the high ground on the other side. At the Barrio of Misinsiman, just as the leading battalion was going into perimeter for the night, another fanatical Banzai attack occurred, in which fifty-eight of the enemy were killed in an hour's fighting.

The next day, May 2, 1945, the 124th captured Kibawe and held up while engineers repaired the airstrip and improved the road behind them. Sometimes, in order to move howitzers or trucks across the yawning gorges, the engineers stretched steel cables between huge trees on either side of the ravine. The heavy equipment was then hung on the cables with a pulley arrangement and winched over. Wounded men on stretchers were also hauled across the dizzying ravines on these primitive cable spans, and it was an experience most of them would never forget.

While the engineers worked, advance elements of the 124th continued to probe northward along the Sayre Highway, crossing another three bridgeless ravines and again outdistancing the artillery. On May 6, with the 1st Battalion on point, the Americans encountered a very heavy and completely camouflaged Japanese position that straddled the road just inside a heavy stand of woods.

These woods, later called "Colgan Woods" after the Catholic chaplin who was killed there, became the scene of the heaviest fighting ever encountered by the 124th. In a battle that was to rage almost without letup for the next eight days, American forces pressed forward and were pushed back in the relatively small wooded area by a desperate contingent of enemy troops who were ensconced in spider pillboxes that could not be seen from more than a foot or two away.

Despite continual mortar fire, little damage was done against the deeply entrenched Japanese. Heavy artillery was needed, desperately needed, and yet it was not available. Almost the only weapon available that had any effect upon the pillboxes was the flamethrower, and these weapons were

THE DEPARTURE OF A FRIEND

used extensively to force the enemy out of the ground. But they were close-combat weapons, and their use extracted a heavy toll of American lives.

Three days into the fighting, "E" Company was pinned down by heavy Japanese machine-gun fire. As the Americans that had fought on Morotai under Ben Bennett crawled and fought and dug in against the withering fire, Lieutenant Nick Kastanas finally spotted the machine-gun nest hidden beneath a large tree. Unable to point out the location to his desperately fighting men, he grabbed up a flamethrower dropped earlier by one of his casualties, and alone he charged the nest. But the discarded flamethrower did not work. He was killed almost instantly.

THE MAN

While operating the LVT and Dukw Company, Ben followed with interest the progress of the 24th and 124th Divisions as they fought across Mindanao. He also had the opportunity to meet and work with several guerilla leaders, including Colonel Fertig, Major Masa, and Lieutenant Thomas S. Sajar. As Ben and his men worked their vehicles farther and farther into the interior, they began to see more clearly the strength and importance of the guerilla leaders in the freeing of Mindanao from the Japanese. Ben also grew better acquainted with the Filipino people and gained a healthy respect for them as well as for what they had been forced to endure during the Japanese occupation.

In his writings, Ben thrilled to the surrender of Germany, but with the rest of his men he felt somewhat left out as far as relief was concerned. He was also excited when Russia announced plans to attack Japan, and every further Allied advance across the Pacific brought paragraphs of joy flowing into his journal.

He also discussed in detail the lengthy conversations he had had with his men about obedience to the commandments, including the Word of Wisdom. Some willingly accepted what he taught them, and others inexplicably resisted every word he spoke. Regarding these resisters, he wrote:

"I [am] convinced that some people are more inclined to disbelieve things than they are to believe them. Such people are lacking in faith. If they would put forth the same effort to believe that they do to disbelieve, they might find themselves believing many of the things they now think they disbelieve!"

Then he added: "We should be [questioning], but we should not be skeptics. It will lead to shallowness of life and unhappiness. We should remember the statement of Thomas Huxley about the bar of steel floating in the air [showing to Huxley that he had encountered a law of which he was, as yet, ignorant]."

On June 15, Ben wrote that it was Infantry Day and that 116,000 of the 174,000 army dead in the war thus far were infantrymen. Only a few days after that, he received word that one of his Dukws was stranded in the mountains of the interior and that someone needed to go after it. Because it was his responsibility, he determined to go himself . . .

CHAPTER

SEVENTEEN

"Tuesday, May 8, 1945, 1930 hours
   "Dear 'Patty:' "
Ben paused over the blank page, his eyes seeing beyond the tent flaps that were closed against the steady rain, seeing on and on through the unimaginable distance toward America. It had rained every day for a week, and the entire post was a quagmire of mud and filthy men. Even the interior of his tent was a mess, and that was something that he rarely let happen. But now he ignored it, for a letter from Patricia Christensen had arrived this evening, and he wanted to get his answer off as soon as possible.

Only, what should he say? Hers was another newsy letter, rather like his own recent epistles. So how might he possibly write the things that Nick Kastanas had encouraged him to write? He didn't know, but he did know that it wouldn't happen if he didn't stop dreaming and get his pen back onto the paper.

"Patty sounds too much like Willie," he finally wrote by way of a lame introduction, "so in case you don't like the one as much as I cringe at the other, I am still going to call you Pat. But don't be surprised if I call you Patty when I see you one day, for I like that name, too.

171

"Thank you for your recent letter. The way you describe the beginnings of spring in Utah, it must be the most beautiful season the Lord ever brought to pass in that country. How I would like to be there to see and enjoy it with you."

Again Ben paused, suddenly worried that he had already waxed too bold. What if she didn't want to see it with him? What if she didn't—

Shaking his head, Ben grinned. Here he was sabotaging himself after only the first paragraph. Silly. He did want to see things with her, so by cracky he was going to say so— and take his chances that she would like what he wrote, he determined.

"And perhaps that will be soon," he continued. "At least I have hopes of the war ending soon. Of course you will have heard the news of Hitler's death, supposedly at his command post in Berlin. Karl Doenitz, former submarine and navy commander, has reportedly succeeded Hitler. Berlin is now 90% in Russian hands, and we hear that the Russian flag is now flying over the former German Chancellry. Hitler's empire has crumbled and 'ere long will go down in history to an ignominious death. Japan's downfall approaches, but is not just yet. Hopefully soon—"

A sudden chattering caused Ben to look up, and then he grinned and returned to his letter.

"One of my men, PFC Lodge, is on patrol in one of the dukws up toward Lake Lanao, and he has left his pet monkey for me to babysit. Right now it is hanging by its tail from the cross-pole of the tent, scolding me. I think it must be of the opinion that I am awake too long after darkness, and should put out the light and go to sleep. But a monkey's opinion is of little consequence when I have a chance to read one of your letters and then respond to it. So to the devil with a monkey's rest. You and I are going to have a visit.

"My old outfit in the 31st, the 2nd Battalion, has been in some pretty tough fighting in the interior. Reports say nine were killed, but I can't get any names yet. Nor do I know how many were wounded. I feel terrible that I wasn't with them, almost guilty. Why should I be spared, I keep asking myself? Of course I can hear you say that the Lord was protecting me, especially with transfers, and I know He is. But still I feel like somehow I should have been with my friends. Oh, Pat, how I long for this war to end!

"But good things do happen. My orderly, 'Pete' Limberis, has been trying without success for five years to hear from his family in Greece. Today a card from his folks came for him. He said, 'Lieutenant, this is a big day for me.' And it was. No word had come to him from them during the entire period of Nazi occupation, but now mail service has been re-established and he knows they are alive.

"Pete is an interesting character, Pat. He is thirty-four years old with quite grey hair. He served in the Greek navy for eleven years and has traveled all over the world. After the Nazi occupation of Greece he made his home in America, where he went into the restaurant business. Then he joined the American army, and three months later became an American citizen. And now he is in the Philippines as my orderly.

"And he is the best, probably spoiling me for the years to come when I shall unjustly expect a wife to do some of the things he does for me. Hardly had he arrived before he went to work. In no time he had a floor in the tent and had it fixed up in good style. He fixed up mosquito bar poles, etc. The best part is that he doesn't need to be told what to do. He thinks of things on his own, and then does them. We even have electric lights now, and with a radio, everything seems quite nice.

"Pat, let me ask your advice. I have been having a difficult time with one of my men, a Pvt. Rish, who did not take the oath of war. He used to write threats against the Government and President Roosevelt in his letters, and I fear that he is still heading for a General Court Martial. Yesterday, a Sunday,

Rish was put on a Q.M. detail, and he objected strenuously, for it was against his religious beliefs to work on Sunday. I tried to work with him, but he wouldn't reason. Finally, though, he did his duty.

"So today I called him in and had a long, frank talk with him. He is a Baptist. I told him I was a Mormon, and then we had a long talk about religious freedom and agency. We discussed the commandment 'Thou shalt not kill' in light of war. I told him that if, in time of war, a soldier is required to break that commandment, he is not held accountable for it, provided that his heart is right. The responsibility rests with those who are responsible for the war. I don't think he had ever considered this before.

"I then discussed the spirit versus the letter of the law, and applied that to the case at hand, namely working on the Sabbath. I pointed out to him that in my company there are Catholics, Jews, Mormons, Prostetants, and some with no religious affiliation at all. As a company commander, it is my duty to treat all men alike, on a fair and equal basis. I then told him that I would assume the responsibility for requiring him to work on Sunday, and that my assumption of that responsibility was between him, God and me. But I also told him that my position in requiring him to work on Sunday was quite similar to his. I, too, was a victim of circumstances growing out of the war, and could assume responsibility only because I knew that the ultimate responsibility before God would rest upon those responsible for the world's terrible condition. This seemed to cause Rish to feel a little better.

"Pat, can you think of anything else I might have said? His spirits are very low, and he feels that the whole U.S. Government is against him. I am sure that is why he espouses Naziism. If you can think of anything else I might say, I would surely appreciate knowing of it."

A commotion outside caused Ben to put down his pen, turn off his small light, and go to the door of his tent. In the darkness water glistened everywhere, though rain was no longer falling. He could barely hear the sounds of the electrical generator in the distance; other than that, all was silent. But what got his attention was the captain's tent, where light was visible through the open flaps. Also visible was a knot of men, standing still just inside the tent, apparently listening very intently to something.

"Hey, Lieutenant Shore," he called softly to one of the men standing within the tent, "what's going on?"

"Turn on your radio, Ben," the man responded urgently. "Germany has just surrendered!"

Turning quickly to his radio, Ben tuned in and listened as President Harry S. Truman concluded his announcement of the unconditional surrender of Germany to the Allies. He also issued and read a proclamation setting aside Sunday, May 13, as a day of prayer and thanksgiving to Almighty God for the victory in Europe, calling upon all people of all faiths to participate.

Following that, Prime Minister Churchill made the same announcement pertaining to the unconditional surrender of all land, sea, and air forces of Germany. Then he stated that the papers had already been signed, and that soon all remaining resistance in Europe would be at an end.

"2230 hours. Dear Pat:" Ben wrote a little later after the news had finally gone off the air, "We have just received the word of Germany's surrender. I had a very difficult time with my emotions when Prime Minister Churchill stated that all Allied strength would now be directed toward bringing about the unconditional surrender of Japan. Many of the men have long felt that we were fighting an 'outsider's' war here in the Pacific, and this news should cause us all to rejoice.

"It is easy to imagine the feelings of the people in Europe and America this night! This is the day we have been looking forward to for years; the day that refused to hurry itself, and it seemed that it would never arrive.

175

"But here in the Pacific there is no demonstration of any kind being made. Not a single shot has been fired to celebrate the occasion. Not a whistle has been blown. There has been no shouting or yelling, everyone taking the news in silence. Of course they are overjoyed, but the truth is that V-Day over here has not yet arrived, nor does it seem likely that it will be making an appearance very soon. But when that day does come, then I do not think that things will be so quiet.

"But please don't think me ungrateful. Three times now that I know of, my life has been miraculously preserved. I have written you of the ambush on Morotai and the night patrol in New Guinea, but I was preserved another time, in a rather different way.

"Perhaps you have heard of Japanese Scrub Typhus Disease? Many people die of it, for it is a deadly sickness. In fact, two of my buddies died of it back in New Guinea. That stuff's deadly. Well, a medical officer in New Guinea diagnosed me as having Japanese Scrub Typhus Disease. I was sent to the medical aid station, many miles to the rear, and from what little I remember, I was a pretty sick fellow. For four days I was under constant surveillance by a medical officer or nurse, with no change. But then on the fourth day, everything became normal. My temperature and all the symptoms of the disease disappeared. The doctors couldn't understand it, and the nurses couldn't understand it, but I could. You see, Pat, I was being blessed. The Lord has promised that if I would live the Word of Wisdom as I have repeatedly tried to explain it to you, then He would preserve my life. I have done my part, and so I know that the Lord is doing His. That is why I would be remiss if I allowed myself to moan or complain about my lot in this distant land.

"Earlier, Pat, I had a very interesting conversation with a Major Masa, one of the native guerilla leaders here on Mindinao. As I recall, the dialogue went something like this.

" 'I have noticed,' I stated, 'that the native people look

very clean. Even with mud everywhere, the women and girls wear gleaming white dresses, with not a spot of mud on them.'

" 'It is a thing of pride with us,' Masa responded, beaming. 'Those clothes were buried or hidden while the Japs were here. But now that the Americans have come, we show them who we really are. Do you notice that none of our women wear shoes?'

" 'I have.'

" 'There, in spite of our pride, you see our poverty.'

" 'Most people understand poverty, Major. So a great many fled to higher ground as the Japanese invasion flooded your land, you say?'

"Major Masa smiled. 'You speak of the Japanese flood, but there was no such thing, Lieutenant. I believe that we Filipinos were the flood. We were in it and we were it, while the Japs were just the rocks and walls sticking up that the flood flowed around. When the Americans left and the Japs came, none of us could seem to stand still. Whatever we found to stand on crumbled away, and we became part of the flood again.

" 'You would see buqwees, what we call the people who evacuated our homes, going north and south on the same road. There were long lines of families of us, none of us knowing where to go, but going, keeping on going in all directions, just like a flood. There was much bravery, but plenty of us were losing our nerve, too. Not from any real danger, really, but just from the pressure of knowing that some real danger might crop up the next moment. But then, many of the Americans who were left behind also lost their nerve over the same thing. One time I was sleeping on a cot next to an American officer, and in the middle of the night he put a gun in his ear and killed himself. The gunshot was so loud that even the next morning when I was burying the fellow I couldn't hear the dirt I was throwing into his grave.'

" 'Then did the Japs ever come?' I asked.

" ' Oh, yes, sir, they did come.'

" 'So what did you do then?'

" 'Why, sir, I stood by and let them do as they wished. In the village where I was they came once, and that is all. They searched the houses. Then they made a speech, and then they went away.'

" 'What kind of a speech?'

"Major Masa smiled. 'That we were brothers.'

" 'And did the people accept that?'

" 'There was no one in that village who was a brother to the Japs, or a cousin or a friend or anything else. No one liked them. But the Japs came with guns, they searched with guns, and when they made their speech, they held their guns pointed at us. So we were quiet to make them go away.'

" 'Good idea. So the people like the Americans, do they?'

"Major Masa smiled again. 'If you were to come among us without guns, you would be safe. No Jap would be safe without guns. Need I say anything more?'

" 'That sounds good enough to me,' I replied. 'Imagine, a people without fear. No wonder the guerilla movement is so strong here.'

" 'Oh, sir,' Masa protested, 'I did not say that. About two thirds of the people feared the Japs, and while they did not deny hospitality to those of us who fought them, they would have rather seen us on our way. The other third, though, they laughed at the Japs, and they helped us all the time. If the Japs came near, no matter whether or not the local people knew us, they would run to us and tell us that the Japs were coming. Then they would show us the safest way out.'

" 'But didn't the Japs hurt the people for concealing you?'

" 'Not at first, sir. At first they only talked. "Where are the guerillas?" they would ask.

" ' "No understand," one of our people would answer.

" ' "You understand. Where are the guerillas?"

" ' "They are gone."

" ' "Where have they gone?"

" ' "Back there, sir."

" ' "Well, we have come to rescue you from them."

" ' "Oh, thank you, sir."

" ' "We have come to liberate you from the bandits."

" ' "Oh, sir, you flatter us, you despise us, you are too good to us only, sir."

" ' "It is our pleasure to welcome good neighbors into the Greater East Asia Co-Prosperity Sphere."

" ' "Viva Hapons! Banzai!"

" ' "Now where are the guerillas?" the Japanese pressed.

" ' "They are gone, sir."

" ' "Where are they gone?"

" ' "Oh, sir, back there only."

" ' "Will you help us to find them and thus aid your own liberation from the bandits?"

" ' "Oh, sir, who can find the guerillas? They are gone only. There is no finding them in the hills."

" 'Thus went the conversations of our people, Lieutenant. It was impossible, sir, for a Jap to hide anywhere to spy on us, for no one would hide him or help him conceal his movements. He was in the house of his enemies. But wherever we went, on Mindanao or any of the other islands, we were in the house of our friends.'

" 'Why don't you Filipinos like the Japs?' I asked.

" 'We are afraid of them, afraid of what they would do if they got their foot in the door of our land. That is mostly what we don't like about them.'

" 'You mean the atrocities and the cruelties?'

" 'Oh, no, sir,' Masa responded emphatically. 'Such things are of little consequence, for people always suffer and die, whether the Japs are here or not. What we feared was what the Japs did in such places as Korea and Formosa. It was told to us that the Japs had forbidden the Koreans or the

Formosans to marry each other. If those people wanted to get married, they had to marry Japs. In that way the Japs made sure to incorporate their conquests into their empire. Well, sir, we did not want to marry Japs, we did not want our women to marry them, or our daughters. To the Japs, women are less than cattle, and what is happening now in the war proves this is so.'

" 'What is happening?'

" 'Why, sir, the Japs are now fighting with women, so that they can stay behind and be protected.'

" 'Women?'

" 'Oh, yes, sir. Japanese and Korean women, and, sadly, even some of our own. At first they were used only as whores, but lately we have begun to find women, after they had been killed by our fire, wearing uniforms and fighting as men.'

" 'And you believe the Japs forced them into battle?' I asked, appalled.

" 'Oh, yes, sir, thank you, sir. And then last week only, sir, naked women appeared on the front lines against our forces in Bukidon, women with no clothing on at all. Naturally our men held their fire, sir, but as the women got close, grenades the Japs had attached to their backs, exploded. Of course the women were killed, as were some of our men who were trying to clothe them to preserve their modesty. Naturally, sir, we are now forced only to shoot the women as well as the Japs, for sir, one never knows.'

" 'How tragic!'

" 'Yes. But that is why we do not want them around at all. That is why we do not like them.'

" 'Did the Japs bring any prosperity at all?' I asked then. 'At least at the beginning?'

"Masa shook his head. 'Oh, no, sir, there was no prosperity. The Japs take only, sir. They do not give. That is, they do not give except for one thing. They give our people the chance to be brave, and to be heros as we die. Many of us died making the Japs afraid of our hills. There are hundreds of heroes among us, sir, and their stories will never be known, for they are heroes only in very small and lonely places, where the only witnesses were those who were soon to be dead and their Jap killers. Our hill people took to carrying two bolos, a long-bladed bolo and a shorter one under their shirts. When they were caught and couldn't run, they would drop their big bolo as ordered and then wait for the Japs to come to them. Then they would snatch their small bolo out and work with it until the enemy was dead. Our people have found many ways to fight the Japs. Until now the Japs live in fear of us and do not go anywhere alone. Perhaps this is a good thing that the Japs have given us.'

"And so the conversation went, Pat. These native people are truly remarkable, and I am thankful for the opportunity of getting to know them a little better. But it is late, and I must close. I will conclude this letter tomorrow . . . "

CHAPTER

EIGHTEEN

"0700 hours—continued from last night.

"Dear Pat:

"I must tell you of a rather unusual experience I had this morning. I was awakened about 0600 by the jabbering of Filipinos standing and looking down at me. Both men and women were there, and they would not leave even when it was time for me to arise. It was a bit embarrassing for me to get up and dress myself with several women standing there looking on, but I finally had to do it, for they would not leave. They seemed to think nothing of it, but I am glad I was reared where a little modesty and privacy existed.

"Then a little later I was shocked to see a young Filipino woman standing about 25 feet from an open latrine that the men were using. Then to my surprise she walked directly to the latrine and questioned the men about doing their laundry, and the men thought nothing about it. Maybe that's the way things should be, but I still think I want a little privacy.

"Even as I write, a middle-aged woman, her young daughter, and a young woman are seated on a log about ten yards from me. They have a G.I. knife in hand, and every few minutes they will squeeze and squeeze upon their own arms and legs. From what I am told, they are killing lice, which have become a terrible problem since the war began.

"A little while ago I spoke with the mother and daughter, and perhaps made the mistake of telling the daughter that I thought she was very pretty. She replied, as nearly as I can remember, as follows: 'Oh, sir, you despise me, sir, you flatter me, sir. sir, I do not like this. I am unaccustomed to it, sir.' Needless to say, I was startled.

"Then, when I referred to her mother as a lady, I was even more surprised. She said, 'Oh, no, sir, I am no lady, sir. I have a husband.' Apparently here in the Philippines the word 'lady' describes only unmarried girls. When a girl marries, she loses the title. Interesting, don't you think?

"But it is very sad, Pat, what these people have been put through. Yesterday along the road we passed many people, all returning from the hills. I saw a child being carried by its father. The child was just skin and bones. Its little legs were like toothpicks, and its ribs could be counted at a distance of 25 yards. The little tummy stuck out as a spokesman for malnutrition. And the older people were not much better off. At our base they come and stand in line with little pails to take the leavings from the men's mess kits, and they consider it a privilege to do so. Oh, Pat, how blessed we Americans are, and yet I fear that not one in ten knows or appreciates that fact. How thankful I am to have seen this, for it has made me aware of how greatly God has blessed me.

"But on the other hand, last night I was given a real treat. A little Filipino boy, who was twelve but looked seven, sang some songs for me. He was dressed in pure white — a short-sleeved blouse, knee short pants, and a cute little white cap on his head. He was a good looking boy, and he had a marvelous voice. He sang 'Santa Lucia' 'God Bless America,' 'Pistol Packin' Mama,' 'Paper Doll and others. He would sing first in English and then in his own Filipino dialect. It was one of the cutest things I have ever heard. He has an uncle in the American army in California, and his desire is to go to America and become a lawyer. For three years he and his folks have lived in the mountains, but now they are going home to Cotabato. His name is Rudy Colampagna, and he has two brothers and three sisters: Eddie, Virginia, and I can't recall the others.

"I also met Colonel Fertig, the leader here. He is a full Colonel, and a very rugged looking individual. He wears one of Dr. John A. Widtsoe's goatees, and he looks very distinguished in it. His face is weather worn, his eyes are bright, and his step sprightly. Prior to the war he was a mining engineer, and his home is Denver, Colorado. General MacArthur assigned him to handle the guerilla activities here on Mindanao, and as soon as he can get all of the bands united, MacArthur will start giving them more aid. But he says there is too much monkey business going on right now, so MacArthur will not give them official recognition.

"Pat, Fertig keeps the most mobile headquarters I have ever seen. He has the kind of place where he can jump through a window and be off any time of the day or night. He keeps all his maps and codes in a little suitcase, and all he has to do is grab that and go. His records, files, and other impedimenta are stored in holes in the ground, kept carefully covered. It is a curious filing system, but under the circumstances, it seems eminently practical.

"He is in daily contact with 'Souwespac,' as General MacArthur's Southwest Pacific Headquarters are called. But before that, he had to make contact with the continental United States. That wasn't accomplished until late in 1942, when Fertig appointed three Americans as his signal corps. These three scrounged around and improvised and invented and did without and finally went on the air, and reached San Francisco. It was strictly hambone, but it worked, both sending and receiving.

"The more I see and the more I hear, Pat, the more I am

impressed with this Colonel Fertig. He is a real businessman, a true executive. Prior to the war he had never been a guerilla, but he ran his organization as if it were a corporation—a shoestring corporation perhaps, but with all the shoestrings there could possibly be.

"One thing he told me that makes me feel very badly. There is suddenly a serious venereal disease problem among the American troops since they have been in contact with the Filipino women, some of whom seem to feel that it is their duty to 'pleasure' the Americans. I had heard reports of this, but Colonel Fertig showed me some of the sad results of it, the open sores on the faces of the people, and so forth.

"Our army has a curious policy towards this problem, one that I very strongly disagree with. If a man contracts a venereal disease and fails to report it immediately, he is subject to court-martial. However, the army does not consider illicit sexual activity 'not in line of duty,' and so nothing is ever said about the cause of the problem. Nor does our Regimental Commander intend to do anything about it—not unless the problem grows much more serious than he now considers it to be.

"Needless to say, Pat, I do not approve of such loose morals being encouraged, as I feel the army does. Further, I am thankful for a father and mother who practiced and taught chastity and virtue in their home. What a great advantage that has given me over most of the people I have met in our army.

"I must tell you about one other thing, Pat. The other night I saw the most beautiful sunset imaginable! It was simply gorgeous. The world was in technicolor. My vantage-point was good, too, and from where I was I could look across the bay into the sunset, while between could be seen the ships in Polloc Harbor, and the waving coconut palms to my immediate front. It was truly a grand sight. As the twilight deepened, the air became filled with large bats; I'll swear some of them have a wingspread of over three feet. As night comes on, and they take to the air, they fly northward — always north, never south — just like a salmon going upstream to spawn and die. I have no idea where they all come from, nor where they go, but while they are above us they fairly blacken the sky. There are, without exaggeration, thousands upon thousands of them. Curious, to say the least.

"Well, Pat, breakfast is being served, so I must again conclude. Last evening we ate corn that had been boiled in the husks — very tasty. There was also dried squid, pork, and a dish made out of the upper pear part of the cashew nut. We also had mango fruit, both ripe and green. I ate some ripe, but the Filipinos preferred it green, spreading on it a sort of sauce made from dead fish that must be like anchovies. I smelled a dab of it, and that was enough for me. Now we will see what new culinary adventures come with breakfast.

"I wish you were here, Pat, so we could see these things together. But perhaps one day that will change, and I can conduct a guided tour of this land just for you.

"I will write again as soon as I can —"

Ben was interrupted by a soft knock on his tent pole. Inviting the visitor in, Ben sat in silence as the message was given. For an hour afterward he continued to stare into space, his father's counsel to keep his crying on the inside ringing in his ears. Finally, however, he gave a long sigh and picked up his pen once again.

"0930 hours. Dear Pat," he wrote, "I hope you do not mind that I am using you as a sounding board. But perhaps if I talk with you, the suffering in my heart will be lessened.

"I have just been informed that Company 'E' had no men killed in their recent battle, though Sergeant Tiffin and Matthews were both wounded by shrapnel when the Japs dropped mortar shells on them out of the trees. Draper was also wounded, as were Hall and Ivey. There are several others with minor wounds, and almost a dozen severe shock cases.

"But the hardest news of all, Pat, is that my good friend, Lieutenant Nick Kastanas, has been killed. He was serving as 2nd Bn. S-2, and I understand he was killed when a flame-thrower he was trying to use didn't function.

"This has hit me very hard, Pat, and suddenly I feel very depressed in spirit. Nick and I have worked together as fellow officers in Company 'E,' and in the 2nd Bn. for nearly three years now. He is a Greek, and had a way about him that was all his own. But everyone liked him, myself included.

"He had a premonition that this would happen. We spoke of it one night recently, and now it becomes my duty to mail his Purple Heart and other things to his wife, Penny, and to discuss the gospel of Jesus Christ with her at my first opportunity, for that is what he asked of me.

"He was very much in love with his wife and baby daughter, and was sorely vexed that he might die and lose them forever. But after I had explained the principle of eternal marriage to him, he accepted it immediately and seemed to find peace."

Again Ben paused, but this time only to take a deep breath and to organize his thoughts. Then boldly he proceeded.

"Pat, Nick Kastanas also encouraged me that last night we were together to tell you how I feel . . . about you. Now that he is gone, I feel somehow bound to do so. This is hard for me, for as I have explained in other letters, I am by nature quite shy. But putting shyness aside, I would like you to know what a wonderful thing it has been, corresponding with you. In fact, and please don't think worse of me for this, I told Nick that you were 'my girl.' Does that meet with your approval? Please don't be shy in telling me if it does not.

"If you approve, however, you will make me a very happy fellow, for I have come to feel that you are exactly the type of girl I would like to spend my time with. One day soon I will show up on your doorstep in person and tell you that. I'll have my car then, and we should be able to find plenty of things to do. Maybe an Aggie football game or a track and field meet, or perhaps even a picnic if the season is right. Please don't say you are all dated up—it would make me very disappointed.

"Time to say goodby again, Pat. Please don't be too long in writing. Your letters are some of the best things to have happened to me over here, and I surely appreciate them. When I am depressed in spirit, as I am today with the news of my friend Nick Kastanas' death, you seem able to lift me back up. Thank you for that, and thank you for being you."

Ben signed his name and nodded solemnly. Then he leaned back in his chair.

"Well, Nick," he said aloud as he stared toward the top of the tent where the monkey now swung by its tail and one hand and one foot, watching Ben intently, "I'm sorry things happened this way, for I will miss you a great deal, as will Penny and your daughter Andrea. But I am certain that this was how it was to be, for otherwise God would never have prepared you as He did. Therefore, my tears are only tears of loneliness and not of sorrow, for I know you will be fine over there."

Smiling through tears that he could not quite manage to hold back, Ben continued. "Nick, take a minute and read this letter before I fold it up. There. You see? I have shared my feelings with Pat as you suggested and so have begun the tasks you charged me with. Nor will I stop until all of them are finished, including telling Penny and your daughter of our last visit. Now, you get to studying the gospel over there, old man, for you have a great deal to learn before I can enter the water for your baptism."

PART FIVE

BRINGING IN THE COLONEL

May 1, 1945 — September 24, 1945

THE WAR

On May 7, 1945, in the War Room at Allied headquarters in Reims, France, Colonel General Alfred Jodl of the German High Command signed Germany's unconditional surrender document. The day before, Admiral Mountbatten had declared that the Burma campaign was over, and the day after, on May 8, Prince Olaf and British representatives accepted the surrender of German troops in Norway.

On May 9, Germany surrendered the Channel Islands, the only British territory occupied by Germany during the war. On the 10th, the U.S. announced the withdrawal of 3,100,000 American troops from the European theater; and on that same date, all German forces in Czechoslovakia capitulated to the Allied forces.

Through the remainder of May, mop-up operations continued throughout most of Europe. Here and there, individual members of the German High Command either committed suicide first or were captured and then committed suicide afterward. Those few who did not, including William Joyce, a British fascist who had become a radio propagandist for Hitler and who was known in England as "Lord Haw-haw," were imprisoned at Flensburg and later executed.

189

On June 29, Ruthenia was formally ceded to the Soviet Union by Czechoslovakia. Russia had thus acquired, since 1939, a total of 300,000 square miles in Europe, land greater in size than the state of Texas.

In the Pacific arena, however, the war dragged on. The U.S. Marine 5th Division and the U.S. Tenth Army were engaged in a bitter struggle on Okinawa, while the 6th Australian Division occupied Wewak on New Guinea. The Balete Pass on Luzon in the Philippines was cleared by U.S. forces, while the U.S. 8th Army launched new attacks on the islands of Mindanao and Negros.

On May 16, U.S. planes began one of the most intensive napalm (jellied gasoline) bombing operations of the war, against Japanese units defending the Ipo Dam, east of Manila. Fifth Fighter Command dropped 110,000 gallons of napalm on the well-entrenched Japanese in a three-day period, after which the U.S. 43rd Division was able to take control of the dam.

On the 18th, Sugar Loaf on Okinawa was taken by the Marines, who suffered 2,662 casualties in ten days and lost another 1,289 men to combat fatigue.

On the 21st, the Japanese supply base at Malaybalay in Mindanao was captured by units of the U.S. 31st Division. On the 23rd, Japan's largest port, Yokohama, stopped functioning because of Allied air and sea attacks, and, on the 27th, Tokyo was closed to all maritime shipping, its facilities almost totally destroyed.

On the 28th of May, Japan launched a massive attack on Okinawa, but after more than a hundred of her planes were shot down, the attack faltered, and the U.S. Chiefs of Staff set November 1 as the date for the U.S. invasion of Japan.

By the first of June, Japanese resistance on Luzon was reduced to rear guard delaying actions, and Marines on Okinawa had cleared about half the Naha airfield. But on the 5th, nature hurled a typhoon almost as destructive as the kamikazes against the U.S. ships around Okinawa, severely damaging four battleships, eight carriers, seven cruisers, eleven destroyers, and a host of auxiliaries. Had Japan been in position, they could have seriously impaired U.S. strength in the Pacific, but they were not, and nothing further came of the typhoon.

On the 9th, Japanese forces on Okinawa's Oroku Peninsula were trapped by the 4th and 22nd Marine regiments, and Mandog on Mindanao was captured by the U.S. 24th Division, thus eliminating the final Japanese defense position on the eastern side of the island.

By June 12, Japanese forces on Okinawa were either surrendering or committing mass suicide, and all resistance ended on the Visayan Islands, where Japanese losses were estimated at 10,000 dead.

The U.S. Joint Chiefs of Staff, on June 15, issued directives to the top military leaders in the Pacific to prepare plans for the occupation of Tokyo in the event Japan suddenly capitulated. And on the 17th, Admiral Minoru Ota, Japanese commander of the Okinawan naval base, was found dead, having committed hara-kiri, or religious suicide.

On June 22, Lieutenant General Mitsuru Ushijima, commander on Okinawa, followed suit, and Okinawa was declared secure. Thus ended the eighty-one-day campaign in which the Americans suffered their heaviest losses of the Pacific war. A total of 12,520 U.S. soldiers and Marines were killed, and 36,631 were wounded. About 110,000 Japanese were killed, and 7,400 were captured. Okinawan action virtually eliminated Japanese air defenses, as 7,830 planes were either shot down or destroyed as kamikaze attackers. Eight hundred Allied planes were downed. The U.S. Navy lost 4,970 men and 36 ships, while about 180 Japanese vessels were sunk.

But U.S. officials were alarmed by the ferocity of the Japanese on Okinawa and feared even greater resistance on the

Japanese home islands. Okinawa, therefore, became a key consideration in the decision to use the atomic bomb against Japan.

On June 27, a kamikaze hit the U.S. carrier *Bunker Hill,* killing 373 men. On that same date, hostile action on Luzon effectively ended, though 11,000 Japanese were still hidden in the Sierra Madre Mountains and another 12,000 were holed up in the Ifugao-Bontoc area.

By July 1, the 7th Australian Division had invaded Balikpapan, Borneo, one of the richest oil-producing areas in Asia, and only 200,000 people remained in Tokyo, the remainder having been evacuated to safer areas.

On July 4, U.S. forces and Filipino guerilla units began clearing out pockets of Japanese resistance on Luzon and Mindanao, and, shortly thereafter, Japan asked Moscow to serve as a mediator to bring about a cease-fire with the Western Allies.

On July 16, the first atomic bomb was exploded at the test facility in Alamogordo, New Mexico. In Potsdam, Germany, Truman was notified of the successful test with the tersely coded message, "Babies satisfactorily born."

Also in Potsdam, between July 16 and August 2, the Big Three—Truman, Churchill, and Stalin—met in the final conference of the war. There they drew up plans for the surrender of Japan. The thrust of the conference was political, however, with the first indications of suspicion and mistrust manifesting themselves. In a real sense, Potsdam was the termination of World War II and the onset of the Cold War.

On July 17, Allied aircraft and Third Fleet ships began an attack on Tokyo and encountered no resistance whatever. In this operation, British fast carriers joined the attack, the first joint American-British naval operation in the Pacific.

On the 24th, Truman told Stalin that the atomic bomb would be used against the Japanese, and on the 25th, the Allied leaders called on Japan to surrender or face "utter destruction." Radio Tokyo indicated that Japan would accept peace terms but not unconditional surrender.

The next day, in British elections, Winston Churchill was ousted as prime minister, and Clement Attlee succeeded him. Atlee flew immediately to Potsdam and took over for Churchill.

On the 27th, leaflets were dropped on Japan's major cities, warning of their destruction if Japan did not surrender. But on the 30th, Tokyo rejected the Potsdam ultimatum. Yet in Japan, conditions were pitiful. Food shortages had become so acute that the government called on the civilian population to collect 2.5 million bushels of acorns to be converted into eating material. The average Japanese had to survive on a daily intake of 1,680 calories, or 78 percent of what was considered necessary for survival.

On July 31, the Allies responded to Tokyo's rejection of the Potsdam resolution by warning Japan that eight of its cities would be leveled if she did not surrender. On August 2, this began with the bombing of Toyama, when 6,600 tons of bombs nearly obliterated the city.

On the 3rd, Japan was totally blockaded in a joint army-navy operation called STARVATION, and on August 6, a U.S. B-29 named the *Enola Gay* dropped a 9,000-pound atomic bomb on Hiroshima at 8:15 A.M. The bomb seared the center of the city for a fraction of a second with a heat of 300,000 degrees centigrade, and it is still not clear how many thousands of people perished in that instant.

On August 9, a second bomb was dropped over Nagasaki, and on the 10th the Japanese stated that they were willing to surrender. However, they wanted the status of the emperor Hirohito to remain unchanged.

Finding this unacceptable, 1,600 Allied aircraft attacked Tokyo, and throughout the rest of Japan, other aircraft dropped millions of copies of Japanese translations of the

Potsdam ultimatum, calling on the people to follow the path of reason or face utter annihilation.

Finally, on August 14, after Japan had assessed the damage done by the atomic bombs and realized that they faced the distinct possibility of more nuclear blasts, Japan agreed to unconditional surrender.

Meanwhile, on the island of Mindanao, the 124th Regiment of the U.S. 31st Infantry Division, finally victorious at the battle of Colgan Woods, pushed north along the Sayre Highway toward Malaybalay. The night after the battle finally ended, a Japanese banzai attack against the 2nd Battalion was met with effective retaliation, resulting in hundreds of enemy dead and earning the battalion special recognition from General Eichelberger.

After securing the Kibawe-Talomo Trail and the Sayre Highway, the 124th moved on to Malaybalay, where they met units of the 108th Combat Team of the 40th Division. These units had landed to the north near Cagayan and had then pushed south. From Malaybalay, the 124th was ordered to make a two-pronged attack on Silae, which was the escape point for all Japanese caught between the converging American forces on the Sayre Highway. It was decided that the 3rd Battalion should move east on the Silae Trail, while the 1st Battalion would drive southeast through Managok, Maglamin, Imbatuh, and thence to Silae. Meanwhile, the 2nd Battalion and Company "E" would remain in Malaybalay and patrol to the west.

These movements were horrendously difficult, both east and west of Malaybalay, with mud so thick that not only jeeps but also water buffalos bogged down, and with hills so steep that, as one GI said, "even the goats needed skid chains to stay up there." And on every ridge, in every cave, in many trees, in carefully prepared positions in the most unlikely places, Japanese soldiers waited. Their express mission, of course, was to delay the Americans as long as possible and then to die. Each of these had to be blasted or burned out, until yard by bloody yard, mile by tortuous mile, the 2nd Battalion of the 124th cleared the jungles to the west or converged on Silae and the headwaters of the Pulangi River to the east, which location the 1st and 3rd Battalions reached on July 16.

Attrition in these campaigns was terrible, however, and so by the 20th of July all units of the 1st and 3rd had reassembled in Malaybalay with the 2nd. There they were all reinforced and assigned to patrol throughout all of central Mindanao, which messy, disagreeable, dangerous work continued until the end of the war.

THE MAN

For Lieutenant Ben Bennett, the summer was as busy as it was tedious. Still at Parang on the western coast of Mindanao, he continued to serve as C.O. of the 31st's LVT and Dukw Company, seeing that supplies and equipment were removed from incoming ships and forwarded to various American positions throughout north-central Mindanao.

He also censored mail, filled out continual reports, conducted courts martial on several of his men for various reasons that usually involved the native women, kept up an amazing amount of correspondence with family and friends in the states, and conducted an investigation when one of his men, McBurnett, was killed in a Jeep accident. He also did all of the follow-up work to McBurnett's death, served as monthly paymaster for himself and all the men of his company (he was making $212.67 per month at the time), participated in continual athletic workouts and games, attended many movies, counseled numerous soldiers both in and out of his company on a variety of personal problems, held lengthy discussions with chaplains and others concerning Mormonism and his stand on the Word of Wisdom, and in his spare time served as one of the leading forces behind weekly LDS services on Mindanao. For all this work, he ultimately received a rating of 6.5 out of a possible 7.0, which was Superior.

Yet, rather than faltering under the pressures of such numerous activities and demands, Ben wrote at the time: "Do you really know how to live, and to live more abundantly?

"So many of us do not, because we let the pressure of little routine things swamp us into a forgetfulness of the inherent bigness to be found in all things.

"How invigorating it is, and how illuminating, to just stop, look, and listen every once in a while to the story that each little task, duty, trial, or hardship has to tell. It makes no difference who you are or what your life brings — nor the why or the wherefore of it — there is a story there for you. If you will just stop long enough to look about you and to listen, you will hear it.

"It will impress you greatly, and all at once you will find that you have had a glimpse of the true purpose of life. Thereafter you will become very susceptible to its beauties. When that happens, and only then, will you know just how much fun living a life can really be."

On July 6, 1945, Ben was startled to be relieved of his duties with the ducks and buffalos and be sent back to his parent organization, Company "E," 2nd Battalion, 124th Infantry. Truly pleased to be back with his old friends, Ben flew by Piper Cub to Malaybalay, and at his request the pilot flew over the battle-scarred Colgan Woods where the 124th had suffered so many casualties and where his good friend Nick Kastanas had been killed.

Enthralled with the beauty of Malaybalay and Bukidnon Province, Ben described it repeatedly in his journal, as he did the Filipino people he found there. His reunion with old friends such as Tom Dabbs, "Tiff" Tiffin, Lieutenant Richester, Leslie Milam, and others was especially thrilling to him, and though they were exhausted by the terrible rigors of their continued campaigns, his comrades overwhelmed

Ben with how they went out of their way to see that he was made comfortable.

For almost three weeks, he was with "E" Company as they sent out patrols and recuperated from the same, enjoying old companionships and doing his best to settle back into the almost forgotten routine of working with his men as they patrolled the area to the west of Malaybalay.

And then on July 26 came another surprise transfer, this time to Company "A" of the 1st Battalion, 124th Infantry, 31st Division. Company "A" was a rifle company, and Ben was once again made commanding officer. They were also being moved to a new area, and so Ben's duties would consist, at least initially, of once again establishing a base camp with perimeter posts, bunkers, latrines, showers, and so forth— all of this while his friends in Company "E" continued their dangerous patrols to the west.

Ben was not pleased with his new orders, however, and he wrote in his journal that he had not been consulted about the transfer and that the army was treating him like a checker on a checkerboard. Yet, of course, he went, for within the army there is no such thing as choice, and within days, according to his nature, he had extended to his new men the firm hand of fellowship and leadership. For many, the changes that then occurred would be eternal.

For two weeks, Ben applied himself and his men to establishing a satisfactory bivouac area, and then came the orders to take his company into the hills to route out the remaining Japanese pockets in the interior of Mindanao. Ben and Company "A" were on one of these patrols when, on August 15, they were radioed the momentous news that Japan had surrendered unconditionally to the Allies.

CHAPTER

NINETEEN

"Malaybalay, Mindanao — 1300 hours
  "Friday, September 7, 1945
  "Dear Pat:
  "I feel somewhat despondent this afternoon and thought perhaps if I told you about it, you might be able to cheer me up. For I have been handed an assignment, Pat, that I truly don't want to accept."

Ben paused and looked for the umpteenth time at the orders on his table, the difficult orders that had sent his emotions into such a tailspin. Never had he wanted so badly to disobey, to disregard orders from a commanding officer.

"Here the war is over," he continued writing, "but this morning I was called in to Col. Hardenbergh, who informed me that my company has been ordered back out into the hills. It seems there are some 800 Japs out there who do not know that the conflict has ended. Our job is to go to Silae with some Jap prisoners, and, while we wait, we are to send them off into the jungle to find and bring back out to us their 800 desperate comrades. Of course if they don't want to come out, they could make real trouble for my 165 men.

  "Oh, Pat, now that this war is over, a mission like this

seems so unnecessary. It would be hard to forget if we should lose any men. Reports indicate that the Japs have moved right in with the natives, and they might very easily put up a fight, rather than submit to us.

"Needless to say, Pat, I do not relish this assignment, nor do I favor going into the hills again after the Japs. In fact, I feel very much disgusted with everything military. I feel my temper flaring up in the way it did when I was a young boy, and I would like to take hold and tear things apart. Of course I will not do that, for I feel that I am past such things. But someone needs to be jarred. If I were a civilian, they would be. Our immediate superiors are more concerned with showing themselves off than anything else. This army is afflicted with too much I-sight, and not enough insight or foresight. If this were not so, how else could be explained the silly things that are done, the orders that are constantly changed, the lack of planning, the inefficiency and waste of time, energy, and materials?

"I am convinced that many army officials are public parasites in the worst sense of the word. They are not only unproductive, but they waste and divert into selfish channels the productive efforts of others.

"And now I find out that our fearless leaders, who never went to the front lines during the entire Pacific campaign, are promoting themselves so they can go home early, while many junior officers who stood in the thick of the fighting have been completely ignored and passed over. I was informed yesterday that I had even been appointed to Bn. S-4 so that I could go home early, which appointment I instantly declined. Not only is it very irregular, but it is a form of dishonesty that I want no part of. I will not be party to doctored books, receiving Purple Hearts even though I was never wounded, or submitting false reports for the sake of looking good.

"Perhaps this is the usual thing in the army. I am inclined

to think that it is, and that is why I want no more part of it. I want to live my own life—in the right way. At least I want to make an attempt to apply those things that I have been taught and have come to know are fundamentally right, and that are essential prerequisites to my happiness.

"So yes, I want out; but unfortunately I do not want out at the expense of my own personal honor. Of a surety, Pat, a day of reckoning will come for those who are responsible for these things. May that day find that I have done my duty as a man, no matter what the conditions are or may have been."

Ben paused, looking west toward the huge quinine plantation that extended to the north and west of Malaybalay and Alanib, while his mind examined his soul. "There," he wrote then, "I knew you could do it, Miss Pat. Already I feel better about things.

"But I must assure you, Pat, that on this coming mission I do not fear for myself but for my men. Throughout this conflict Heavenly Father has protected me, and I have no reason to believe that He would abandon me now.

"In fact, only recently I received confirmation of another instance of what I believe I must call 'protection by transfer.' Only one day after I was moved from "E" Company here to "A" Company, the men in "E" Company ran into forty or more Japs. "E" Company had several casualties and at least one killed, but once again I was not a part of it. One day it will be interesting to add up all the incidents of divine protection that have been manifested for myself and my men.

"Thank you, Miss Pat, for the letters and the news clippings. My Aunt Margaret had already sent me the *Church News* articles regarding the deaths of President Grant and the calling of President George Albert Smith. But I appreciated so much the articles on church statistics and your alma mater, Snow College. I was pleased to learn that your great uncle, C. N. Lund, had helped with the founding of Snow College.

That is a wonderful school. While I have not had the privilege of attending it as a student, I have visited the campus numerous times and have been favorably impressed on each occasion. I do not wonder that you enjoyed your years in attendance there. Nor do I wonder at the love you express for the people of Ephraim and SanPete County. I have always found them to be warm and caring, and they helped make my work for the extension service just that much more pleasant.

"Imagine! 952,000 members of the Church world-wide. Isn't it wonderful how God is allowing His kingdom to grow and roll forth. I also found it interesting that 100,000, or 10 percent of us, are in the Armed Services, and that 936, or 1 percent of us LDS armed forces, have been killed or are missing in action. Such a low percentage indicates tremendous divine protection, but I find myself wondering why the 1 percent were not protected as myself, my friend Les Milam, Brothers Doxey, Fackrell, Neal, and a host of others, have been. But the Lord is at the helm, and He knows far better than I when a man's mortal life is to come to an end.

"Of course, we who have been protected do have our problems. For instance, Sergeant Milam has been in the 106 Clearing Station Hospital for the past two weeks with malaria and swollen glands. Lt. Kempainen and I went to see him yesterday, and it was a grand reunion. Leslie looks quite ill, but thinks he will be up and around very soon. I gave him the *Church News* clippings you sent, for which he seemed very grateful.

"I don't know if I ever mentioned, but Kemp and I visited the U.S. Cemetery at Parang before I was transferred to Malaybalay. Lieutenant John G. (Nick) Kastanas was buried there, grave #88, and when Kemp and I looked at the grave I cried like a baby. I don't know why I became so emotional, for that is not my way. But I just felt such a great sorrow for

his wife and baby daughter. How they must be longing to
see him again.

"Then I was going through my papers the other day and
came upon some feathers that Nick Kastanas had given me,
that he had taken from a parrot he had killed on Goodenough
Island. They were green, red, and black—very colorful. Then
that very day I received word that he had been posthumously
awarded the Silver Star, which I will forward to his wife,
Penny.

"I also got word that Tom Dabbs, my former platoon
sergeant on Morotai, had been awarded the Silver Star for
bravery. I had recommended him for this medal, and I feel
that he truly deserves it. My four men who were wounded
in that ambush on Morotai were also awarded medals, which
I also recommended. Interestingly, a Bronze Star was also
recommended for me by Captain "Woody" Wilson, which I
never knew about. He told me about it the other day after
he learned that it did not go through. But not receiving it
relieves me, for I feel that I have done nothing beyond what
I swore an oath to do when I was inducted.

"Perhaps my most cherished honor, however, and one
which I am quite anxious to accept, came a few weeks ago
in the form of a carbon copy of a report sent to Salt Lake City
regarding LDS services here in the Pacific. I hope that you
don't mind, Pat, if I share this with you. The report is posted
'Somewhere in New Guinea,' and details the four sacrament
meetings held during June of last year. Brother Frank N.
Terry, a Seventy from Ogden, presided at these meetings,
and writes in his report, 'The privilege of gathering together,
renewing our covenants through the Sacrament, discussing
Gospel principles, and enjoying each others' fellowship, is
really appreciated by the men, and spiritual feasts have been
experienced by all.'

"Pat, those spiritual feasts have continued for myself and
the other brethren throughout the war. Truly our gatherings,

small and sporadic as they have been, have been blessed with the Spirit of God. I sometimes think that the army is in league with the devil, who desires that we not hold these meetings, for it never fails that major movements and important meetings are invariably set up for Sunday. But notwithstanding that opposition, we LDS have been blessed with almost weekly opportunities to gather, partake of the Sacrament of the Lord's Supper, and bear sweet testimony to each other of the divinity of Christ's gospel.

"But back to the compliment paid me. Brother Terry writes: 'We regret that Lt. Bennett's movement does not permit him to be with us further. He is a fine, spiritual leader, and one of the faithful servants of the Lord in these latter days.'

"Truly, Pat, there could ne no higher compliment paid, nor a greater title bestowed upon man, than to be recognized as a 'faithful servant of the Lord.' I would rather be called that than president of the United States or commanding general of the armed forces world-wide. You may bet that my desire is to be worthy of the title 'faithful servant of the Lord' to the end of my days. With His help, I will be.

"But enough on that. Of course, all the news here is concerning the end of the war. I talked to one of the airmen who saw the atomic bomb blast over Hiroshima last month, and he described tremendous sheets of white flame shooting skyward. His description made me think of the tongues of flame mentioned in the scriptures. Smoke columns rose to a height of 20,000 feet in a very short time, and some fires could be seen raging even through the dense smoke cast. It is difficult to imagine such awesome power, but what a blessing it will be if and when that power in the atom can be put to beneficial, peace-time use. But how horrible it is when put to destructive use. We must guard our secret carefully as a nation, and not let it get into the hands of our enemies, or even of our allies. Another war could very likely wipe the human race completely off the globe.

"You asked where I was when I heard that Japan had surrendered. On patrol in the hills above Silae, in the upper Pulangi River country, where we are going again tomorrow. We received a radiogram from 'Pappy,' (Col. Williams, acting regimental commander) at 0945, stating, 'The war is officially ended. Return to this area by the most expeditious route.'

Ben grinned at the morbid humor and then continued. "Sadly, Pat, just before we received that message, another message came in from one of my patrols, worded thus, 'Jap attacked man in swimming. Jap killed in struggle, man unhurt. Jap in good condition.'

"Also, the first fourteen Japs who surrendered to the guerrillas west of Malaybalay were killed on the spot. No doubt the guerrillas have suffered much at the hands of the Japs, and it will not be easy for them to forget and to extend the hand of peace to these former enemies.

"So yes, the war is over; but the killing, it seems, goes on. Thus tomorrow, of necessity, we will go forward very carefully.

"I must tell you of a very strange experience I had recently. I was riding in a Jeep when I felt something start up my leg. I made a grab for it but missed, and it continued climbing. I couldn't tell whether it was a snake, a toad, a rat, or a centipede, all of which seem more than plentiful here. I jumped almost out of the Jeep as I made another grab, but it was nearly as wild as I, and I didn't get it pocketed until it had reached my knee. Then with my free hand I pounded it to death. In the meantime it had scratched me terribly, and I thought it had bitten me on the knee. Lt. Filas had a pocket knife with which he then cut through my trouser leg—and out fell a dead rat! That concerned me, for rats carry typhus fever and bubonic plague, so I immediately had some iodine put on it. But believe me, Pat, I will never again laugh at stories of women who fear mice running up their legs, for now I know how they feel!

"Well, by this time, Pat, you must think me a terrible bore, I run on so. But it means a great deal to me, sharing my feelings with someone as understanding as yourself. I too wish, as you wrote in your last letter, that at five *p.m.* today I could meet you at the west entrance of your office building, hold your hand, and take you on that stroll down the boulevard."

Ben paused, pen in hand, while he thought about his next words. He feared saying what he wanted to say, but nevertheless they fit the situation perfectly. So, by gum, he suddenly concluded, he would say them!

With a flourish he penned the words, and then, grinning widely, he signed his name, addressed and sealed the envelope containing his daring epistle, and posted it.

CHAPTER

TWENTY

"Ben," Lieutenant Sid Wright asked, "I heard you were single. Is that true?"

"Why do you ask?" Ben quipped back. "Don't I look single?"

Instantly Sid Wright was embarrassed. "I . . . uh . . . "

Laughing, Ben clapped him on the shoulder. "Say, Sid, I'm sorry I embarrassed you. I know I look too old to be single, and, worse, I *am* too old. Now that points are looming up in importance as far as rotation home is concerned, I wish I had a wife and sixteen children. But, sad to say, I don't."

"I don't, either. But I've sure got a great little gal waiting for me. I expect we'll be married the day after I get back."

"That's wonderful, Sid."

Sidney Wright looked up. "Do you have a girl, Ben?"

"You bet I do," Ben responded enthusiastically.

"She must really be something, the way you say that."

"She is, Sid."

"Any marriage plans?"

Ben grinned. "On her part, or mine?"

"Oh, so you haven't talked about it yet."

"Tell you the truth," Ben replied, "I only saw her once,

and that was three years ago, long before we got acquainted through the mail."

Sidney laughed. "So she's a mail-order bride, huh? What a great story!"

"It would be, wouldn't it. But I'm not bold enough to propose through the mail, Sid. It took all the courage I had in the world just to ask her to be my girl."

"And she said yes?"

Ben nodded and tapped his chest. "She certainly did! I carry that letter right here in my pocket and read it about once an hour just to make certain I didn't dream it."

Again Sidney chuckled. "She must have said yes in a pretty exciting manner."

"She did."

"And?"

Ben looked at him. "And what?"

"And what did she say? For pete's sake, Ben, you can't leave me in the dark like this."

Ben grinned. "No, I guess that wouldn't be very gentlemanly of me. She called me her dearest and told me that she would be thrilled and honored to be my girl."

"That's it?"

"How much more do you want, Sid?"

"Just more. I'm looking for clues, man. If I'm going to get you engaged, I must know where her heart is."

Ben looked at him. "Engaged? Sid, what the devil are you talking about?"

"I'm engaged, Ben, and its great! Knowing that, I think it would be wonderful if you were engaged, too. Besides, I've been looking at your eyes, and if I've ever in my life seen true love, it's there. That's why I need to get you and your girl engaged."

"But . . . but I haven't even met her."

"Details, details! Makes no difference at all, and you know it. Now tell me what else she said."

Ben colored a little but finally stammered it out. "Not
. . . in that letter, but in one I got the other day, she . . . she
said, 'My dearest, I'm lonesome for you, honey. Wish you
were going to pick me up at five o'clock tonight, west door.' "

"Yes?"

"Well, she said she felt like walking off the job and taking
a stroll down the boulevard, hand in hand, with the one
she . . . she . . . uh . . . "

"Loves! Right?"

"Well, yeah," Ben replied, embarrassed.

"There! You see? Does she put all those Xs and Os at the
bottom of her letters?"

Ben nodded.

"Hugs and kisses. Man, Ben, what else do you want? Do
you want her to propose to you? Do you think this is leap
year or something?"

Aghast, Ben looked at his companion. "You think she's
going to do that? Propose to me?"

"She might, if you don't hurry and get the job done yourself. And I wouldn't blame her, either. I never saw a guy act
so stupefied about a little thing like being in love and getting
engaged. You'd think you were sixteen or something."

Ben grinned sheepishly. "Yeah, I guess I am sort of shy."

"Sort of! Ben, you'd make shrinking violets look like tulips
and crocuses popping out of an early April snowbank. No
wonder you aren't married."

"Say, I'm not that bashful. In my last letter I closed by
telling her that I was too shy to ask for a kiss, so I would just
take one without asking."

"Well, whoop-de-doo and good-for-you! I'm proud of
you, old man. So in your next letter, why don't you just pop
the question? It can't be any harder than telling her you are
going to steal a kiss from her."

"How would you know that?"

Sidney grinned. "Because that's how I proposed to my

girl, is how. That's what mail is good for. In case she wants to, she can't slap you. And if she feels the other way, she can't smother you to death with kisses, which might also give you a cold if she had one. So you see, the mail is the perfect way to do it."

Shaking his head, Ben grinned. "You're really something, Sid. I'm just glad I wasn't in your outfit before this. Why, I'd likely be married now, and still not have ever seen her."

"Say," Sidney Wright responded, "what a great idea! Do you suppose, Ben, that they do marriages by mail?"

Grinning, Ben slugged the man in the arm, and for the next hour and a half he continued to grin. For in his mind, over and over, was running the thought that maybe he should propose to the amazing Miss Patricia Christensen.

After all, he had had witness after witness from the Spirit that Pat was a perfect match for him. His sister Lila had told him in every letter she had written, including the one where she had announced her own marriage to Francis Spencer, that Pat was an incredible girl and that he ought to marry her. Cliff and his wife, Edna, had written, encouraging him to hurry and marry as soon as he found the right woman. Jim and his wife Dolores had done the same. Den, Ray, and Ruth had begun teasing him about not being shy with Pat in his letters. And even his mother had written that Pat seemed like the right sort of girl for him.

So maybe, by golly, he *would* propose.

CHAPTER

TWENTY-ONE

"Lieutenant Bennett, Draper's got a problem."

Ben looked up. "What kind of a problem, Sergeant Cannon?"

"Well, sir, I think it's battle fatigue. You know he's been wounded once, and I guess he still suffers quite a bit of pain. Besides that, he's a good soldier—none of this shooting-him-self-in-the-foot sort of thing, like we saw with Compton and some of the others. Draper has even been decorated a couple of times for bravery. That's why I think he's just suffering from battle fatigue. Seeing those poor dead buqwees this afternoon sort of rang his bell, and he's going through the whole war all over again in his mind. But maybe if you talked with him . . . "

Hurrying to the man's position, Ben was startled to see Draper weeping copiously, while Sidney Wright looked helplessly on.

"I don't know, Ben," Sidney said. "He looks to be in a bad way."

Squatting, Ben took hold of the man's arm. "Draper, what is it? My goodness, old man, buck up. Nothing can be that bad."

"Y-Yes it can, sir. I d-don't want to be in this w-war any more!"

"But the war's over, man."

"Not as long as we're here in the Pacific it isn't. I just want to go home . . ."

"But you're going home soon," Ben said, startled.

"Not soon enough, sir. I . . . don't want to chase Japs any longer. I don't want to be in the Philippines any longer! I'm tired of this war, I'm scared, and I want to go home! Only . . . I don't have enough p-points, and . . . and they won't let me go with the rest of the outfit! All the guys with points are going, but I . . . I can't . . ."

Carefully Ben regarded the young man, wondering what he should say. He had seen cases of battle fatigue before, and he knew how serious they were. The man needed rest, and that was obvious. But first he had to get back to the bivouac area, and he could do that only by going forward.

Worse, he was right about not going home. The entire 31st was being shipped home, with the exception of a few men who simply had not acquired enough points. Draper was one of those. He would have to stay in the Philippines for an indefinite period of time, doing nonsense work and busy work, waiting for the war department to lower the number of points required.

So what should he say now, Ben wondered? How could he encourage the man? How could he help him see that even the darkest clouds most always have silver linings.

"You say you don't have enough points?" he finally asked.

Draper shook his head. "I'm not married, Lieutenant, and they say my w-wounds weren't serious enough to keep me out of action. So I don't have enough p-points to go home. But . . . I've been wounded bad, sir, and I . . . I know how it feels to be sh-shot . . . It hurts, sir, it hurts something awful!

And it's going to happen again! I know it is! But it wouldn't happen again if . . . if I could only go home . . . "

After the man had shed more tears and then composed himself somewhat, Ben sighed and spoke.

"Have you ever seen a weasel, Draper?"

"A . . . a weasel, sir?" the man asked, sounding confused.

"That's right. A long, thin, ferocious animal that turns white in winter. Have you ever seen one?"

Draper nodded. "Once, I think."

"Are you aware of their reputation for being fast?"

"Yes, sir."

"Good. Now let me tell you about the time my mother outran one of them."

"Is this serious, sir?" Draper asked then, still trying to understand how his fears and problems added up to a woman's outrunning a weasel.

"Very serious," Ben replied. "On our farm in Canada, we had a dugout cellar where we kept our milk and cream and other such perishables. One day a weasel went down a gopher hole and ended up in that cellar. My father fastened a snare on a string, put it around the mouth of the hole, and told Mother to pull the string if the weasel poked its head out. Then he went down into the cellar to force the weasel back into the gopher hole, which he somehow managed to do.

"When the weasel poked its head out of the hole, Mother yanked the string so hard that the snared weasel landed almost on top of her. Terrified, she started to run, but in her fright she forgot to let go of the string. Of course, the snared weasel followed right after her. She always claimed that it was chasing her, but it wasn't. She was moving so fast that if she hadn't been dragging that poor weasel to death, it could never have stayed in her dust."

The tearful man chuckled with Ben at the story, and then

Ben concluded. "Draper, like my mother, you may be dragging your weasels behind you. You are holding so tightly to
the string of your pain and fear that they can't possibly go
any other direction than right after you. Let them go, stop
thinking about them and worrying over them, and you'll be
free from them. Then you can be at peace with yourself."

"But . . . but I'm not going home . . . "

"No, not yet. But what's so awful about that? Look around
you, look at the country, learn from it, enjoy it—"

"That's easy for you to say, Lieutenant!" Draper snarled,
suddenly shouting. "You're an officer, and the minute the
outfit leaves, if not before, you'll be on your way home. They'll
find a way to see that you have enough points!

"Besides, officers never have to do the dirty work! That's
left to poor Joes like me. Look at all the men here who have
been wounded, not an officer among them. You're all educated and stuff, everybody does what you tell them, and I'll
bet you never had anything difficult happen to you in your
whole lousy lily-soft life!"

Startled, Ben almost yelled back at the man. But then,
with an effort, he controlled himself and looked at Sidney
Wright, who simply shrugged his shoulders helplessly.

"Well," Ben finally said, "you're wrong about one thing,
Draper. I have been shot at, and I've spent plenty of time out
on the front lines, sleeping in muddy foxholes and wondering
when the next Jap was going to slip his bayonet into my
gizzard."

Surprised, the man looked up at Ben. "Yeah? You have?"

"That's right. Sometime why don't you talk to some of
the men in "E" Company. They'll tell you a few stories."

"Well," the man sputtered, still unconvinced. "You're still
an officer, and mostly all officers do is the cushy stuff. 'Silver
Spoon Sammys,' I call you guys—every one of you born with
a silver spoon in his mouth. Why, if I'd had half the chances
you've obviously had . . . "

Thoroughly taken back by the man's bitterness, Ben let him continue until finally he had run out of things to say. After that, the two sat in silence for perhaps five minutes, Ben relaxed but thinking furiously and Draper decidedly uneasy. Finally, though, Draper broke the stillness.

"So, doggone it, say something, sir!"

"Like what?"

"Like denying everything I just said. That's what I would expect you to do. Lie and deny it."

Draper was treading on perilously thin ice in talking to an officer the way he was, and Ben knew it. But he also knew that Draper knew it. So why was he doing it, Ben wondered as he pondered the situation? Was the man truly that bitter against officers? Or was he just frustrated to the point of exasperation? That, and exhausted by the pain and fear that Ben could see so clearly in the man's eyes.

Deciding that it was probably the latter, Ben determined to take a softer approach and see if perhaps he might be of a little help to the man.

"Well, are you going to deny it?" Draper pushed.

"Not at all," Ben replied.

Draper was stunned. "You mean you admit it? You mean I've finally found an officer with the guts to admit that he and every other strutting peacock of an officer in this man's army is pampered like a baby? I told you you'd never had to go through anything that was hard. That's why you can spout all that stuff about me letting go of my 'string of fear' nonsense! Because you don't even begin to understand—"

"I used to live on a farm," Ben said, once again derailing Draper with his unexpected statement. "Every day when I came in for lunch, I would strip down to my gym shorts and go out into the road in front of our home and practice throwing the shot and the javelin. You see, I had every intention of going to Berlin to participate in the Olympics."

"So?" Draper asked almost sarcastically.

"Let me finish, my friend, and you'll have your answer. The summer finally came when they held Olympic tryouts in Montreal, and I was tremendously excited. There was no place I would rather have gone that year than to Montreal. The president of the Taber Amateur Athletic Association approached me with the idea of sponsoring me and my cousin, who was a sprinter."

"It figures."

Ben nodded. "It does. In order for them to raise money for us to go, however, they wanted me to go to different towns in the area and put on demonstrations. My cousin couldn't do it, but they still wanted me to go. Though it meant giving up my badly needed income, which I was using to attend agricultural college, I agreed.

"Several times I went with them and put on these demonstrations, and of course I was never paid for doing so.

"Finally, as a last effort to raise more money, the association decided to sponsor a carnival, and again I was asked to make an appearance. Because my father did not believe in games of chance, which they had at the carnival, most of my family didn't attend. But I went alone, and, if I do say so, I did quite well."

"Naturally," Draper said in a voice laced with continuing bitterness and sarcasm.

"A funny thing happened, though, Draper. At the end of the carnival, the association counted the money it had raised, largely, if not totally, through my personal appearances. There was only enough money to send one man to Montreal, and since I lived out on a farm while my cousin lived in town, and because most of the association were townspeople, my cousin was selected to go instead of me."

Draper didn't say anything, but Ben could see the sudden interest in the man's eyes. And so he continued.

"Needless to say, I was almost sick with disappointment. I felt that I had been used and misused, and, worse, I was right. I had been. My whole family was upset by it, but one of them did something about it.

"My younger brother Den, the hard-working, thrifty, stay-at-home one of us, came to me and said, 'I've enough money for you to go to Montreal; and I want you to use it. You don't need to worry about paying it back until you're through school. I can manage without it.' "

Draper settled back then with an "I told you so" expression on his face. But ignoring him, Ben went on.

"As Den and I were making plans, my bishop, Harold Wood, drove up. After Mother brought him in, he said, 'Bill, I want you to know that even though I was a member of that committee, I don't like what they did to you; and I'm here to tell you that I'll lend you the money so that you can go to Montreal.' "

Draper nodded knowingly.

"I broke down over my bishop's generosity," Ben said quietly. "But then I thanked him and told him I already had the money and was certainly going to Montreal.

"Well, Den and I had decided that I should leave a day early so I could get in a little extra practice; but when we went to the bank to get Den's money a few days later, we met my cousin's mother, who pleaded with me to wait a day and travel with her son, who had never been away from home. I asked her why he didn't leave with me a day early so he could do a little practicing, but it turned out that she was reluctant to let him be gone from home for such a long time. Anyway, she was so worried that I finally agreed to wait and go with him.

"Outside the bank, I ran into the president of the association, who tried his best to dodge out of my way. But I cornered him and told him just what I thought of the way I had been treated. That way, though we didn't exactly part friends, I at least got rid of a little bitterness. In other words, I did about what you've done this afternoon.

216

"Needless to say, I finally got to Montreal with my cousin, but with no extra time for either of us to practice, which was sad for him. At the tryouts he got so nervous that he jumped the gun and was disqualified. On the other hand, even without practice, I was blessed to do better than I had ever done in my life, and I set one or two new Canadian records in the process." Ben grinned. "Of course I had to pay for them myself."

"I'd say it was worth it," Draper exclaimed with no sign of his former anger. "Did you do any good in Berlin?"

Ben smiled. "No, I didn't. In fact, conditions at home and abroad prevented me from going at all."

"Gee," Draper said sincerely, "that's tough, Lieutenant. I'll bet you were disappointed."

"Yes," Ben said as he stood to go, "I was. Now buck it up, Draper. Put your fears behind you, and you'll be just fine."

Ben walked away, and Draper, watching him go, suddenly grinned. "Well I'll be doggone," he said aloud. "That son-of-a-gun just got me to admit I was wrong about him being pampered and mollycoddled and never having hard times. And got me feeling sorry for him, to boot."

"Well, you don't need to feel sorry for him," Sidney Wright said from the side, where he had stood unobserved, listening to the whole affair.

Draper grinned even wider. "I'll say I don't. Lieutenant Bennett may have had to pay for his trip to Montreal, but by setting those records he sure got the last laugh on those jokers back home in his athletic Association. What I wouldn't give for a last laugh on the army like that!"

"Would you like to hear how he got that last laugh, Draper?" Sidney Wright asked slyly.

Still grinning, the man nodded.

"While his cousin and he returned to Taber on the train,

Ben sat down and composed a letter to the local news-paper—"

Draper chuckled. "What a great idea! What'd he say? Come on, Lieutenant, tell me how he nailed those bums."

Sidney Wright smiled. "All right, I'll tell you. In his letter, Ben thanked the people of the community for all their support, and then he closed the letter."

"What? But those people didn't give him one red cent."

"I know," Sidney Wright said, nodding. "And Ben knew it, too. But, as he explained to his father, who apparently felt like you and I do, the people in Taber thought they were giving to both him and his cousin, and so Ben felt that they should be thanked by both of them. He did so, and that is how he got his revenge."

"But that's not revenge," Draper fumed. "That's . . . that's . . . "

"That's letting go of the string and leaving his weasels behind him," Sidney Wright concluded. "You see, Draper, those weren't just words Lieutenant Bennett spoke to you. Officer or not, Lieutenant Bennett is a man who knows."

CHAPTER

TWENTY-TWO

"Are you all right, Ben?"

Looking up from the letter in his hand, Ben smiled thinly. "I'm fine, Sid. Just a bit tired of waiting, is all."

Sitting down on the log next to Ben, Sid Wright gazed off into the hills and then sighed. "Five days is a long time, all right."

"Too long. Worse, there is still no sign of Kenouchi or his men. We sent them off with no arms, and there is no telling what might have happened to them. Maybe they were killed by Filipinos, maybe they were killed by Japs, maybe they got lost, maybe they went back to their own ranks and are even now sneaking up for a last banzai attack. Who knows? How are the men doing?"

"Getting ready for the daily rainstorm. But the stockade is completed, and except for the men on guard—who are doing a fine job, I might add—the rest of them are over swimming in Silae Creek."

"I don't blame them. That's delightful swimming. Have you tried it yet, Sid?"

"Three times," Sid Wright replied, grinning. "And I'm ready to go again."

Ben nodded in agreement, but neither man moved, and so at last Sid Wright continued. "Do you think this will work, Ben?"

"If you mean will the Japs come in, I would say yes. If you mean will they come in peacefully, I don't know. Our Filipino guard, Juan Siberia, saw that Jap yesterday, and instead of surrendering, the Jap took off into the bushes. So, who knows? Maybe they will all do that."

"But you have the Jap general's order to his men to surrender, and now they'll have copies of it. Don't you think that will help?"

Ben shrugged his shoulders. "I wish I knew, Sid. That order the cub plane dropped to us the other day was the real thing, all right. So it should work. Handwritten and signed by General Gyosaku Morozumi, commander of all forces here on Mindanao, it is a direct order to every Jap on the Island. They are told that the war is over; that they are to surrender to the nearest U.S. force unconditionally; that all commanders are to see that their men all leave the mountains; that they are to approach with a white flag and with their hands over their heads; that all arms are to be left one kilometer from our encampment; and that they are to approach only in daylight. Those sound like wonderful orders to me, and I pray with all my heart they will be heeded."

"Amen, my friend. Where was Morozumi when he signed it?"

"At Cagayan. Of course, our Jap patrol has the original of his order right now; but when they bring it back, I'm going to save it. Some day it could be valuable. So might the copies of it, for that matter, and right now there are thousands of them scattered out in the hills. I just hope that one of those orders falls into the hands of the right Jap commander, who has the sense to obey it and come in without a fight."

"It would be nice if we could get one of those angels you

Mormons believe in to go out there and bring the Japs in peacefully."

"Yes," Ben said with a wry grin, "it would."

"Have you ever seen any angels or visions, Ben?"

Ben's smile widened. "Not hardly, though I expect to see both when I get back to the states."

Sid Wright looked startled. "What? But . . . but . . . "

"When I meet my girl," Ben said quickly, smugly. "That is, if she'll still be willing to see me."

Sid Wright grinned knowingly. "Ah-hah! Angel; vision. Very clever, Lieutenant Bennett. But I warned you, didn't I— about your girl, I mean. Women only put up with so much foolishness and tardiness. If you don't hurry up and propose, she'll take the matter right out of your hands and either dump you or propose, whichever happens to suit her mood at the moment."

Ben waved the letter he held, the letter that had been dropped by Cub plane that very day. "It seems she is getting ready to do that very thing, Sid. What a chastisement I received. Now I must determine how best to respond."

"Tell her you love her and want to marry her, you big lug. How tough can that be?"

Ben nodded. "You're right, Sid. How tough can it be? Tough as old boot leather, I think. And much tougher than fighting the Japanese. Come on, let's head back. Maybe I'll work on it now, before it gets dark."

"Good thinking," Sid declared as he stood. "And Ben, do you have that Word of Wisdom revelation written down anywhere? The one you're always harping about? I'd like to read it."

"And pray about it?" Ben pressed.

"I didn't say that! I said—"

"For me to do the hardest thing I've ever thought of doing," Ben finished for him. "If I write that letter, Lieutenant Wright, then you had better have the courage to pray."

For a moment Sid Wright looked at the ground. But then, grinning, he lifted his head and put his arm up around Ben's massive shoulder. "You've got a deal, Lieutenant Bennett. But I get to read your letter . . ."

" . . . and I get to listen to you pray!" Ben concluded. And laughing together, the two men moved toward Ben's poncho tent and his worn and often-lent copy of the Doctrine and Covenants and Book of Mormon.

CHAPTER

TWENTY-THREE

"September 17, 1945

"Upper Pulangi River Country, 1630 hours

"Dear Pat:

"Well, it has happened again. I had another opportunity to explain my beliefs concerning the Word of Wisdom. Pat, it is almost like my whole purpose in coming to the South Pacific has been to serve a Word of Wisdom mission. From my first days at Camp Shelby right on up to today, almost every private conversation I have had has focused on our belief in not smoking or drinking or otherwise wilfully abusing our bodies. Pat, I have explained these things to officers and enlisted men, chaplains and atheists, and the doctrine comes as a great shock to all of them. The Lord called it a doctrine of wisdom, adapted to the capacity of the weak and the weakest of those who could be called Saints. But if that is so, it is like nearly every man in the armed forces lacks rudimentary wisdom and cannot qualify to be even a weak Saint. I find it very perplexing, to say the least.

"By the way, remember Lieutenant Mitschele, who was going to stop smoking for ten days just to give it a try (and to prove to himself and the world that he wasn't addicted to tobacco)? Well, I have it from two different men that he only made it seven days and was nearly a raving maniac by the time he inhaled, in one long breath, an entire cigarette. And he told me he wasn't addicted.

"One night when Mitschele and Lt. Shore and I were talking about whether or not tobacco was harmful, Shore saw my open D&C. He asked if he could read section 89. I let him, and by the time he finished reading an hour or so later, he had jumped back to the front and was all the way through 1 Nephi in the Book of Mormon. I remember when he came to the account of Nephi slaying Laban, he said, 'Nice guy — just picks up his sword and cuts his head off. If God really meant that stuff about it being better for one man to perish than for a whole nation to dwindle in unbelief, then why didn't he have someone stop Hitler, instead of letting him lead the German people down to destruction?'

"You know something, Pat, I didn't have an answer for him.

"Another man who read some in my scriptures was Chaplain Woolcott, who told me he hoped someday to have time to read all of them. I too hope that he does.

"Last night we realized that we could no longer listen to 'Tokyo Rose' and the wonderful music she played over Radio Tokyo, and I will miss that. The Japs designed their programs to discourage and dishearten the Americans, Pat, but so far as I have ever been able to tell, it had the opposite effect upon us. I found 'Rose's' comments humorous, her claimed but unheard-of land and sea victories laughable; and her very up-to-date American music outstanding. I swear, Pat, according to 'Rose,' the entire U.S. fleet was completely sunk once a week, and no one has ever heard of the islands she claimed we had been driven from by superior Nipponese forces. Every one of her programs ended with 'I'll Never Smile Again,' which was supposed to make us homesick but which seemed to have the opposite effect. Once Radio Tokyo even went off the air playing 'The Stars and Stripes Forever,' which I thought was great. So we will miss 'Tokyo Rose' and 'Princess Anne.'

"Speaking of radio programs, did you hear the program aired the day after Japan signed the peace papers, September 3? Bing Crosby, the incomparable Bing, was the master of ceremonies and announcer. It was marvelous to listen to him. The chief of army chaplains opened and closed the program with prayer. Dinah Shore sang 'America.' Bob Hope recited one of Ernie Pyle's favorite pieces (Ernie Pyle was killed by Jap bullets on Okinawa). Frank Sinatra sang (the best he ever did); also Frances Langford. And then to top it all off, Bing sang 'I'm Dreaming of a White Christmas.' President Truman was then presented and spoke for perhaps fifteen minutes.

"I shall remember that program for a long time, Pat, not only because it was a wonderful program, but also because it was a special V-J Day program. I think only after I listened to that program was I really convinced that the war is over.

"But after the other day, I had my doubts again. On our way here to Silae we came upon the bodies of three Filipino people who had been killed and horribly mutilated by a Jap patrol. I have managed quite well to keep this war in what I think is the right perspective. But after seeing those bodies, Pat, I felt for a time as though I would never be able to look upon the Japanese people again without feeling a horrible revulsion and even hatred for their race.

"But knowing that the gospel teaches us otherwise, Pat, I prayed diligently that the Lord would somehow soften my heart. He has heard my prayers, and I feel much better about things now. In fact, I intend to use this opportunity to get to know the Japanese a little better as a people. Of course, there is not much time to do that, especially now that the 31st has been rotated back to the states. In fact, it looks as though I will be coming home . . .

"2130 hours.

"I am sorry for the interruption, Pat. Kenochi's Jap patrol, accompanied by five other Japs (one an officer) arrived. Apparently they have managed to accomplish their mission. They took General Morozumi's order directly to the Jap commander in this area, a Colonel Nanami. Then and only then did he and his men know that the war was over. The five men who came in with Kenochi today were sent by Col. Nanami to arrange for the surrender of the entire force.

"From what I gather, the original strength of the Nanami force was about 630 men when it went into bivouac along the Upper Pulangi River. The force had been fleeing the Americans, who were pushing down from the north. Only 271 men are now left alive, the remainder having perished either from disease and sickness, or through suicide. Many of the 271 who will be coming in are suffering from malaria, beri-beri, and malnutrition, their chief diet consisting of wild vegetation.

"Knowing that, Pat, makes it easier to understand why those Japs stole the produce from the three natives we found murdered. "The officer in charge of this advance party of five is named Lt. Kitano, and he seems a very intelligent chap. I got along well with him. He is a jujitsu expert, and with another of the Japs presented a demonstration for us, which was very impressive.

"I must go now to order in supplies for the entire force and will add more to this letter at my next opportunity. I would also like to discuss certain things you stated in your letter but will wait on that as well."

"September 21, 1945, 2145 hours
"Dear Pat:
"Yesterday the main Jap force finally began to arrive. The first contingent consisted of a group of officers. Lt. Wright and myself, accompanied by Lt. Kitano, went unarmed to

greet them. Of course, we were escorted by two tommy gun-
ners and four platoon sergeants, so it was not the foolhardy
venture one might suppose.

"The Japs were carefully searched, and all ammunition,
knives, pistols or other firearms, field glasses, sabers, etc.,
were taken from them in accordance with our orders.

"Groups continued to arrive until on into the night, and
as fast as they could be searched and checked over, they were
led to the stockade and placed under guard.

"It had rained heavily during the afternoon, leaving the
trails muddy. The Japs had been marching for several days
in a weakened, under-fed condition, and many of them were
exhausted. Yet by the time they stopped coming in, 258 had
arrived. Nine had died along the way, six by suicide.

"There were a total of twenty-nine officers who reported
in—one colonel, two captains, nine first lieutenants, eight
second lieutenants, and nine warrant officers. A meal per
man of K rations was issued immediately after they arrived,
which was probably the first substantial meal they had had
in months. Nothing could have won them over more completely than food. From there on out, we had no trouble with
them.

"My men had cut shelterhalf-poles prior to the arrival of
the Japs, and in a matter of minutes we had a thriving Jap
community right in our midst. Fires were burning brightly
and clothes were being dried in the good old-fashioned way.
As night wore on, some of my men dickered for and obtained
souvenirs, which I was not inclined to discourage.

"Colonel Nanami proved to be a full colonel but is just a
little old man, fifty-one years of age, who seems to be in his
second childhood. He is suffering from malaria, and I do not
think he weighs more than ninety pounds.

"The colonel had not brought in his saber but had broken
it. From what I understand, it had been in his family for over
four hundred years and was very beautiful, valued at 20,000

yen. These sabers are known as Samurai swords, and they are made in secret by members of the Black Dragon Society, a murderous secret band whose secret rites and doings no doubt resemble those of the Gadianton robbers of Book of Mormon days.

"Today, Pat, we are waiting for the stragglers to arrive and for more supplies to be dropped to us so that we can eat as we march back to Malaybalay. But I must tell you about the unusual sight the Japs presented us this morning.

"They arose before we did, and when I awakened I could hear sharp commands being given. It proved to be a sort of reveille-worship ceremony combined with a bit of calisthenics. Many of the men were so weak that they could not properly perform the exercises. But they bowed toward the east and the rising sun, and then prayers were offered and commands given. Whenever it became necessary for them to obtain firewood or water, they asked permission of their leaders, and then a non-com officer would fall them into ranks and march them off. Everything was strictly GI, and I had the idea they were trying to impress us, even in defeat.

"So yes, I am finding them a proud and interesting people, though not a people I particularly relish becoming better acquainted with.

"Well, Pat, I have put off talking about your most recent letter for long enough, though if I could think of anything else to say, I would probably do so. But it is time for me to respond.

"I appreciate your account of Elder Richard L. Evans's talk, especially the portions about chastity and virtue. I have seen much of the wrong side of that during the war, and I agree with Elder Evans when he tells men to let their eternal needs, and not their base desires, rule their actions. And I also agree with him that the greatest contribution a woman can make to a successful marriage is to bring to it her own chastity. To my way of thinking, it would not be possible to depend on a husband or wife who could not even depend on themselves, and what marriage could ever survive without dependability?

"You write: 'I wonder how young people feel, when they have not lived a clean life, and then listen to a talk like that? It must be hard to know you have sinned and cannot go back to the day you were clean and pure. Oh, yes, I know that repentance exists, but I can't imagine that you would ever feel quite the same about yourself. Perhaps you could, but I for one would not want to pay the price to get there. It seems so much easier to remain pure. I'm so thankful for the guidance of my Father in heaven, my folks, and what I have done for myself in keeping my body chaste and pure. We are so blessed, aren't we?'

"Yes, Pat, we have been blessed, especially to have the understanding of the gospel that we have been given. I also rejoice that you feel the same as I do regarding absolute personal purity and the value of it in building a successful marriage.

"There. That is the easy part. Now I must address something that is far more difficult for me to discuss.

"In your letter you also write (and I will quote it in case you have forgotten): 'Bill, I may not have the basis to say this, but it has been in my mind recently, so I'm going to try and explain it to you.

" 'I have wondered so many times why, if you felt for me like I feel for you, that you didn't tell me so. I have wondered why you could seem so indifferent at times, while I was feeling so much the other way, wanting you and needing you—oh, so much!

" 'But now I can reason with myself that you just don't feel as I do. It may be because you are so busy with your interests there, but I have so much time to think about you, and the more I do, the worse I feel, for your letters do not indicate that you feel about me the way I feel about you.

" 'Bill, why haven't you told me that you were not in-terested in my attentions? I'm slow in catching on, and I am sorry for that. You mean so much to me, and I feel that you care for me, and always have. But with all your other interests, I have been trying for the impossible to happen. I know that I have brought most of this hurt on myself, and my heart aches for you, Bill, because you were trying to be kind to me, while I just kept pushing. I hope you will forgive me, and let us continue being "best" friends.' "

Sighing, Ben lifted his pen, twirled it slowly between his fingers, and gazed into the compound, where Lieutenant Wright was processing three new Japanese arrivals. One was obviously very ill, and the other two had carried him in on a makeshift litter, thus explaining their delay.

In a tent nearby, a sudden roar of laughter accompanied what Ben was almost certain was another game of cards be-tween several of his men. There were a few, he knew, who were perpetually broke due to the vice of gambling, which Ben had concluded was at least as addictive as smoking or drinking. Yet the men would not acknowledge that, and so he had quit trying to get them to see it. If they wanted to spend their lives bankrupt and in bondage to others, that was their affair, and he would leave them alone to wallow in the tragedy of it.

Looking back down at his letter and at Pat's blue stationery lying next to it, Ben smiled humorlessly. After all, he had some fairly major problems of his own to worry about. What could possibly make him think that he might have the capacity to help others out of their problems?

Especially Pat. Look what his own personal problems had done to her. She was deeply hurt because of his ridiculous shyness, and she had every right in the world to chastise him severely. Yet here she was, placing the blame for her suffering upon herself and excusing him of all blame in the matter. More and more he could see clearly who Miss Patricia Christensen really was, and more and more he knew what he wanted to do about it; no, what he should do about it. Only he didn't do it—didn't even know if he *could* do it, even with Sid Wright's encouragement. Besides, he felt as though he was being pushed into something, and he had never been one to take very well any sort of pushing by another. So what should he do?

"Pat," he finally wrote, "in your letter you scolded me rather severely for the way I have treated you, saying that I had left you hanging as far as a future was concerned.

"Well, Pat, I certainly hadn't been looking at things in exactly that light. I felt things were coming along quite happily, and there was no reason why they couldn't continue that way. Maybe I have been a bit slow, but I've been pretty slow for a long time, and so maybe I wasn't going so slowly for me at that. I'm not trying to rationalize or excuse myself, but it bothers me to think that I have hurt you. Surely you don't think that I would try to hurt you or purposely be unfair. I admit that I have been slow and hesitant about making commitments or asking you to make them, but is that being unfair? Maybe it is. If so, then I am sorry, but you must know that it isn't in my nature to be otherwise than what I have been.

"I think the world of you, Pat—you know that even though I may have been slow in saying it in words. I look forward to the time when I can see you, be with you, talk to you, and plan things together. I've thought a great deal about our future together, but a decision concerning that requires patience, Pat. If you've got to have action now or else, then maybe I'm not the one for you to spend any more of your time with.

"Well, this is a heck of a letter, isn't it. I've made a mess of it. Please understand that I am not angry. Neither do I want you to feel bad about anything I have said. I feel the same way towards you that I always have. I think you are tops, Pat, and I hope that I may have the opportunity of calling on you when I get home, and that you aren't going to tell me that I'm through.

"I miss you, Pat—very much . . . "

CHAPTER

TWENTY-FOUR

"How are the men, Sid?"

Lieutenant Wright hurried forward to where Ben sat on a boulder that jutted out above the rushing stream. Since 0700 he and his company, along with the 262 Japanese prisoners, had been pushing to get out of the mountains before dark. For the past two hours, they had been wading the stream channel in knee-deep water over an uneven, pebbly bed, and so the going was doubly difficult.

"The men are spent, Ben."

Ben nodded slowly. "I know, Sid. But every hour we take a ten-minute break, and we take more than that when we've been on the steep hills. Are they going to make it all right?"

"Oh, they'll make it. But I don't know if the Japs—"

"Sid, the Japs don't have a choice. They have to make it."

"But . . . we have one boy back there that is ill, Ben, and he is being beaten pretty severely by his superiors because he can't keep up."

"They have litters, Sid. Why don't they carry him?"

"I don't know."

Ben shook his head. "Well, see if you can find out. If I

were you, I'd encourage the Japs to take better care of him. If they won't, then see if the Filipinos will do it. But whatever you do, Sid, don't bother me with it."

For a long moment Sid Wright looked at Ben, wondering at the tightness, almost the hardness, in his voice. But then he turned away. "Our order of march is holding up," he finally declared. "The squad from the first platoon is still able to lead. The Filipino carriers are making it with the Jap sick and infirm, and they don't seem to need prodding. I forget the next squad, but they are leading about thirty Japs, with another squad and that many more Japs behind them. That order is being maintained all the way to the rear, where Lieutenant Freeman's third platoon is positioned."

"Good. Is PFC Cone still with Colonel Nanami?"

"He was a few minutes ago. He's helping the colonel over the rough spots, all right. But then, he's big enough to help two or three colonels that small."

"That he is," Ben agreed. "Now let's get this outfit cracking again, or we'll be in real trouble come nightfall."

"Yes, sir."

Sid Wright did not move, and after Ben had stepped back down into the water, he looked up at his executive officer. "Something else, Sid?"

"Ben, are you all right?"

"Of course I'm all right! Now let's get moving!"

"Uh . . . if you want to talk . . . "

Ben took a deep breath. "I don't, Sid. I want to get out of these mountains before dark, and that's all I want. Do I make myself clear?"

"Yes, sir!"

"Good. Then let's go!"

For the next two hours, the company moved steadily forward, resting when necessary, but never for longer than the briefest time possible. Ben, who was near the front of the procession, walked alone and was thankful that it was so.

Never had he been in such turmoil, not in his entire life. One moment he was congratulating himself for his firm stance with Pat, and the next moment he was castigating himself for playing the absolute fool with her. Here he was, quite madly in love with a girl he could not even remember seeing, and absolutely convinced through prayer that she was the one who was to be his wife. Yet with all that, he was probably throwing her over simply because she had the temerity to suggest that he might consider not dragging his feet so deeply in his relationship with her.

Slowly Ben shook his head as he unconsciously stumbled forward through the stream. What was the matter with him? Why on earth was he reacting so ridiculously? Was it pride? What was it something in his makeup that made him bow his neck like an old mule when somebody started pushing him? It made no sense, no sense at all—especially when she was trying to push him in the very direction that he really wanted to go.

But did he? Was he really ready for all the responsibility that marriage to Pat would entail? Well, he didn't know, at least not with absolute certainty. But if he wasn't ready, then would he ever be? Further, how had he managed to do so well with all the responsibilities he had carried throughout the war if he wasn't ready for responsibility? Or before the war, for that matter?

So then, responsibility or the fear of it couldn't really be the problem. Might it, instead, be the fact that he had never actually seen Pat, or spoken with her? That might have something to do with it, all right. But on the other hand, he knew very well what she looked like, for he had several photographs of her. Also, he could vividly imagine her voice, and he knew exactly what her conversations would be like, for her letters reflected her thought processes perfectly. So it wouldn't make sense that that would be it.

On top of that, he had always prided himself on his

obedience to the principles of the gospel. Frequently he had told himself and others that he would be willing to do all that the Lord asked of him, even to laying down his life if that became necessary. But now he found himself wondering if he really meant what he had said. After all, he had prayed about Pat on numerous occasions, and if he had ever received clear direction about anything in his life, it was that the Lord approved of his desire to marry her. Yet he persisted in resisting that prompting, and for the life of him he couldn't understand why.

And now he had as much as told her that he wasn't interested in her written advances, and that if they persisted, he would just as soon walk away from his relationship with her. In fact, he would rather walk away, he had told her, than bother to change.

So how would the Lord feel about that, he wondered? Would He be pleased with Ben's wonderful strength and willpower in the face of such innocent feminine persuasion? Would He be pleased that His servant, Ben Bennett, was resisting so strenuously the promptings of the Holy Spirit?

Ben ground his teeth with frustration. Put that way, the answers were obvious. But if looked at from his own perspective, which, he felt, was how he should look at it, then he was resisting pressures from very fallible people to do things he wasn't actually certain he should do. And as to the promptings of the Spirit, they might be nothing more than the strugglings of his own frenzied mind, made frenzied by the incredible pressures of his numerous assignments.

Of course, the words "frenzied mind" caused him to think of Korihor, the Book of Mormon anti-Christ who categorized all spiritual events as the effects of frenzied minds. But that was anciently, while this was now in the midst of the horrendous pressures of a tragic modern world war—

"Lieutenant, ahead is the bivouac area!"

Looking up, Ben was startled to see that they had emerged

from the steep mountains. Further, there was still ample day-light to set up an effective bivouac, though doing so would not leave enough time to erect a stockade.

"S-Sid," he called as he stumbled from the stream, "bi-vouac the men on this first ridge, and see that the Japs are bivouacked at least a hundred yards away from us."

Sid Wright looked at him. "Are you sure you don't want me to continue running the show?"

Ben's head came up sharply. "What's that supposed to mean?"

"Nothing," Sid replied emptily. "How many guards for the Japs?"

"No guards. If they have enough energy after today's march to make a break for it, then I say good riddance."

Ben grinned thinly. "Besides that, Sid, we don't have a man who isn't dead tired already. The war's over, so let them all get their rest and make it back to Malaybalay in reasonably good health. I can pretty well guarantee that the Japs will do the same."

Sid Wright nodded. "Very well, Ben. And do me a favor. Please—get some rest. Maybe that'll help resolve whatever's bothering you."

After Sid Wright had walked away, Ben spread his pon-cho, built a fire, and ate his K rations. Then he tried his best to shut his letter to Pat Christensen from his mind. Actually, all he wanted was a little peace and quiet, and he hoped that by keeping off to himself, he might get it. But the events of the night seemed destined to prevent him from any such thing.

First, Colonel Nanami tried to kill himself with his straight-edge razor, and Ben was forced to get caught up in the furor that existed among both the Japs and Americans as they all worked together to stop him. Then Corporal Nix, Ben's orderly from Georgia, spotted a Jap crawling up a ridge on the other side of the valley. Through field glasses, he could see that the man was armed, and though the POWs shouted at him in Japanese to come in because the war was over, the man ignored them and disappeared into the trees.

Of course, a whole perimeter had to be established then, and Ben had just settled back from that when three other Japs were spotted on a different ridge, not more than five hundred yards away. Again, in spite of the shouted invitation by Warrant Officer Kenouchi to come in and surrender, the three backed out of sight and did not appear again. So, all night long Ben worried about the possibility of an attack on one or more of his men, or upon his prisoners, by the recalcitrant Japanese hide-outs.

Finally, of all nights for the weather to turn cold, that one did; and the men, chilled already by several hours of exposure to the icy stream, shivered all night. Ben, huddled under his poncho and as close to his fire as he dared get, and he almost swore when the wind whipped up.

But whip up it did, and for the remainder of that long and terrible night, he lay awake as the cold gale tugged at the edges of his poncho and worked its icy fingers in around him. He shivered, he pondered, and he justified himself for saying what he had said to Pat. And then he chastised himself for having said it. Ultimately he prayed, pleading for God to show him the way he should go to find peace for his troubled soul.

But with the dawning of a gray, rainy morning, he still felt no better than he had the day before.

CHAPTER

TWENTY-FIVE

"Leslie," Ben said with a sigh as he lay his head back against the truck cab, "I can't tell you how glad I am to see you!"

Leslie Milam smiled. "We do seem to run into each other in the strangest places, Lieutenant."

"Maybe it's more than fate. How did you get the assignment to drive this truck?"

"Dumb luck, I suppose. I got out of the hospital and caught a ride back to 'E' Company's bivouac area, and I stepped out of the Jeep just in time to get caught up in a general order for all men who did not have specific assignments, to assist in hauling 'A' Company and your prisoners back into town. It was only by accident that I spotted you."

"A great accident," Ben said thankfully. "You can't imagine the horror I've been through the past two weeks."

"Tough go, huh?"

"Was it ever! This accident a few minutes ago is just the latest episode in an assignment that never did go well. Poor old Malcom Brown. Here he's gone through the entire war unscathed, and now because that Filipino sideswiped him with that old Jap truck, he will very likely lose his leg. Sergeant Buschofsky got a wicked gash in his arm, and PFC True's

nose will never be the same again. I'm telling you, Les, everything has gone wrong."

Leslie Milam looked at his friend. "Why do you think
that's so, Lieutenant? I mean, things have always gone so
well for you before this."

Ben stared ahead as the truck rumbled on through Malaybalay and out toward the stockade area. "You're right,
Les, things always have gone well for me. But now . . . "

He sighed and grew still, and Leslie Milam fidgeted, wondering what he could say to comfort his dearest friend.

"How's Pat?" he finally asked, thinking that discussing
her would cheer Ben up a bit.

"She's probably fantastic," Ben responded bitterly. "At
least she will be when she gets the letter I mailed a little while
ago."

"My gosh, Lieutenant, what's wrong?"

Ben shook his head. "I don't know, Les. Everything, I
suppose. All I know is that when the division is rotated back
to the states, I won't be meeting any girlfriend."

Leslie Milam said nothing but steered the truck carefully
to the stockade, where the Japanese prisoners he carried in
the back were unloaded. On their way again, he finally spoke.

"Lieutenant, I don't know if I can help you or not, because
you're a lot older and wiser than I am and have had a lot
more experience. But on the chance that I can see something
you can't, I'd truly appreciate hearing what's troubling you."

"That's good of you, Les. Really it is. But I don't know,
I just don't know . . . "

Leslie Milam smiled. "That makes sense, Lieutenant. I
know you well enough to know that if you did understand
what the trouble was, you'd take hold of it and do something
about it."

"Thanks, Les."

"I mean it, sir. That's who you are. So if you don't know
what the problem is, why not start at the beginning? Just tell

me everything that happened on your whole patrol, and on the off chance that I can spot something you haven't, I'll just hair up and tell you what I see, exactly as I see it."

Ben smiled his first real smile in days. "Hair up, huh. That must be a Louisiana expression that I missed out on."

"It was my father's, when he was trying to get us boys to be men. How about it, sir?"

"Fair enough, Les. But do me a favor, will you?"

"Yes, sir?"

"Call me Ben, and not lieutenant. After all, you're about my best friend, and the war is over, you know."

Leslie Milam nodded seriously. "So it is. All right . . . Ben. Now, where did all this start?"

"I guess it started with a letter I got from Pat, Les. That, Sid Wright's playful pushing for a mail-order engagement, and three dead buqwees we found above Silae who had been butchered by the Japs. I'm telling you, Les, that was the worst . . ."

For the next two hours, even long after they had arrived at "A" Company's bivouac area and parked the truck, Ben talked. He told everything he could think of telling, including the thoughts he had struggled with. And through it all, Leslie Milam said nothing. He listened carefully, nodded occasionally, and once or twice tapped the steering wheel with his two index fingers. But not once did he make a comment or express an opinion.

"Well," Ben finally sighed, "that brings it to now, Les, and the wreck of the truck. So, tell me, what do you think?"

"And you've mailed your letter to Pat?" Leslie asked.

Ben nodded. "I have. When we first came into Malaybalay today, I passed a mail truck, and I gave it to them."

Leslie Milam shook his head. "Well, that's too bad. It surely is."

"Why?"

"Because I think you're making a big mistake, Ben. And

if you had just thought about it, you would be able to see that for yourself."

"If I had thought about it? Les, I haven't been thinking of anything else for days!"

Leslie Milam looked earnestly at his friend. "Let me re-phrase that," he replied slowly, his southern drawl dragging the words out even more than usual. "If you had thought about it clearly."

Slowly Ben turned away, his eyes misting over. "But I . . . I can't think about anything clearly," he replied in al-most a whisper. "Nor do I know why!"

"Do you want to know?"

Ben looked at his friend, his eyes pleading. "Do you know why, Les? I've surely been praying that somebody would know. Can . . . can you help me?"

Leslie Milam nodded. "I . . . I think, Ben, that that is why I ended up driving this truck today. This might sound pre-tentious, but I have a feeling the Lord answered your prayers by . . . by bringing me along. I don't hardly know why it would be me, for I don't think I have ever been anybody's answer to prayer before. But I can see your problem plain as day, and I can even tell you what to do about it."

"Then tell me, Les! For pete's sake, I can't go on like this very much longer. So, tell me what to do."

"All right, Ben, here goes. First of all, I don't know who you are exactly, or who Miss Pat is, but I have the feeling that you're both pretty special to the Lord. I mean, in His eyes, the two of you are supposed to be together."

"Now Les—"

"Ben, I listened to you, and now it's your turn. Just hear me out, and then you can say what you want. For some reason, the Lord isn't going to allow you the luxury of making a mistake as far as marriage is concerned, so He is stepping in and giving you some very clear direction."

"What are you getting at?"

"What you are experiencing, Ben, sounds very much like a loss of the Spirit, which you taught us about in a church service not more than six months ago."

"Do you mean me? A loss of the Spirit?"

"That's right. Anger, bitterness, hatred, animosity, hardness of heart, and so forth. Who is the author of those emotions, Ben?"

"Why, the devil, of course. But—"

"Bingo!" Leslie Milam said, grinning.

"Ah-hah," Ben said thoughtfully as he sat back, "I think I'm beginning to see what you're getting at. It's the timeless issue of not being able to serve two masters, isn't it. Or Nephi's 'two churches only' doctrine. Either I am harboring the Lord's emotions and spirit, or I am harboring Satan's emotions and spirit. I cannot possibly contain both at the same time."

"That's how I see it, Ben."

Slowly Ben nodded. "That's a good point, Les, a very good point. The question is, why is it happening?"

"A good question, Ben. And it brings us to the issue of Miss Patricia Christensen. As I understand it from what you told me, you have, in so many words, told her to back off and stop pushing you into marriage. Right?"

"Right."

"And you have been praying about that decision?"

"For about three days straight. But I can't feel anything, Les. I'm all confused and in a turmoil, and no matter how I try to work through it, I can't seem to find any peace. Instead, I'm filled with all those emotions you described a few minutes ago. I don't know what's wrong with me, but something surely must be."

Leslie Milam grinned. "You're getting the answer to your prayers about Miss Pat, is all that's wrong."

"I'm getting my answer?" Ben quizzed in surprise.

"Sure you are. I've never seen such a classic example of what the Lord calls a stupor of thought."

Ben blinked. "A stupor of thought? But I—"

"I call it a 'stupid of thought,' Leslie Milam said, interrupting his friend. "That's because when it happens to me, I always feel absolutely stupid because it takes me so long to recognize it. The Lord tells us in Doctrine and Covenants 9:9, Ben, that if we make a decision that is wrong and then pray about it for a divine confirmation, we will get a stupor of thought, which will cause us to forget what we originally decided to do. If we fight that feeling, of course, then the Spirit departs, and confusion and despair and a sense of frustration will mount until we either go nuts or finally recognize what is happening.

"If we recognize what is happening, then we only need to go before the Lord and acknowledge His help with the direction we are to go. Of course, we accept that direction by repenting of our former desires. Once that is done, then almost instantly the stupor will be replaced by the peace that comes of the Holy Spirit."

"And . . . my decision was to . . . resist Pat's desires for an . . . an eternal marriage?"

Leslie Milam nodded. "That's right, Ben. Or at least for one in the near future."

"Hmmm," Ben said quietly. "An interesting theory, Les. An interesting theory, indeed. Now, I suppose I must take all this before the Lord and put it to the test."

"I'd certainly recommend that."

"And if it turns out that you are right?"

"Well," Leslie Milam said with a smile, "I would guess you will want to write another letter to Miss Pat."

"Yes," Ben said, nodding thoughtfully, "I would suppose I should. But only, as I said, if it proves that you are correct."

CHAPTER

TWENTY-SIX

It was late in the afternoon, and Ben stood alone in a remote area of the quinine plantation. Idly he examined a large palm, discovering by its reddish color that it was a hemp tree rather than a banana tree. Without thinking, he tore some fibers loose and rubbed them between his hands, thinking that the binder twine he had used in Canada might have come from this very area.

Walking forward, he noted other varieties of vegetation, such as sugar cane, coffee and cocoa beans, betel nut trees, guava trees, and so forth. But even though he saw and mentally cataloged the flora he passed, his mind was elsewhere. For Ben could hardly stop thinking of the things Leslie Milam had told him.

Correct or otherwise, Leslie's ideas were certainly provocative, and he was to be admired for having had the courage to share them with Ben. But then, he was perhaps Ben's best friend in all the world, so he should have felt free in expressing them. The question was, was he right? Ben didn't know, but he was amused that he felt such a reluctance to get on his knees and find out.

Finally, however, on a hill overlooking a vast grassy area

245

over which hundreds of cattle grazed, Ben dropped to his knees. Feeling curiously self-conscious, he looked around him carefully until at last he was certain that he was alone. Then and only then did he lower his head and close his eyes.

"Dear Father in heaven," he prayed, "according to Les Milam, I have offended Thee, and if that is so, I am deeply sorry. Dear Father, wilt Thou please forgive me if I have ignored the answer Thou gavest me? But Father, I must know if Les is right. Is it a stupor of thought Thou hast given me concerning my decision to not be hurried into marriage with Miss Pat Christensen? Father, if this is a stupor of thought, and if that is what I have been struggling with these past several days, then wilt Thou please remove it, that I might know that I am to . . . to m-marry . . . Pat Christen . . . sen . . . "

Suddenly overcome with emotion, Ben sank sobbing to the earth, for his answer had come.

It was gone! The turmoil, the anguish, the despair, the doubt, and the confusion were gone! And in their place, overshadowing Ben like a huge, downy-soft blanket, was the sweetest feeling of peace he had ever felt in his life.

Les Milam had been right! He must thank him, but first he had to find a way of thanking his Father in heaven. And he could only do that by repenting—by apologizing for the way he had been talking to the men around him, for his written response to Miss Pat, for the feelings he had been harboring against the Japanese, whom he knew were children of the same God he worshipped and served, and, finally, by coming back before God and apologizing to Him.

PART SIX

A NEW LAND TO LOVE

August 27, 1945–January 31, 1946

THE WAR

On August 27, 1945, victorious U.S. Navy ships steamed into Tokyo's Sugami Bay. Admiral Halsey led the force, which was probably the greatest display of naval might in history. It included 23 aircraft carriers, 12 battleships, 26 cruisers, 116 destroyers and escorts, 12 submarines, and 185 other smaller ships.

The Allied occupation of Japan began three days later, on August 30, when units of the 1st Marine Division landed at the Yokosuka naval base while units of the army's 11th Airborne Division landed at the Atsugi air base.

Two days later, American newsmen in Tokyo located Iva Toguri d'Aquino, who was known throughout the world from her propaganda broadcasts as "Tokyo Rose." The American nisei graduate of UCLA was eventually arrested, tried, and convicted on charges of treason.

On September 2, the official Japanese delegation to surrender ceremonies arrived on the deck of the U.S.S. Missouri. Wearing top hats, standing very formally and appearing very grim, Foreign Minister Mamoru Shigemitsu and Army Chief of Staff Yoshijiro Umezu (who had hoped for "one last battle" with the Americans) signed the instruments of surrender. For the Americans, General of the Army Douglas MacArthur signed the documents, while the emaciated Generals Wainwright and Percival, both former prisoners of the Japanese, looked on. Also signing were Admiral Chester W. Nimitz for the United States, General Hsu Young-chang for China, Admiral sir Bruce Fraser for the United Kingdom, Lieutenant General K. Derevyanko for the Soviet Union, General sir Thomas Blamey for Australia, Colonel L. Moore-Cosgrove for Canada, General Jacques Leclerc for France, Admiral C.E.L. Helfrich for the Netherlands, and Air Vice-Marshal sir L. M. Isitt for New Zealand.

World War II had ended.

But the work was by no means finished. Japan, a thoroughly defeated nation, had to be rebuilt, but in the eyes of the Allies it had to be rebuilt along lines that would promote individual freedom while eliminating militarization. SCAP, Supreme Commander, Allied Powers (which in effect was General Douglas MacArthur) headed the rebuilding efforts, which began within hours of the signing of the instruments of surrender.

SCAP also focused on instructing the Japanese in how to build a government (though no particular form was selected by the Americans) that would guard individual rights and then go on working to strengthen that government. Americans also encouraged the Japanese to develop a strong economy that would be adequate for peacetime needs.

The early months of occupation saw SCAP move swiftly to remove the principle supports of the militarist state. The armed forces were demobilized; state Shinto was disestablished; nationalist organizations were abolished and their members removed from important posts. Also removed from active roles were all persons prominent in wartime organizations and politics, including commissioned officers of the armed services and all high executives of the principal industrial firms.

In Tokyo, an international tribunal tried General Tojo and other war leaders, sentencing seven to death, sixteen to life imprisonment, and two to shorter terms. Millions of Japanese were repatriated from the former colonies in the Pacific and from Southeast Asia. The Home Ministry, which had controlled wartime Japan through its appointive governors and national police, was abolished, and the Education Ministry was deprived of its sweeping powers to control compulsory education.

Between October 1945 and February 1946, a cabinet committee headed by Matsumoto Joji prepared revisions to the Japanese constitution, but these were so superficial and so few that SCAP rejected it and rushed through a draft of its own, which included a thirty-one-article bill of rights, an elected house of representatives, and an emperor who was not divine but who derived his power from the will of the people. Approved by Emperor Hirohito and passed with wide support in an election in April (in these elections women voted for the first time in Japan's history), the constitution went into effect in November 1946. Thus Japan was launched on her way toward the modern economic nation that she has become.

THE MAN

Once out of the hills above Silae on Mindanao, Ben Bennett prepared, with the rest of the 31st, for ship loading and the return to the United States on what they were told would be about October 10. It was a busy time, for the 124th was transferred to Del Monte, near the Del Monte pineapple plantation, where once again Ben took charge of establishing a bivouac area that met military standards and at the same time pleased his own aesthetic tastes.

Finally settled, he fell into the routine of reviles and

retreats—flag ceremonies at the beginning and ending of each day—that had been reinstated following Japan's surrender. Further, with the aid of Sergeant Cannon, Ben established an intricate series of athletic competitions that would keep the inactive soldiers busy.

Continuing his program of personal development, he began a study of the Japanese language as well as subscribing to military correspondence courses in botany and agronomy.

And then on the morning of October 5, a personal "bomb" exploded in his life. He wrote, "I just learned that I am being transferred to the 24th Division, which at present is at Davao. In a few days it will leave for Japan. Instead of going back home with the 31st Division, I'll soon find myself on a ship or plane going north instead of east. Horace Greeley was wrong when he said, 'Go west, young man, go west.' I want to go west, but I have only sixty-nine points, and the decision has been made that an officer must have seventy-five before he can go home with the division. It is a bit of a disappointment.

"A few years ago, I was none too diligent in laying the groundwork for a few 'twelve pointers' (the army gives thirty-six points for three children, and twelve for one). Now it looks as though Uncle Sam intends keeping me for so long that I'll never have a chance to make amends for it. Sins of omission, and remorse of conscience, someone might call it. If so, then I am fast getting in the mood for repentance. But how in the world can a man 'bring forth fruit meet for repentance' way over here?"

By the next day, October 6, Ben had bid good-bye to Sergeant Milam and Lieutenant Kempainen, who were going home. He was then on his way to the islands of Japan.

250

CHAPTER

TWENTY-SEVEN

"Are you going down to eat, Ben?"

Looking up, Ben shook his head. "Not today, Art. I'm a little seasick again, so I think it would be best to give my stomach as little ammunition as possible."

Art Lambkin nodded. "Seems wise, all right. See you a little later, then."

He disappeared down the hatch, and Ben was left alone on the deck of the *Griggs,* ship no. 110. Shortly he found a sunny spot on the afterdeck that was in the lee of the wind, and there for perhaps thirty minutes he simply watched the distant shoreline. The temperature was cool but not cold, and more than anything else it reminded him of late fall days back home in Alberta. Speeding forward, his mind took firmer hold of the thought of summer, fall, and winter, and at last he knew he was ready to write the letter he had been putting off for so many days.

Opening his writing tablet, Ben positioned the paper on the arm of his chair; then carefully, thoughtfully he began.

"Sunday, October 21, 1945

"Inland Sea, between Shikoku and Kyushu, 1230 hours

"Dear Pat:

251

"How are you? Well, I hope. Are you still living at your same address and working at your same job up at Fort Douglas? What are you doing? If I remember correctly, you had a speech to give this past week. How did it go? I'm sure you did very well. Wish I could have been there for the occasion. Please tell me about it.

"Well, here I am just a day away from setting foot in Japan! I don't believe I ever thought I would have this experience, but now it is upon me and I am excited about it. Did you know that I had been transferred to the 24th 'Victory' Division and assigned with them to occupy Japan? Here I thought all along I was to be sent home with the 31st, and at the last minute my props were knocked out from under me, so to speak, and I am here instead of there. We are scheduled to land tomorrow on Shikoku, and I will be stationed at Matsuyama, which is directly across the Iyo Sea from Hiroshima. As you will remember, that is where the world's first atomic bomb was dropped.

"I have been assigned to the I & E (Information and Education) Department and will be in charge of organizing Japanese language classes for all American servicemen stationed on Shikoku. I feel better suited for this line of work than leading infantry patrols, and I am positive that it will be somewhat safer, as well.

"Due to the waters still being heavily mined, we are traveling very slowly, and it gives me an opportunity to examine the shoreline. Shikoku seems extremely rugged, with the steep mountains rising directly from the sea. In spite of this, I have been amazed to discover that every hillside is terraced and cultivated. Every so often we pass a town or village, with factory smokestacks and numerous high, white towers, which might be radio towers. The country is very green, and from here it seems a beautiful land.

"As we sail along, I have been wondering what sort of reception we would have received here had we arrived before the war ended. Gun batteries in caves appear all along the shore, and they would have given us a mighty hot reception, I can tell. They would have been very difficult to knock out with our bombers and naval fire because of their positions, and so it would have been rough. And we probably would have been making such a landing along about the first of the year, if the war hadn't ended. Thank heaven it did!

"I am traveling with a man by the name of Art Lambkin, whom I knew back in my Aggie days. He is a good man and a Mormon, and we have had several grand conversations regarding the good old days at Utah State Agricultural College. I have been saddened to discover, however, that he now uses tobacco and drinks beer. He is quite self-conscious about this and apologizes to me regularly. Yet somehow, though I believe he truly wants to, he cannot find within himself the strength to change. What a terrible hold those things place on a man!

"Also, word has come down from Major Howitt that all women and girls on Shikoku have been advised by their leaders that when the Americans come, they are not to resist the advances of the American soldiers but should submit without making any outcry. This, if it be true, is one of those things that would be termed 'something awful.' How thankful I am for the teachings of my mother and father, who have shown me that personal cleanliness is the only way to exaltation and eternal lives.

"I have given a great deal of thought, Pat, as to why I am here going north instead of going east with the 31st toward home. Of course, the pragmatist would say that it is due to the fact that I did not have enough points, and nothing more. But I must look beyond that, Pat, for I believe that the Lord is directing my course as much today as He was when I was in New Guinea or on Morotai or Mindanao. Of course, He may have many reasons for sending me to the home of the Nipponese instead of to my own home, and I won't pretend

253

to understand all of them. But one, which I think I do understand, has to do with a letter I wrote you a few weeks ago, wherein I displayed great pride and stubbornness. It seems that the Lord may have also been displeased with that letter, Pat, and so has granted me additional time to reconsider not only my words but my solitary and lonely position in life.

"I had a thought along those lines today, Pat, that I would like to share with you. It is sunny where I am sitting, but the nip of fall is in the air, telling me that winter is coming. This, I believe, is earth's oldest romance.

"As summer says good-bye, the first fall breezes touch gently the cheek of Mother Nature. She stirs, then awakens from her warm and pleasant sleep of laziness to enter a newness of life. Hastily she dons her gayest garments. Then, in all her dazzling splendor, she takes a last fling before Old Man Winter arrives to woo her, dress her in the purest white, and claim her as his bride.

"For four long months they live as one. At first they are happy, but as the days come and go, Old Man Winter turns out to be a cold and heard-hearted individual. Romance is killed. Mother Nature refuses any longer to be subjected to this cruel, austere mate. With a supreme effort, she breaks forth from his clutches, discards her white garment, and once again puts on gay attire.

"But you know, Pat, it's funny. They are separated, but they are never divorced. Every year at the same time, Mother Nature responds in the same way to those fall breezes. And every year at the same time, penitent Old Father Winter returns to woo and win her again. Just means, I guess, that a man can't get along without a woman in this world, nor a woman without a man.

"I fear, Pat, that I am a bit like Old Man Winter, for I have likely killed a romance, and it is time for me to become penitent. I hope that you will be like Mother Nature and listen to me again. As I said, it has been over a month since I wrote you. I've wanted to write before but have felt that maybe it didn't make much difference to you anymore whether I did or not.

"Then I received your last letter, and its tone indicated that you weren't quite sure that you were doing the right thing by writing me. I even wondered if you had forgotten how to spell—you started out with 'Dear.' I was certain you knew that the spelling had been 'Dearest,' but I suppose I gave you reason enough for making the change.

"I guess we have just been acting like a couple of adolescent kids, Pat. I know I have acted like a teenager at times, and I am sorry for that. I do hope you will forgive me and grant me another chance. I suppose Dr. Bee at Utah State might call what I have shown "emotional immaturity," and maybe he'd be right. You would think that at my age I would know better. But hopefully, like Old Man Winter, I have learned that a man cannot get by without a woman in this world. Dearest Pat, would you consider, once again, being 'the one and only' for me?

"Please write soon. Knowing now that I feel as if I would like to spend eternity with you, I will be more than anxiously waiting for your decision . . . "

CHAPTER

TWENTY-EIGHT

"Ben, you look beat!"

"You're right, Captain," Ben sighed. "I'm bushed!"

Captain Reynolds pushed back from his desk. "You should be, Ben, the way you run yourself to death. Your cold any better?"

"Not much, sir. I can't seem to shake it."

"Didn't you have malaria once? Might it be that, acting up again?"

"I didn't have malaria, sir. I had Japanese Scrub Typhus Disease. But I don't think that's what it is."

Captain Reynolds shook his head. "It's a wonder you aren't dead, Ben. Are you sure that isn't what you have?"

"I don't think so, sir. It feels altogether different. I'm certain it is only a cold."

"Have you tried steaming it out down at the bath house?"

"Haven't had time. I've been too busy with this education program. But it has really hit me this afternoon. Oh, lawsy, as one of my sergeants used to say . . . "

"Come in, Ben, and sit down."

"Thanks." Ben sighed as he stepped into the cubicle and took a chair.

"Are you able to keep up your training for the Olympic tryouts in Nagoya next week?"

Ben smiled. "In a way, sir. I'm putting the shot a little every day, and throwing the discus as well. But I don't have much strength in my arms right now, or any of the rest of me, for that matter. I think this cold has just beaten me down."

"Well, keep working, Ben. You'll be representing all of us, you know. We're counting on you to make it all the way to the Philippines, and to win two gold medals there besides. Do I need to make that last part an order?"

"If you'd like," Ben replied with a smile. "I've never disobeyed an order yet."

"Then consider it done. Are you on your way to the hotel?"

"Not for another few minutes."

"It's past quitting time, you know. More troubles with your language classes? Are they going to be concluded by next week when you leave for Nagoya?"

Closing his eyes, Ben clasped his hands behind his head and leaned back, stretching his aching muscles while he formulated his answer. He and Captain Reynolds were on the third floor of the library building in Matsuyama, which had been converted into division headquarters. It and the Bank of Japan, which was also made of concrete, were the only buildings left standing in an area of rubble and destruction that stretched for miles, the entire devastation the result of one single Allied fire-bombing raid.

Outside the area of destruction, life for the Japanese seemed hardly to have changed. Narrow streets, narrow-gauge electric railways, canals with rocked-in walls, massive crowds of people that appeared as if by magic after the restrictions had been lifted, agricultural use of every square foot of earth, including the shoulders of the roads—all these Ben noted with interest again and again. Rice paddies were everywhere, and so were sweet potatoes and taro, and all were a very healthy green.

Practically all the Japanese buildings had tile roofs, and, though close together, they were well arranged. Flower pots and shrubbery surrounded most of the houses, and they uniformly presented a neat and clean appearance.

But looking out the window of the library, on the other hand, while awe-inspiring and unbelievable, was discouraging in the extreme. Never had the Americans seen or even imagined such destruction. Time and again as Ben walked through it, he tried to picture how it might have looked before the raid. But he could not do it, nor could he imagine how it might ever be rebuilt.

"You look like you're thinking deeply, Ben."

"I'm sorry, sir," Ben said, opening his eyes. "I still haven't grown used to what lies around us. My mind seems to consider the destruction all the time."

"I do that, too. I find myself wondering what it was like during the raid, how many people suffered and died."

Ben nodded. "Me, too. It seems to me, sir, that we hit an awful lot of residential areas while missing far too many industrial and military targets."

Captain Reynolds smiled thinly. "I see that you and I think alike, Lieutenant Bennett. For right now, though, we hadn't better think too loudly. By the way, I enjoyed the summary of our educational efforts that you wrote and put in the '24th V Week' paper last week."

"Thank you. I think we're making progress."

Captain Reynolds nodded. "So do I. Now how about your classes, Ben. Are they all running smoothly?"

"I'm certain they are. I tend to lose track when X Corps keeps calling me to those meetings in Kure. I just can't seem to do both things at once."

"I understand."

"As for details, Captain, I have met on several occasions

with our interpreter, Mister Kawada, and his wife. She has been doing a bang-up job with the class she teaches. Did you know, sir, that Mister Kawada holds a B.A. from the University of Nebraska and an M.A. from Stanford in political science? He also has a year and a half in the law school at the University of Nebraska. And as for his wife, whose name I can never remember, she was born in New York and has attended Columbia University. She is very cultured and strikingly beautiful, and that fact alone has enhanced enrollment in her class."

"Yes," Captain Reynolds said, smiling, "I suppose it has. And she was born in New York? I wonder that she would rather live here."

"Well, sir, besides the fact that her husband is from here, she loves the land and the people. I don't blame her, either. The Japanese are so polite, and everything is so well organized. Of course, they tend to carry that organizational characteristic to the extreme, but there are things that I find very appealing about Japan."

Captain Reynolds nodded. "They are hard workers. Did you happen to notice how their carpenters refinished this office?"

"Did I! At first, Captain, I thought they were going to be like some of our students back at Utah State, all talk and no work. But when they started, they really went to town. Every one of those Japanese carpenters knew their jobs, and once they got going, there were no breaks and very little talking. I was amazed at how quickly they finished the job."

"As was I. What about your other instructors? How are they working out?"

Ben smiled. "Mister Takino, who is chief of the Labor Section, Japanese Liaison Office, lined them up for me, and they are doing fine. We met last week to go over the conclusions on the lesson outlines, and I gave them all a general orientation on how to end their classes and prepare for the next series. Our interpreter, Mister Yokosawa, was a great help to me in this. He graduated from the University of Utah in 1923 and took his M.A. out there. He was well acquainted with Doctor Thomas, Doctor Kingsbury, and Doctor Pack, and he has many fond memories of the United States. Truthfully, Captain, I am amazed at how many Japanese people I have met who were educated in America."

"I've noticed that, too, Ben. It's almost like we educated them so they could fight against us more effectively."

"That's true, Captain. But we couldn't stop educating the people who come to us from around the world, not and remain the great bastion of freedom and democracy that we are."

Captain Reynolds sighed. "How true, how true. I understand that you met with Colonels Pearsell and Drake?"

"I did."

"What did you think of Drake?"

"I'd rather not say, sir."

"This is off the record, Ben. I want to know if my perceptions are the same as yours."

"If they're negative, sir, then I suppose they are."

"Go on, Ben."

Drawing a deep breath, Ben leaned forward. "I think he is a pompous fool, sir. He had his ribbons and campaign stars and badges and medals spread all over his chest so we would all take notice and sit up and listen to his majesty while he rumbled."

Captain Reynolds chuckled as Ben leaned back once again in his chair. "The trouble, Captain," he continued more seriously, "is that he has very definite fascist tendencies and ideas. He seems to think that the army and its policies should never be questioned, and that anyone who dares do such a thing is undisciplined, ignorant, and low.

"But, sir, we are Americans! We have been fighting for freedom. Included in that is freedom of expression, freedom of speech. Most of us can understand why strict censorship of news and information had to be maintained during the time we were fighting a war. But with the return of peace there should come a return to freedom of expression, and Americans should not stand for anything else.

"I believe it is dangerous, Captain, when one man who controls the lives of fifteen thousand others takes steps to deprive them of their freedom, which is what he is doing. Silly, asinine restrictions are being imposed when they are neither necessary nor desirable. The men are being made miserable rather than happy, and he is the one who is largely responsible. I am sorry, sir, but this is what I thought of him."

"Ditto," Captain Reynolds replied with a grin. "And we aren't alone, Ben."

"Well, I hope not. Captain, listen to this quote of his. I jotted it down during the meeting, in case I ever needed ammunition. Colonel Drake said: 'We are not interested in training men for return to civilian life—we are interested in training them for the job here.' "

"Why, that's as incorrect as it can be!"

"I know, Captain. Incorrect, and very stupid. Listen to this one. He said: 'Our job is not to raise the standard of the Japanese people—our objective is to keep it down.' "

"Hummph! The man's a fool, Ben."

"I know, and I'm telling you, sir, that my spirit rebelled, and I wanted to reorient him with a hefty tip on the chin. One man bringing misery and hardship to fifteen thousand Americans plus who knows how many Japanese civilians. That is just wrong! The situation ought to be busted wide open and the whole thing exposed."

"I think it will be, Ben. Chaplain Keilty, who as you remember was accused by Drake of black-market activities with some Christian missionaries—"

"Charges that were proven groundless, as I remember."

"That's correct. Anyway, Keilty took your secret desire

to heart and delivered his Sunday punch against Drake's chin in the latest issue of *Stars and Stripes*. We'll see what comes of it, but I suspect that the new chief of staff, Colonel Lester, might make things a bit hot for our man Drake."

Ben grinned. "They should be made a bit hot. Governments have done enough damage in this war. Now we ought to be working to set things right, for us as well as for the Japanese."

"I understand you went to Hiroshima when you were at Kure for the meetings. What did you think?"

Ben's face grew very serious. "Captain, I shall never forget that trip. I had heard a lot about the atomic bomb's destruction, but what I actually saw stunned me. For miles and miles, everything was destroyed. A number of buildings were still standing—those made of stone or such—but everything inside had been blown out or burned out. I saw glass bottles fused together from heat. I saw cement bridges destroyed. I saw steel girders twisted and broken; press drills blown apart; and lamp poles blown to the ground. I saw a skeleton in the rubble—a backbone and a few ribs. I touched one of the ribs with the toe of my shoe, and it turned to powder. I saw people with scarred faces, indicating that they had been burned. At several points, as we drove along, a terrific odor greeted us, the odor of putrefying flesh.

"We tried to determine just where the center of the explosion was, and we believe we located it, at least approximately. Captain, it is incredible that one single bomb could cause such great destruction. Surely the people of Hiroshima must have thought that the world was coming to an end when all that destruction came in a matter of a few seconds. I cannot even begin to comprehend the horror they must have felt."

"It's interesting, Ben, that you should think of the people rather than of the fact that the bomb helped immeasurably to bring an early end to the war. But interestingly, I had the same experience. When I looked at the devastation in Hiroshima, or see it around us here, for that matter, my mind sees only the people — the poor, innocent men, women, and children who suffered so terribly because of the greed of their leaders."

"Do you picture your own family here, Captain?" Ben asked quietly. "I do. I keep thinking of how it would be for my folks, or for my brothers and sisters, if this bomb had hit Alberta instead of Hiroshima. I just got word that my brother Ray is getting married, and my sister Lila just got married this past summer. Two families just starting out, and in a few seconds, annihilation for all four of them. Add to that my parents, my brothers Dennis and Jim, and my youngest sister Ruth, and I can't even comprehend the horror that occurred that morning in Hiroshima. How many families no longer exist, Captain? How many sacred loves, how many innocent hopes and dreams, were vaporized that morning? How many innocent sons and daughters of a just God will one day stand at His judgement bar and with steady but accusing fingers point out the warmongers whom God will surely hold responsible for the agony and devastation they have caused."

Captain Reynolds looked at Ben for several seconds before he responded. "I think," he finally replied, his voice quiet, "that will be a terrible day of reckoning. You know, I have never thought of it in quite that way, Ben. But now that you have nudged my thinking, I intend to commit myself more than ever to help rebuild for these people a quality life, where such unrighteous men will no longer have power to hurt them."

Ben nodded. "That's certainly my own goal, Captain. Because the war has been so terrible, I think it has been hard for most of us to think of these folks as people. But the other day I had the chance to visit several schools in the area, and at the Eoruya School I had a rather precious experience.

"As I came out of the school, several of the kids were playing baseball. I couldn't resist the temptation to get in on it, so I talked them into letting me knock a few flies. Instead of a baseball they were using a medium-soft rubber ball, and the bat they handed me was so light that I missed the ball completely my first ten or eleven swings. They were all trying very hard to be polite, but I could see that those kids were on the verge of laughing at me. So I decided to impress them and got a heavier bat. Then I put all my weight into my swing, and away the ball went, over the fence. When one of the boys brought the ball back to me after that, I said 'arigato,' which is 'thank you,' and that really cracked them up. You should have heard those kids laugh.

"But you know, Captain, boys in Taber would have laughed the same way at a Japanese man struggling to do something western and then trying to be polite about it in an unfamiliar language. They might not have been so polite, but they surely would have laughed. So you see, former enemies or not, we truly are all children of the one true God, and brothers and sisters of His Son, Jesus Christ. Knowing that, how can we do otherwise than to love these people and do all in our power to help them put their lives back together?"

"Well," Captain Reynolds said as he rose to his feet, "I'm glad you are on my team, Ben. You're a better man than I think even you know. Could you use a ride home?"

Ben stood. "I'd like a ride, sir, but I was going to go look for a kimono to send my mother."

"Wonderful! Let's do it together. First, though, let's hit the bath house and see if we can knock out that cold of yours with a little hot water and steam."

264

CHAPTER

TWENTY-NINE

"Ahhh, this feels *great!*"

Ben, his eyes closed in absolute relief and pleasure, nodded in agreement.

"You give yourself a fifteen-to-twenty-minute soaking in this naturally hot water, Ben, and then pour two wooden buckets of cold water over your head, and I guarantee that cold of yours will never come back again."

"I hope you're right, sir."

"I am. Believe me! Then you can wow them at the Olympic tryouts. I understand you did quite well in the Olympic tryouts in Canada a few years ago."

"I was truly blessed, sir. I just never expected to have the chance to do it again."

"Good people have a way of being rewarded, Ben. I'll be looking forward to the results. By the way, are you still living with Kirk and Selby at that hotel?"

"The Toyora? Yes, sir, I'm still there, though Lieutenant Schwab is now my roommate."

"What's it like—your hotel?"

"Very Japanese, Captain. It's about two miles from headquarters, on a little side street. The first time I went there, a

Japanese boy and girl met me at the door with their customary bow. The boy told me to remove my shoes and put on the pair of sandals that were waiting for me at the entrance. I did, and I soon found that the sandals were only to get me from the door to my room, and that I could only go into my room in stocking feet."

"Seriously?"

"Absolutely. You see, Captain, the floors are covered with beautiful, clean mats that would quickly be ruined by shoes or sandals. These mats are about six feet long by three feet wide and are all the same size. In fact, the Japanese indicate the size of a room by stating the number of mats on the floor."

"I didn't know that."

"Neither did I, until the boy told me. My room is very beautiful, very oriental. The beds, which consist of a thick pad or mattress, are not even there during the day. They are only placed on the floor at bedtime by the maids. The comforter that covers us is very warm but a little short for me, so I end up sleeping with my legs bent. The pillow is a neck rest, made of flax and beans or something like them. I worried that I would miss a head pillow, but to tell you the truth, I don't think I have ever slept better in my life."

"Do you . . . uh . . . get in on the parties, Ben? Oh, you needn't be surprised. We know about the parties the men have in these hotels. They are actually quite famous. Do you get in on them very often?"

"Sometimes," Ben stated rather coolly, "I don't have much of a choice, especially when the participants force themselves into my room. Then I do get somewhat involved."

"What do you mean?"

"Oh, like the night the nurses from the 229th General Hospital gave the officers a party at our hotel. I looked in on it for a while, but frankly, I was disgusted by some of the things I saw going on. The nurses looked worn and spent and dissipated, and practically all of them drank and smoked."

"Ah, yes, I have heard about your views on those things."

"Yes, sir, I expect that you have. And I feel very strongly about them, too. Anyway, the nurses furnished all the liquor that night, and there seemed to be plenty of it. The party turned out to be a pretty wild affair, and so I left. It was a good thing I did, too, because a little later some joker hit one of the nurses over the head with a plate, and two different fights broke out. Finally about fifty M.P.s arrived and broke up the party."

"Sounds like a fun time."

"Fun, sir? I was asleep when a bunch of officers came into my room carrying a Navy man who was completely out. He had fallen down some stairs, and his face was a real mess. I'll bet he required surgery just to patch it back together. My room happened to be closest to where he fell, so they brought him in and laid him on a bed. He was dead drunk, sir. I watched him groaning for a while, and then one of the nurses came in and checked him over. She told me he would be all right, and then she left. A couple of hours later, some other Navy officers came and took the poor guy away. To me, sir, it was all very disgusting. How people can think of such idiotic behavior as being fun is beyond me.

"Night before last was another case in point. When I arrived at the hotel, I saw a rather good-looking Geisha girl standing at the entrance. She was dressed fit to kill in a beautiful sky-blue kimona with flowered design. Her face was pretty well camouflaged with rouge, powder, and so forth, and I knew immediately that something was in the wind. Shortly my suspicions were confirmed. Colonel Ross, the ordinance officer, had a party in his room, and I hear it also turned into a pretty wild affair. I didn't even look in on that one, though."

"Have you ever seen Geishas entertain, Ben?"

"No, sir, I haven't."

"Some of them are very graceful, and many have out-standing voices."

"They don't have to be Geishas to qualify in that regard, sir. My maid, Setsui, has a lovely voice, and she is a very graceful dancer."

Captain Reynolds grinned. "Maid, huh? You married, Ben?"

Ben shook his head.

"Ever . . . uh . . . well, are you still a virgin, Ben?"

His eyes flashing, Ben nodded.

"You mean you . . . uh . . . haven't even been with your . . . uh . . . maid?" the captain asked sarcastically.

His face coloring slightly, Ben again shook his head. "Captain, she is en—"

Captain Reynolds held up his hand, stopping Ben's pro-test. "Well," he stated confidentially, "you don't need to tell me any more. However, if you want a chance at a real woman, Ben, now's the perfect opportunity. Some of these girls here are quite stunning, especially the geishas, and I could take you to a place only a few of us know about—"

"No, thank you, sir."

Captain Reynolds looked at Ben for a moment, and sud-denly smiled. "Ah, yes, you have heard the medical reports. Good thinking, Ben, good thinking. Why, just today an order came out stating that the supply of prophylactic kits is almost exhausted, and that 100 percent of the prostitutes are infected with disease. This morning our division surgeon told me that two thousand kits are used per day by the fifteen thousand men of our division, while an untold number don't even bother with the kits. So you are wise, Ben, in avoiding places like Geisha row."

"I went there one day," Ben stated frankly, "and when I saw all the young fellows there throwing away their futures, it made me quite ill. I see no need to ever go back."

"Throwing away their futures?" Captain Reynolds questioned. "Oh, yes, you mean with the diseases and so forth."

Ben shook his head. "Partly. But there's so much more to it, Captain, that so few seem to understand or care about. I just wish the men would avoid the situation altogether."

"But such relationships are so freely offered, Ben," the captain argued. "Everywhere one goes, women make themselves available—"

"Captain Reynolds, that isn't so. Except for the day that Lieutenant Schwab and I went to Geisha row, not once has a Japanese woman made herself available to me."

The captain was stunned. "Are you serious, Ben?"

"Absolutely."

"Then you must not go where everybody else goes."

Ben smiled thinly. "I go to work, I go shopping, I drive around the countryside studying the agriculture, and I go to my hotel where my maid Setsui has things all ready for me to study or retire, whichever I prefer."

"And you have nothing going on with this Setsui?" Captain Reynolds questioned slyly.

At that, Ben laughed aloud. "My goodness, Captain, as I started to tell you earlier, she's engaged to be married. Besides that, she's a fine girl and would never even think of prostituting herself. Her interest in Schwab and me is strictly platonic and economic, though I will say that I think she has come to like us a little."

"What do you mean?" the captain asked with a grin.

"Well," Ben hastened to explain, "the other night she and another maid showed us a little bit about Oriental customs. They put on a dance and singing routine for us, and they did quite well, I believe. It was all very strange, but I enjoyed watching them, as did Lieutenant Schwab.

"Afterwards we tried to get them to dance with us, American style. They were very bashful and shy but finally did try a few steps before they retired from the room in embarrassment. Now, sir, does that sound promiscuous to you?"

Captain Reynolds shook his head. "Maybe you're right, Ben."

"I am right."

"And she made no further advances?"

Ben shook his head. "Absolutely not! Of course, she can get to be a real nuisance, I will admit that. Last night Lieutenant Schwab stayed somewhere else, so I had the room to myself. Except, of course, for Setsui. She truly does like our room, and last night she hardly wanted to leave at all. We talked back and forth in Japanese and English, insofar as my limited Japanese would allow, for several hours. She brought up little tangerines and kept the charcoal on the pots all heaped up to keep the room warm. She even disappeared once and came back a few moments later with a complete new outfit on—obie and all. She was also wearing quite a bit of paint and looked quite attractive.

"I had a lot to do last night, though, and didn't feel right about squandering the entire evening with silly chatter. I'll admit, however, that I had a devil of a time trying to send her away without offending her. I think her room must have been very cold or something, because she really didn't want to leave."

Captain Reynolds guffawed. "Her room! For crying out loud, Ben, open your eyes! It had nothing to do with her room, or the cold, or anything else. She was offering herself to you, and in the process making herself as attractive as she could. And you really didn't see that?"

"I still don't see it," Ben replied quietly.

"Then you're blind, man. What's with you, that you don't . . . don't . . . Ben, don't you . . . uh . . . like women?"

"Like women? Oh, yes, sir," Ben replied with a smile, "I

do. One in particular. I have asked her to marry me, and I am waiting quite anxiously for her answer."

"Why Ben, I didn't know. That's wonderful."

"Well, it will only be wonderful if she says yes. I offended her, though, and I have not heard from her in some time. Frankly, sir, and it breaks my heart to say this, I fear she might have written me off."

"And you would like to be married to her?"

"Yes, sir," Ben replied, nodding. "I would like that very much. In fact, my friend back in Utah has purchased an engagement ring for me and has presented it to her in my behalf. I just hope she accepts it."

"I hope so, too. I'm married, you know."

Ben smiled. "Yes, sir, I've seen the photograph of your wife on your desk."

"Marriage is great, Ben. My wife's a good woman, too. I could never ask for a better companion. Only . . . well, she's ten thousand miles away, which makes my nights very lonely. Thank goodness I can enjoy a little feminine company here while I'm waiting to go home to her. As I said earlier, Ben, if you would like, I would be very happy to show you where you can enjoy the same pleasure quite safely—"

"And your wife, sir?" Ben asked, purposely interrupting his superior officer.

"My wife?"

"Yes. While you are having illicit relationships with these Japanese women, what about her?"

"Why, what she doesn't know won't hurt her," the captain replied with a chuckle.

"Or you either, I presume," Ben responded.

"What?"

"I said, what you don't know won't hurt you either. Referring, of course, to the illicit activities that your wife will also be participating in back home."

"She hadn't better be having any illicit activities," Captain Reynolds growled. "She tries that, and so help me, I'll—"

"But Captain, isn't she as lonely as you?"

"Well, yes, I suppose so, but—"

"And aren't you ten thousand miles away from her?"

"Now see here, Ben—"

"No, Captain, I think you should listen to me. My mother used to say, in referring to the immorality of some of the men in our community, that what was good for the gander was just as good for the goose. And she had a point, sir. Why should you have the privilege of adultery and immorality but deny that same privilege to your wife?"

"Because it isn't right! That's why."

"And what you are doing is right?"

"Well, it's . . . it's at least normal," the captain sputtered.

Ben nodded. "Sadly, sir, you are right. But so were the sins that drove Noah to build his ark and climb aboard. Sinning was the normal, accepted way of life. But it also happened to be wrong, and God destroyed the people for it."

The captain's head came up. "Are you saying that God will destroy me?"

"No," Ben replied gently. "I'm not. In fact, He probably won't need to. You seem to be doing a fine job of that all by yourself."

"What . . . what do you mean?"

Ben shifted position in the very warm water. "First of all, sir, as you pointed out, there is the problem of disease."

"But I'm healthy. I was just checked this morning by the division surgeon."

"That's fine for today," Ben replied. "But what about tomorrow, or next week? I have a man from my old company who, at this very hour, is in a hospital down in the Philippines. He should have been rotated home months ago, but several weeks after his last immoral 'conquest,' the army doctors discovered his disease. Immediately they declared him too great a risk to send home, and he will very likely spend the next several years on Mindanao, ten thousand miles away from his wife and children. Are you certain you are healthy, sir?

"And speaking of destruction, let's discuss the issue of trust. Do you trust your wife, Captain?"

"I do."

"And can she trust you?"

Captain Reynolds didn't reply, but slowly he dropped his eyes until all he saw was the steaming pool.

"You see, sir," Ben continued quietly, "the day you got married was the happiest day in your life. The next happiest was the day you took her to the hospital so that she could give birth to that son whose picture stands on your desk beside that of your wife. Am I right?"

"You . . . uh . . . yes, you are . . . right . . . "

"But Captain, by this gross deception of yours, you have destroyed the trust you and she had for each other, the trust that is the only 'glue' capable of binding a marriage together for an entire lifetime."

"I . . . I hadn't thought of it like that."

"I'm sure you hadn't, sir. Sadly, few do. People are told that committing adultery or fornication is against the commandments of God, and that He will be angry with them if they do it. But what does that mean? Wow, God is angry. But so what? Does He make thunder rumble, or lightening flash? Or tornados, pestilences, and earthquakes hit the earth? So what, they ask? That doesn't do much to motivate them to keep the commandments. Does it you, sir?"

Captain Reynolds smiled weakly. "Not hardly, Ben. It isn't personal enough."

"Exactly, Captain, and in my opinion, that's why so few people bother to keep the commandments. They simply don't understand how God operates, and how personal He has caused everything to be.

"You see, sir, by being immoral you have destroyed your wife's trust in you, and as dominoes fall one after another, so her lack of trust will most likely end in the dissolution of your marriage. That's terribly personal, don't you think?"

"I do. But as I said, she doesn't have to know."

Ben shook his head. "Captain, she will know. You can't hide it from her. The scripture says that all sins will be made known, and this is one of those sins. If you don't tell her with words, then your actions will reveal your dark secret. And if by chance even that doesn't happen, then your spirit will find a way to communicate to her spirit that you have betrayed your vows, and her trust."

"Well, Ben, it may not be as big a deal for her as you seem to think it will be."

"Perhaps not, sir. But if your wife feels anywhere near as strongly about your fidelity as you seem to feel about hers, then I would guess that what you have done will be a very big deal for her."

"But . . . but isn't there anything I can do?"

"Of course there is, sir. You can repent. You can confess your infidelity to her and together work your way through it until she feels that she can trust you again. It will be a long, hard experience, which you can understand better if you reverse your roles and think about how you would feel if it were her who had betrayed you. But still, it can be done.

"But the point, Captain, is that a commandment has been broken, and therefore some very personal suffering must be endured. Do you see what I mean?"

"I think so," the captain replied softly.

"As another example, which we discussed briefly a little earlier, we could consider smoking or drinking."

"But there's no commandment against those things, Ben."

Ben flicked away a little water, then turned to his superior officer. "Do you admit, sir, that smoking is dirty?"

"Dirty, yes. Sinful, no."

"And drinking. Do you agree that alcohol impairs a person's ability to think, to use good judgment in what he does from moment to moment?"

"Yes, I will agree with that."

"And will you agree that in the New Testament, the human body was referred to as a holy temple? And that we were exhorted to treat that temple with piety and respect?"

"Hmmm. Yes, I recollect something of that scripture."

"Captain, have you seen pictures of our Mormon temple in Salt Lake City?"

"I have, Ben. I've even seen the building, when I visited there a few years ago. It is a beautiful edifice."

"I think so, too. How would you feel if you saw someone open a window and begin shoveling dirt into that temple?"

"I'd stop them."

"So would I. What would you do if you saw a busload of people who had lost their sanity cavorting in the hallways of the temple, smashing windows or doing balancing acts upon the spires. Or suppose such people were simply drunken and were participating in an orgy such as occurred in my hotel the other night. What would you do?"

Captain Reynolds laughed. "I'd stop them if I could. And I see what you are getting at, too. If my body truly is sacred, then I am being worse than foolish to intentionally pollute it with tobacco, or damage it by losing my reason to alcohol. In fact, I'm sinning. So what . . . uh . . . blessings do I lose by doing this?"

"Specifically, Captain, and this is according to the Lord, you lose good health, you lose divine protection and a long life, and you lose the right to receive great and hidden treasures of knowledge."

"Knowledge regarding what, Ben?"

"Probably heavenly things, sir. I suspect that a deep and thorough understanding of the gospel of Jesus Christ is denied people who choose not to live this law. Thus they do not have the power to come to know God and Christ, which, as you remember, we were all commanded by Christ to do."

"Fascinating. And that's certainly personal, all right."

"And so is every other commandment God ever gave, Captain. Personal and very individual, for each of us will one day answer as to how we responded to each of God's commandments. Joseph Smith, a modern prophet of God, was told by the Lord that laws affect every phase of our behavior, and that we can only obtain blessings or happiness by being obedient to the laws that are applicable to that particular blessing or form of happiness.

"Frankly, sir, that is why I choose to remain morally clean and pure. I want a marriage that will last for all eternity, and my understanding of the scriptures leads me to believe that God cannot grant me such a happy or lengthy state of wedded bliss unless I have earned it through personal purity. So I am doing my best, sir, to pay the price, by starting with moral trustworthiness."

"But . . . you aren't even married yet, Ben. You have made no commitments to that girl."

"Not to Pat, Captain, but I have to my God. I made those commitments when, as a child eight years old, I was baptized. One day soon I will face Pat, if she accepts my proposal of marriage, and report to her on how trustworthy I have been before the Lord. And then, together, we will help each other continue in purity until one day future we will report, hand-in-hand, to the Lord Himself. Then, sir, in that one area at least, we will know the meaning of true, eternal happiness."

"What an amazing concept!"

Ben shook his head. "Not when you think about it, sir. Christ in the New Testament said everything I have said, only He said it better and with less verbosity. And that was two thousand years ago."

"Ben, I don't remember that He said any such thing."

"Why, certainly He did. Consider the list of commandments we call the beatitudes, sir. If we are peacemakers, then according to Jesus we shall be rewarded by being called children of God. What a wonderful title!

"If we are merciful to others, then God will reward us with mercy. If we are meek, then one day we will inherit the earth in its purified state. If we are poor in spirit, meaning I think, humble and submissive to God's directions, then we will be given the kingdom of heaven. You see, sir, those are very personal promises that Jesus outlined.

"Let me tell you of another. Christ said that lusting after another sexually was the same as committing mental adultery and would be treated as such by the Lord in the day of judgment. To Joseph Smith, God further clarified the penalties for mental adultery, and made them more personal, when He told him that such people would lose the Spirit, meaning the Holy Spirit or Holy Ghost.

"You say, 'So what?' I reply, each of us needs the Holy Spirit every minute of our lives. Why? Because the Holy Spirit is responsible for protecting us in times of danger—"

"Such as the remarkable experiences I have heard that you had?" Captain Reynolds asked.

Ben nodded. "Yes, sir, such as those remarkable experiences. Further, the Holy Ghost comforts us when tragedy strikes; He reveals to our minds information that is critical to our day-to-day living and progress; He strengthens our will when we are tempted beyond what we might normally be able to endure; He quickens our understanding of God and His heavenly ways; He teaches us how to develop faith so that one day we can be enabled to endure God's presence; and I could go on and on. But the point, sir, is that every man, woman, and child on earth needs the presence and influence of the Holy Spirit if they are going to experience meaningful, eternal success and happiness.

"Only, once we begin committing either mental or physical adultery or fornication, then that invaluable Spirit departs, and we are left alone to stumble and grope through the darkness of life.

"Do you see, Captain Reynolds, why I insist on seeing only goodness and purity in the women around me, including my maid Setsui? If purity doesn't happen to be there, then I choose to remain ignorant of the fact and go on about my business as if purity were there. Thus my own heart and mind will remain clean, and I will continue to enjoy the companionship and influence of the Holy Spirit."

Captain Reynolds shook his head, thought deeply for a moment or so, and then climbed from the bath. "You know, Ben," he said as he poured cold water over his head and body to close the pores of his skin, "you are a remarkable man. I don't believe I have ever heard a sermon quite like what you just gave me. You certainly have given me some things to think about."

"I'm glad that we could visit," Ben said as he toweled himself off. "But remember, sir, that what is truly remarkable isn't me. Rather, it is the love of God for all of us that is remarkable. We are all sinners, sir, and yet He has shared with us not only the information we have discussed tonight, but He has also shared His beloved Son, who came to die for us. Through Christ's atonement, sir, we can all repent and become clean, no matter how dirty we may have become. That is truly remarkable."

"Yes it is, Ben, though I fear I give too little thought to it."

"Perhaps that too will change."

Captain Reynolds smiled. "Perhaps it will. Ben, I surely hope that things work out between you and your girl."

"So do I, Captain."

"She'll be a very lucky woman, my friend."

Ben smiled back. "But not as lucky as I will be, sir. Not as lucky as I will be."

CHAPTER

THIRTY

With a smile on his face, Ben gazed out the window of the speeding train. In every respect it had been a wonderful two days, and as he lay alone in his Pullman berth watching the darkened Japanese countryside slip past, he felt as happy as a child.

Smiling widely, Ben once again sorted through the events he had just experienced. First had come the weather the day before, which had dawned clear and sunny, the perfect sort of day for the Olympic tryouts. For two solid weeks prior to the meet, it had rained and snowed, so the fine weather had been a real break.

Secondly had come the news, just after breakfast, that point quotas had been lowered again. And that would mean, absolutely, that he would be on his way home within the next few days. Ben could hardly contain himself, he was so excited about that.

Then had come the actual meet itself, which, while making him nervous at the start, had turned out to be a terrifically enjoyable affair. He had been allowed six puts with the shot and, as it turned out, had needed all six of them. For his sixth put had been his longest and had given him first place in the meet. Of course, he had also competed in the discus throw but had not done as well and had placed only second. Still, the ribbons would make fine mementos, and his placing in the meet had guaranteed him a position on the thirty-man team who would go to Manilla, the Philippines, for the actual Olympics.

Now, of course, he was on his way to Yokohama and then by air to the Philippines, but this time to take part in a track meet with friends rather than to take part in an amphibious landing among enemies!

But all of these, while wonderful, had done nothing more than set the stage, so to speak, for the main event of Ben's past two days, the event that still had his heart racing.

Rolling over, he reached onto the tiny shelf above his head, groped in the darkness, and finally retrieved the envelope that contained, he knew full well, the opening chapter for the remainder of his life.

Flicking on the light switch, he gazed for long minutes at the envelope, fine stationery that had a small paper "Utah State" banner attached to it. Interesting, he thought, how she always managed to think of the little things that he found so appealing, so compelling.

Finally, unable any longer to resist the actual letter, he reached through the torn opening at the top of the envelope and withdrew it. Slowly he unfolded it, remembering how his heart had been hammering the first time he had done this, only hours before. Now his heart wasn't hammering exactly, but he still felt nervous, somehow certain that the message he had already read perhaps thirty times would no longer be what he found on the letter.

But it was, and in the upper berth of the Pullman car, Ben found himself grinning even more widely.

"My Dearest Bill," the letter began. And once again Bill had to wipe a couple of stray tears from his eyes.

"How's my very best beau? Golly, but I miss you, 'Honey!'

May I call you that, Bill, now that my answer is yes? For it is yes, Bill! Yes, I will consider being 'your one and only' for ever and ever! Yes, Darling, I will be more than honored to become your wife.

"Oh, how I missed you Sunday when I went up to the ward. It will be so nice to have you with me one day soon. Isn't it strange that I can miss you so, when we have never even spent any time together? Yet it is so! Somehow I feel that we have known each other forever, and so the fact that we have never even actually spoken more than a few words of greeting to each other, at least here in mortality, means very little.

"Guess what? Everybody is *so* happy for us. Darling, it all seems like a wonderful dream, and I feel like it's too good to be true. Then I look at my beautiful ring and close my eyes to bring you near to me with your arms around me, and I realize it is reality; that your heart is with me and that some day, soon, we will be together for always!

"Oh, Bill, I *miss you—*I *miss you!* The time must go fast, it must!

"I like the picture you sent me better all the time, 'Honey.' I'm partial to a smiling photo, but this one is so sweet. Guess what? I have an unfinished photo of myself, like yours, so I put it up beside yours on my bureau. Funny, but it makes me feel closer to you! I like the way you look me right in the eyes, 'Honey.' I think we do look alike.

"I have a dream, Bill, or a vision, that is always before my eyes. May I share it with you? I see myself sitting across the room from you, but you are looking over at me. An expression of pure love is in your eyes, and is radiating over your whole face.

"Then you wink at me, and my heart skips a beat—Oh, my darling, don't ever stop doing little things like that! I don't know if men realize the importance of such little things; that's something I will need to learn, among many other things about men — about *my* man. Oh, but it will be fun. The time cannot go fast enough, Bill. I'm surely hoping for an *early spring,* aren't you?

"Everyone is so thrilled for us, Bill, and they all think the ring is just beautiful. How on earth did you manage to buy it and get it to me? Jerry and LaRona, my brother and sister-in-law, just thought it was gorgeous, and then some! I think I have the prettiest ring in the whole world. It's just perfect for my hand. Thanks, 'Honey!' Wish you were here, and I'd give you a big kiss and hug! Would you like that? I really would! You wouldn't even have to take it without asking, as you once suggested that you might. XOXOXOXOXOXO — Oh, Honey, how I wish!

"I called Brother Christiansen, and he said the temple was opening the first part of February, and that it would definitely be open and in full swing for the month of March. I was happy to hear that, and hope the timing meets with your approval, as well as the Army's 'approbation.'

"How soon do you intend to 'make me yours,' Bill? From your letter I decided that you wanted to hurry once you got home, so I called the state about the blood test. If we do it here, 'Honey,' it will take between three and four days. But if you can get tested there, and bring the slip with you, not the white copy, but the colored one, the state laboratory will accept that and push it through for us that same day.

"Oh, Bill, every spare minute I have, I read back over your sweet and wonderful letter. Everything about it was just perfect, especially you, my dream come true! I am so happy, darling.

"Write as soon as you can, Bill. I do hope the point quotas drop very quickly, without causing you too much worry and work. Take care of yourself for my sake, will you? After all, you are going to belong to me very soon!

"Bye for now, 'Honey.' Remember, I love you, I *love you,* I *love you!*

"Goodnight, 'Sweetheart.' "

Slowly Ben lowered the letter onto his chest, and then in the darkness he envisioned Pat as she wrote it. Happy, bubbly, excitable Pat. He could imagine her laughter, imagine the almost instant rush of emotion in her voice. He could see her smile, could see the dancing lights of joy and happiness in her eyes. What a change, what a delightful change, she was going to make in the staid, humdrum course of his life!

Oh, if only he was on his way home to Utah rather than south to the Philippines!

PART SEVEN

ENGAGED

February 1, 1946–February 28, 1946

THE MAN

On February 1, 1946, two weeks after receiving Pat's letter, Ben arrived back at division headquarters in Matsuyama. There he found orders, which had been cut on January 20, directing him to Agusaki and the 11th Replacement Depot, where he would be immediately processed and rotated back to the states.

Hardly able to contain his excitement, Ben spent the next day and a half filling out forms, turning over his office to his replacement (a full colonel), and packing his belongings. Getting a 5.5 rating (superior) on his 66–1, he also learned that he had been in grade as a first lieutenant long enough to be in line for promotion to captain on the first day of his terminal leave back in the states.

Shipping home a large case of souvenirs that included Japanese swords and pistols, he took the train to Tokomatsu and then a ferry across to Agusaki. He was immediately processed, given four shots, and then berthed for several days in a wide-open barn near the airfield, where he and numerous of other officers were kept in "a half-frozen condition" while they waited for shipping home.

285

He wrote: "There is a large backlog of officers at the Depot, and we held a meeting where they asked us to approve a plan whereby officers enough to complete the loading of a Liberty or Victory ship troopstyle would be placed in the troop compartments. A lot of officers objected to going back with only enlisted man accommodations and signed waivers to that effect. There were some of us, however, who really want to go home, and as to the type of accommodation, it is of minor significance. It amused me to find that many of those who objected seemed to be staff officers or service personnel who have never known what it means to go on an extended patrol and live in wet foxholes for a few weeks at a time. It's rather asinine for an officer to object to accommodations for fifteen days that enlisted men have had to put up with for the full period of their military service.

"Curse this army caste system. We are all Americans, and it seems to me that most of us learned at some time or other something that goes like this—'We hold these truths to be self-evident, that all men are created equal . . . endowed with certain inalienable rights . . . etc.' We ought to repeat that more often, and we ought to learn how to practice it."

On February 8, Ben received his orders to ship out on the morning of February 9, in enlisted men's quarters, by the way. And at 0330 hours the next morning he was up and getting ready.

Packed and waiting for departure, he penned two messages. The first read:

"Well, this is the day, but I have begun to feel apprehension stealing over me. For nearly four years I have looked forward to the day when I would be released from the army. And now, with that day approaching, I find myself a little afraid of what that change might bring. I have had friends who were fortunate enough to serve missions for the Church, who have told me they felt the same way upon their release. Now I understand them a little better.

"I'll never forget the first day I came into the army—nor the first weeks and months—I wondered what I had gotten into. But I was part of it for nearly four years, and I may find it a bit hard to let go of some of the things I have learned. New places, strange people, and much traveling become a pretty close friend. Constant change is part of the army, and constancy of places and things may make civilian life a bit dull. Friendships formed have been many, and now I know I shall never see many of these friends again. The losses and delays that have been mine in a professional and vocational way will be a serious handicap for years to come, but perhaps they will be more than balanced by the invaluable experiences that military service has brought. I have a deeper appreciation of many of the blessings I formerly took for granted, such as our American standard of living, my heritage, home in the West, Priesthood activity, and church service. I have a deeper understanding of what freedom, liberty, and the free agency of man really mean, and within me there is a more complete and fuller realization of the difference between right and wrong—good and evil. And there will be greater wisdom resulting therefrom. Such values cannot be measured in usual terms. I will always treasure the experiences which opened my eyes to them.

"I will also cherish my experiences in the military olympics—my winnings in Japan and my losses in the Philippines. I would rather have placed and won, but my health was not good, and besides, all things give me experience and will be for my best good. What more could a man ask or hope for?"

After chow, Ben and the others were loaded into trucks and taken to the assembly point, where for the first time he met those who would be going all the way to Fort Douglas with him. An hour later, he was ready to load aboard the ship *Altoona Victory*, which was to take him back to the United States. An hour after that, the ship had weighed anchor, and Ben was on his way home.

But before that, just as he was ready to step off the dock, Ben posted his final letter home.

"Dearest Sweetheart," it read.

"I am leaving in just a few minutes, Honey, and will soon be with you, Darling! I had a good sleep last night and feel fine this morning. The weather delayed things as I was afraid it would, but I hope we make good time now.

"Ruth sent me a card and said that Mother is home again. I'm surely glad that she is feeling better. We'll see her soon, Honey.

"Darling, the announcements you chose are just perfect. It gave me quite a thrill to receive an announcement to my own wedding reception. Thanks for sending it. This is not like me, you know, to allow my life to be planned when I am not right there to control the planning. But I feel good about this — I feel that it is all right. Besides, it is good to have someone upon whom I can lean with full confidence, as I do you.

"Well, I'll be off and on my way. I'm coming, Darling, and when I arrive we'll be together, Honey — no more to part!

"Love always, your Bill."

CHAPTER

THIRTY-ONE

"Well, Captain Bennett, how does it feel to be home?"

For a moment Ben did not answer. Instead, he stood in the chilly darkness, staring up at the neon-lighted building before him. His heart was pounding, his throat was dry, and he could hardly concentrate on Leslie Milam's half-teasing words.

"I say, Captain Bennett—"

"Cut out the 'Captain' business, Les. You and I both know that's only a separation promotion."

"Maybe so, Captain, but for the next eighty-three days of leave, you're going to be drawing Captain's pay. So again I ask, how does it feel?"

"Are you sure she's here at the Rainbow Rendezvous, Les? We may be in Salt Lake City, but this looks like one of those places in Cotaba, or up in Malaybalay. You know, the respectable places?"

"Yeah, it does, at that."

"Are . . . are you sure she's in there?"

"My goodness, Captain, you're nervous."

Ben looked over at Leslie Milam. "So would you be, my friend."

"Oh," Leslie Milam said with a grin, "I don't think I would be. In fact, being married to my Dorothy is about the most 'un-nervous' thing I've ever done. I'm telling you, Captain, there's nothing quite so wonderful as this wedded bliss."

"So I hear," Ben replied with a grin. "Now, is she in there, or not?"

Leslie Milam sighed with resignation. "Ben, on your instructions I've been following Patricia Christensen for three days. I not only know where she is now, but I also know where she has been every minute for the past seventy-two hours."

"You didn't let her see you, did you?" Ben asked, alarmed.

"Wasn't I one of the best non-scout scouts in the 31st, Ben? Of course she didn't see me. She doesn't even know it was me who picked out your rings and got them to her. Now, how do you want to work this?"

"Who is she with?"

"Another beau," Leslie replied sarcastically.

"Cut the comedy, Les, and tell me. I'm so nervous I'm wringing wet, and here it is mid-winter."

"It's not mid-winter, Ben. It's February 27, and spring is just around the corner."

"You may be taking me around the corner in a few minutes, Les, to that mortuary there. I wasn't as frightened as this during the ambush on Morotai. Why the devil am I so scared?"

Leslie Milam grinned. "I don't know, Ben, but it'll end as soon as you lay your peepers on her. That little lady you've gotten yourself engaged to is a real looker! Not as cute as my Dorothy, mind you—but darn close."

"Says you," Ben replied as he nervously readjusted his dress uniform. "Well, shall we go in and face the music?"

"If you mean Les Brown's Band of Renown, then I'm with you. If you expect me to be your point man, though, while

290

you hide back of the perimeter, you can forget it. This is one battle you've got to fight alone."

"Some pal you are," Ben smiled.

"I know. Let's go."

Together, the two reunited friends entered the dance hall and allowed themselves to adjust to the noisy atmosphere. On the stage to the north, a crooner was singing to the melodious accompaniment of the band. On the floor, couples swayed back and forth to the slow music. To the left, people were having refreshments, while to the right, a large group of young people mingled, many seated on the long row of sofas. It was toward this group that Leslie Milam steered the incredibly nervous Captain William "Ben" Bennett.

Finally grabbing Leslie Milam's shoulder, Ben stopped him behind a group of young women.

"Can you see her yet, Les?" he shouted over the din.

"I can't, Ben," Leslie Milam shouted back. "If I was as tall as you, it would help. I know she's here, though."

"Well, I certainly hope so," Ben replied with booming voice. "I've been waiting well over thirty years for this moment, and I'll be—"

Ben stopped speaking abruptly, his whole body frozen in position. Directly in front of him, not more than three feet away, a lovely young woman had turned and was staring up at him. The expression on her face was so startled and her eyes were so wide that it was almost humorous. Yet Ben could not laugh. In fact, he could not even breathe; for the face before him was the same beautiful face he had worshipped in a photograph for the previous fourteen months, the same gorgeous face that had haunted his dreams and troubled his mind when he had tried to concentrate on other, less important, things.

"I know you," the girl exclaimed after she had blinked once or twice in astonishment. "I . . . I know who you are! Aren't you . . . aren't you my . . . my Mister Bill Bennett?"

"Pat?" Bill shouted over the noise that he could no longer even hear, "Miss Patty, is this really you?"

"Oh, my dear Bill," Patricia Christensen cried as she threw herself into his arms. "You're home! My darling is home at last! Now I know that you are real . . . "

And while a smiling and absolutely delighted Leslie Milam slowly stepped back into the crowd of gaping spectators, the future Elder William H. Bennett of the First Quorum of the Seventy of The Church of Jesus Christ of Latter-day Saints swept his sweetheart off across the dance floor toward an eternity of love and joy.

AUTHOR'S NOTE

While the foregoing story is fictional, it is based upon the experiences and detailed writings of Elder William Hunter Bennett. Drafted into the infantry of the United States of America during World War II, he spent nearly two years in basic training and Officer's Candidate School and then served in the Pacific for two additional years, keeping meticulous records the entire time of his day-to-day activities, thoughts, and feelings. Most of these writings comprised his journals; others became part of a book of themes that ultimately found its way home to his mother; and still others made their way into the many letters he sent home.

More than just a record-keeper, Elder Bennett was a deep thinker, and his writings reflect a keen interest in numerous subjects that might escape the normal observer. For instance, he dwelt at length, during one period of time, on the implications and far-reaching reverberations of the English system of letters, the common alphabet. On another day, he compared the creation of Eve from one of Adam's ribs to "cuttings" used by horticulturists as they crafted one plant out of another. And on a third day, he compared the skunk to the onion, determining that while neither lost a thing by setting free their "scent," nevertheless his whole idea of writing about it "stank."

All these things, written almost thirty years before his call as an Assistant to the Council of the Twelve Apostles, were the more startling to us as we realized, as we read them, that even that far back, young "Ben" Bennett sounded and acted like a General Authority.

Elder Bennett also discovered, for himself, that his war years seemed to have a theme, which of course was obedience to the gospel, and specifically the Word of Wisdom. It apparently began with his miraculous escape from the Japanese ambush on Morotai and the wide-ranging discussions of that escape, and the theme escalated rapidly after that.

Hardly ever did more than a week pass that he did not note in his journal a conversation with one man or another, and sometimes whole groups of men, regarding the Lord's law of health. He lived that law faithfully (as he tried to live all of God's commandments), he believed implicitly in the promise of divine protection that the Lord makes to all who live it, and he was never bashful about declaring his belief to others. Many were positively affected by his teachings, and he developed a reputation as a "non-chaplain chaplain," a person to go and see if one had problems of a personal nature.

Years later, after his call as a General Authority, he spoke in the Sydney, Australia Area Conference, declaring: "Now, brothers and sisters, I have a very personal testimony pertaining to the Word of Wisdom. Let me just say that my life was miraculously saved on four occasions that I'm aware of during World War II. I attribute that to three things. First of all, the teaching I received in my home as a boy from wise parents and my older brothers and my younger sisters and also from my wonderful teachers that I had in the Church organizations. I learned the value of prayer very early in my life, and I want to tell you that I did a lot of praying under combat conditions. Second, I received my temple endowments in the Alberta Temple in Canada before I went into military service. I made up my mind that I was going to keep those covenants, including the wearing of the temple garments, and I testify to you that I received the protection that is promised to those who do keep that covenant.

"The third is the Word of Wisdom. Being interested in athletics, I've never had a problem with the Word of Wisdom. I demonstrated in the classroom and in athletics its value. But in World War II, I learned the meaning of that last verse: 'And I, the Lord, give unto them a promise, that the destroying angel shall pass by them, . . . and not slay them.' We were ambushed on one occasion under conditions that would have annihilated our small patrol group. Not a single man was killed.

"On another occasion, I came down with what the medical officer diagnosed as Japanese Scrub Typhus Disease. I had all of the symptoms and was sent quite a distance back to the rear to the medical aid station. I was there for four days, and for twenty-four hours of those four days I was under constant medical surveillance by the medical officers or nurses. I had all of the symptoms, but on the fourth day everything became normal; I was completely well. Medical people couldn't understand it, but I could. There was only one other LDS soldier in my outfit: Sergeant Leslie E. Milam . . . I wasn't able to make contact with him to be administered to, but I still received a blessing. It means a great deal to me, my brothers and sisters."

These were Elder Bennett's feelings regarding the Word of Wisdom.

In writing the story, we have done our best to bring to life the situations Elder Bennett actually found himself in, and the circumstances he truly described.

Of Elder and Sister Bennett's romance, Elder Bennett stated in the same Australia area conference mentioned above:

"I was a little slow getting married. My wife is ten years younger than I am . . . But I fooled around a little too long; (and) I just about lost her. I'm grateful I didn't. She has been a wonderful mother and a wonderful wife, a great person."

Of Elder Bennett, Sister Bennett writes: "My dear husband never stopped pressing forward, in school, on the farm, in the service of his country, or in the service of his God. Ill health never found him down or out. He was up and dressed, doing whatever needed to be done at that moment in time. He was very kind, tender, and charitable with others when they were ill, but with himself, no. He believed in true, honest labor. He loved to work and he worked hard, and, to the best of my knowledge, he never left a job undone. I feel that he could have used more sleep, more fun and recreation, but to him life was a serious business, too serious to waste frivolously.

"I am so thankful that the Lord spared his life during World War II. His dear mother was suffering with very poor health during the four years that he was in the service, but her every thought and prayer were in behalf of her son. I know how extremely happy and grateful she was when he returned home safe, and more a man of God than he had been four years earlier.

"My husband loved the Lord, and bore a beautiful, strong testimony. He held so many positions in his service to the Lord, and loved so much serving within the numerous wards in which he lived. When he was called to be a General Authority his health was not good. But he pushed forward, fulfilling each and every assignment with a willing heart and mind, never questioning the call he had been given. For you see, he knew with all his heart that that call, as with every single calling in his life, had come to him from God."

As a final note, we found it interesting to learn that while as a soldier Elder Bennett had fought the Japanese, as a General Authority he was called to preside over a stake conference held in Tokyo, Japan. Further, Elder Bennett's only son, Brad, served his mission in the Japan Tokyo Mission and was able to be in attendance at that same stake conference where his father was presiding.

Lieutenant William H. "Ben" Bennett, about 1944

William H. and Patricia Christensen Bennett
at the time of their marriage